Return to Roswell: Book II

Return to Roswell: Book II

Martin A Rosen

Copyright © 2015 Martin A Rosen
All rights reserved.

ISBN: 0988280752
ISBN 13: 9780988280755
Library of Congress Control Number: 2015912563
Silver Alien Press LLC, Woodstock, VT

DEDICATION

To Riley, Jacob, Chloe, Abby, Connie, Wendy, Sally, Molly, Maggie and Hannah

I believe alien life is quite common in the Universe, although intelligent life is less so. Some say It has yet to appear on planet Earth.

—Stephen Hawking—

The only thing that scares me more than space aliens is the idea that there aren't any space aliens. We can't be the best that creation has to offer. If so, we are in big trouble.

—Ellen De Generes—

Who are we? We find that we live on an insignificant planet of a humdrum star in a Galaxy tucked Away in some forgotten corner of a Universe in which there are far more galaxies than people.

—Carl Sagan—

I have not told half of what I have saw!

—Marco Polo—

CONTENTS

Prologue · · · xi
1 Message Outgoing · · · 1
2 Message Incoming · · · 9
3 Retrieval · · · 18
4 Committee Meetings · · · 31
5 Byline, Leah Anne Bailey · · · 44
6 Orbiting Titan · · · 57
7 What's up, Earth? · · · 68
8 Site Selection · · · 80
9 Intelligence Training · · · 89
10 Brother Explorers Returned · · · 102
11 Mother Ship · · · 121
12 Return to Earth · · · 138
13 Ready to Rumble · · · 154
14 London Negotiations · · · 171
15 Moving Forward · · · 188
16 Snatch and Comply · · · 204
Acknowledgments · · · 223
About the Author · · · 225

PROLOGUE

On the evening of July 2, 1947, Newton Foster, a professional newspaper photographer, and his young friend Lone Wolf, a Mescalero Apache, were camping outside Roswell, New Mexico. As the day moved towards its conclusion, an intense summer thunderstorm with numerous lightning strikes lit up the sky. As Newton and Lone Wolf gazed skyward, they observed the lightning strikes repeatedly hit a moving silver disc as it skipped across the sky. A loud crackling sound signaled the breakup and fall to Earth of the disintegrating silver disc. Newton and Lone Wolf decided to explore the unusual event and quickly hurried to the crash site. Before them on the ground, still smoldering, they saw what appeared to be numerous broken silver spacecraft pieces. Newton began to photograph the crash debris while Lone Wolf selected a few interesting objects to keep as mementos. Shortly, they noticed an oncoming line of Army vehicles dispatched from the Roswell Army/Air Force base approaching the crash site. Newton and Lone Wolf moved off into the distance and hid while observing the military personnel picking up all evidence of the crashed silver spacecraft. The pieces were placed in the military vehicles for return to the nearby military base.

Newton decided to continue his surveillance by following the military vehicles back to their base. There he shot additional black and white photographs to document the apparent military investigation of the crash. Newton was discovered at the air base and was warned never to speak of this incident again. As a result, Newton decided to keep quiet about what he had seen. Nevertheless, he carefully documented each of his black and white photographs with dates and locations. He set them aside along with a hand written letter, which remained unseen in a shoebox for over 60 years. Only after his funeral many years later did Newton's wife, Lucy, hand the shoebox containing these special artifacts to their grandson, Casey Foster.

Casey, like his grandfather before him, was a professional photographer. When Casey reviewed the photographs and accompanying letter he was amazed at what they appeared to disclose. Using state of the art computer enhancement equipment at the *Washington Post*, where he worked, Casey uncovered what appeared to be photographic proof that an alien spaceship had indeed crashed near Roswell, New Mexico, in July, 1947. With the help of his girlfriend, Leah Anne Bailey, Casey decide to take an exploratory trip to Roswell to further investigate this major, newsworthy event. Once in Roswell, Casey located Lone Wolf, who gave him his firsthand account of the alien spacecraft crash. Then, with the help of Leah Anne's and Lone Wolf's grandson, Tecote, they located, photographed, and immediately uploaded to the *Washington Post* new photographs showing additional pieces of the crashed alien spacecraft . Knowing that they would soon be discovered, Casey had the presence of mind to re-bury the newly uncovered crash debris.

Through the Pentagon, the United States government had been tracking Casey, Leah Anne, and Lone Wolf. Shortly after they uncovered the new crash debris pieces they were all taken into custody and transported to the Roswell air base. Here they were interrogated and kept in isolation until the Washington administration decided what to do with them. Later, when these events were disclosed to President Obama, he decided to obtain a complete briefing on the Roswell event. At the briefing the President learned that the United States government had, through the years, retained numerous scientific experts to review the facts and make findings concerning whether or not an alien spacecraft had really crashed in Roswell in 1947. The President's conclusion, upon review of all of the facts, was crystal clear: an alien spacecraft with two alien pilots had indeed crashed on Earth. As this review was taking place, the United States government, along with SETI, each recorded an incoming message from space. When decoded, this message confirmed that extra-solar aliens had not only previously visited Earth but were presently on a journey back. As world leaders mapped out a plan for future action, the *Washington Post* received governmental permission for Casey Foster and Leah Anne Bailey to act as the primary news reporting personnel for this unfolding historic event.

Return to Roswell, Book I, ends with the live television broadcast from President Obama beamed to the entire world and out into interstellar space, which went as follows:

Dear fellow galaxy members:

Greetings to you from Earth. We are pleased that our sovereign worlds have made contact. We are confident we have much to share with each other. We look forward to your visit to Earth, and we look forward to a peaceful meeting. May God bless us all! Please advise receipt.

The entire world waits as this story continues to unfold. The most anticipated meeting in history moves towards its culmination. Meanwhile, out in the dark, incredibly cold depths of space, an alien mother ship of immense size continues its long journey toward Earth. The alien spaceship commander seeks the Immediate return of their earlier visiting "brother explorers" and, more importantly, the opportunity to meet with Earth's leadership so that he can implement his plan for Earth's solar system and decide what to do with Earth's humans.

CHAPTER 1

MESSAGE OUTGOING

Casey Foster and his girlfriend, Leah Anne Bailey, were invited guests of President Obama when he informed the world's population that the Earth had previously been visited by extra solar aliens and were about to receive a return visit. This message, broadcast in 15 languages around the world, was also simultaneously beamed deep into the far reaches of space for its intended reception by the incoming alien visitors. Up, up, and away the televised presentation leapt at the speed of light. Out the message went, past the Earth's reflective moon, past Earth's newly-explored sister planet Mars, out past Jupiter with its many orbiting moons, past Saturn with its dazzling array of concentric icy rings, past cold dark Uranus, and beyond the currently catalogued last solar planet, Neptune. The message flashed past Pluto, once the last planet and furthest from the sun, which had been recently downgraded to merely an icy "dwarf planet." The message sped forth past the icy cold asteroid belt and into the imaginary titled "termination shock boundary" where, according to Earth scientists, the speed of our solar winds drops below the speed of sound. Farther and farther, minute by minute and second by second the message sped from Earth at the speed of light towards the heliosphere. Finally, the broadcast traveled far enough to reach beyond the solar system and into interstellar space.

Now the Earth's greeting message sped past *Voyager 1*, our famous and so far most distant satellite, launched in September, 1977, to explore our outer solar system and beyond. *Voyager*, Earth's first messenger to outer space, carried with it into the unknown its famous "Golden

Record" (not exactly a top of the charts Elvis or Lady Gaga super hit), which catalogued the sights and sounds of Earth's little blue water world. *Voyager* continued traveling forth from Earth at over 35,000 mph into what Earthlings would refer to as outer space. So if *Voyager 1* continued successfully on its journey into space, in a mere 14,000 years it would emerge from our nearby OORT cloud and eventually reach Earth's nearest star neighbor, Alpha Centuri, in another 40,000 years. Chugging along at 35,000 mph, hour after hour, seemed fast in Earth terms, but when tackling the huge distances in space, we Earthlings have a long way to go. It's kind of like we are meandering along at horse and buggy speed. Tiger moms to the front. Better get busy, kidlets! Many of those alien guys are plenty smart and have a pretty long lead on their educational achievements.

Casey Foster completed his selection of photographs, which would be published in a story written by Leah Anne Bailey. He wished to confirm his grandfather's documentation of the crashed alien spaceship with its alien astronauts at Roswell in 1947. He wished that he and Leah Anne could fully inform the *Washington Post's* readers about the much anticipated return of the off world aliens. Casey wondered when the message broadcast by the President would be received. He wondered how it would be decoded and interpreted. He wondered, as did the rest of the tuned-in world, what the intentions of these aliens might be. Casey focused on his prime task of reporting on Roswell through his photographs while pursuing his relationship with Leah Anne Bailey with equal intensity. Luckily for Casey, as part of the *Washington Post's* agreement to cooperate with the American government, the newspaper had been granted first rights to act as Earth's leading disseminator of public information on the Roswell event. And so, the morning after President Obama's broadcast, the *Washington Post* published and distributed over 35 million copies of its special Roswell World Edition. It seemed that everyone wanted to read and own a copy . This was a record for a newspaper publication in terms of its issue size. Distributed around the world by the *Washington Post*, humans studied and marveled at the old black and white photographs taken by Newton Foster and updated by Casey. These spectacular photographs clearly showed the initial crash debris field, the Army personnel gathering the evidence, and the onsite alien autopsy. Yep, these guys with big heads and glaring red eyes had visited Earth. Running alongside these spectacular photographs were the written commentaries prepared by Leah Anne Bailey. Now, like other media darlings before them, Casey and Leah Anne were becoming instant celebrities. Job offers flooded in for Casey Foster to work for other newspaper organizations, media outlets, and even filmmakers. He rejected all the offers due to his desire to continue working at the *Washington Post. Why abandon a good thing when all was turning out just right*? he thought.

Not surprisingly, Leah Anne was also under siege to accept new employment. There were government offers to join various congressional and senatorial staffs. Various administrative lobbyist firms wanted her high exposure help. Hillary Clinton stepped up to offer her a position as science advisor for her 2016 Presidential run. Leah Anne was even offered a position to host a TV series regarding the proposed subject "Little Gray Men Coming to Visit Earth." Leah Anne declined all these offers.

The world wondered what Casey and Leah Anne would do next, just as the couple did. And so Casey and Leah Anne decided to do what they normally did. A dinner date was arranged for the Hotel Washington for 8 PM sharp at its rooftop bar on Friday night following the President's worldwide broadcast. Casey arrived first, camera in hand, sporting a new dinner jacket accessorized with a casual smile. Immediately recognized by the previously snotty maître d', Casey was escorted to a prime table overlooking the Washington scene, including the not-yet-broke Treasury Department and the White House beyond. The maître d' handed over the dinner menu with highlighted specials and informed Casey that his waiter, their best, would be with him soon.

Casey had previously labored as the newest recruit in the *Washington Post* photographic department. He was no longer obscure. Many *Washington Post* readers had taken notice of his startling photographs. As he sat perusing the dinner menu, a few of those lofty Washington insiders present at the rooftop restaurant stopped by his table to say hello and offer their congratulations. Maybe would he even autograph a dinner menu to "show the kids", they suggested. Casey was happy to comply. His new celebrity status felt pleasant. *It's good to be king*, thought Casey, *even if it proves to be fleeting.* He hoped to parlay his present success into a long-term career. While he waited for Leah Anne, the waiter brought forth unsolicited, like manna from Heaven, an extra dry martini, a gift from a young admiring society lady sitting at a nearby table who was hoping for a private conversation and perhaps more.

Outside, Leah Anne, as was her custom, arrived by taxi. She hated driving in downtown DC's grotesque nighttime traffic and always preferred her role as a passenger. Alighting from her chariot, she appeared as one might when they are at the top of their game. She wore red stiletto heels, tight black leather pants, a loose but still clinging white silk blouse set off by a strand of faux pearls, and matching dangling faux pearl earrings. The smile on Leah's face seemed bright enough to light the night sky as she delicately walked to the hotel front door guarded by two uniformed hotel footmen. Now, as a local sensation, Leah Anne was met and then escorted by the hotel manager from the front door to the rooftop restaurant. The maître d', as if on guard duty at the Tomb of the Unknown Soldier, clicked his heels, lightly gathered Leah's elbow, and escorted her to Casey's prime location table. "If there's anything else I can do for you," remarked the maître d', "just let me know. I am here to make sure your evening is an enjoyable one." With that, the maître d' bowed low, swiveled on his slick heels, and pranced back to his entryway station, all a-giggle.

Casey, eyes wide open, looked across the short space to the other side of the table and smiled at Leah Anne. *Yippee*, he thought to himself, excited for a delicious dinner, stiff drinks, a little charming talk, and then another ride down Rock Creek Parkway, top down in his adored British racing green Austin Healy sports car. Time for some quiet conversation, pull over to park, and enjoy the view both far and near, a few preliminary kisses, and the anticipated late night rendezvous with Leah Anne at his Georgetown safe house.

"Hi there, sweetheart," he said as his opening greeting. "How goes it?"

"Things are great with me," Leah Anne replied. "So tell me, handsome: what's happening at the *Post*?"

"I'm pleased to inform you that the *Post* has promoted me to senior photographer, now assigned to exclusively cover the Roswell incident. So it looks like I'll be in this for the long haul. And you? What's new?"

"Well, before I start explaining, how about ordering drinks and dinner?"

"That sounds great to me. How about our usual: dry martinis, medium rare New York strip steak sizzling and covered in mushrooms, big baked potato with all the fixings, perhaps a Caesar salad to start, and if were feeling really nuts we can share a hot brownie sundae with rum raisin ice cream for dessert. You likie?" asked Casey.

"Yep, I likie a bunchie. You order, and then I'll tell you what's going on with me," Leah Anne said with a coquettish little girl smile.

Within a blink of an eye the waiter brought a second martini to Casey and a first to Leah Anne. A side dish of assorted stuffed olives, crackers and hot, straight out of the oven, fragrant bread appeared on their flower-adorned white tablecloth-covered dinning space, compliments of the house. Casey smoothly ordered the dinner they had agreed upon.

"Well," Leah Anne started, "the most amazing unsolicited offers have been arriving concerning future employment opportunities. Of course, the Library of Congress offered to upgrade my position to head of the science department in an effort to capture some of my current popularity. I've also had an inquiry from the FDA concerning my availability to serve as an appointed commissioner. Senator Wilson Stone asked me to join him in the Senate dining room to discuss hiring me as his lead legislative aide. And most interestingly, I even received a call from Hillary Clinton herself, to act as her science consultant during the upcoming 2016 Presidential melee. While all of these inquiries are interesting another opportunity has arisen which has my undivided attention."

Casey leaned forward. His tie, which he didn't normally wear, came dangerously close to dipping into his dry martini as he listened to each of her words dutifully.

"I received a telephone call this morning from this wonderful gentleman, a Mr. Charles Evenridge, the editor-in-chief of the *Washington Post*. Mr. Evenridge invited me to his offices to explore a possible opportunity at the newspaper. I'm sorry I didn't tell you, but I wanted to ensure that there would be no inside finagling involving my meeting. I was met at the *Post*'s front entry desk by the ever professional Ms. Billingsly attired in her wire rim glasses, chicken neck to the fore, dressed as befitting one with over 25 years of service as the door-guarding champion. Ms. Billingsley escorted me to the hallowed 10th floor executive suites and seated me in front of Mr. Evenridge for an interview. Mr. Evenridge suggested that, due to my background, education, and experience with you on the Roswell matter, that my most beneficial employment would be to work for the *Washington Post* as a special science consultant and reporter concerning all matters involved in the Roswell story. He further suggested that he could see the *Post* publishing a weekly featured news article covering the historical background of Roswell, the current status of events, and future expected interactions between the approaching aliens and us Earthlings. Mr. Evenridge also indicated I would have to work hand in glove with you, since each newspaper presentation would be accompanied by photographic corroboration. I should also note that Mr. Evenridge offered me a nice 5th floor office with a view, secretarial assistance, a yearly salary in excess of that which I am currently receiving, and the potential for advancement as I accumulate experience as a news reporter. He asked me to think it over and let him know by the end of the week."

"Wow," Casey replied. "We could work together! But you understand, of course, that this will be a professional relationship and there can be no fooling around during work hours," he added with a wink. "So, with that in mind, I'm all in favor of you working at the *Post*."

"What makes you think that I'd be interested in fooling around with you either during or after work hours?"

"Well, I guess the answer to that question might be illuminated by what happens following our dinner and drive on Rock Creek Parkway."

"Dickhead," Leah Anne responded. "I'll call and schedule an appointment for later this week with Mr. Evenridge to accept the *Post*'s offer. Do I need to learn any secret handshakes?"

"Yep; I can show you later tonight. You will love working at the *Post*, as will I," Casey laughed.

With the future employment issue out of the way, Casey and Leah Anne dove into their dry martinis. Dinner was delightful as they ate, talked, and anticipated their current ascendance to the top of the news reporting industry, covering the most intriguing story ever presented to the entire human population of Earth. While they ate and drank, somewhere far out into the dark emptiness of deep space, Earth's responsive broadcast message filtered its way to the incoming alien mother ship. Its antennas gathered in the stream of data which was duly recorded for careful decoding.

All around planet Earth, a lingering question lurked in peoples' minds. Was this really happening? Were these aliens really on the way back? What did they have in mind for humanity? What did they want? Were they interested in attending an NFL game, perhaps an opera or ballet, or were they more interested in serving up humans on dinner plates? Casey and Leah Anne were not immune to these questions, but they smiled, thinking only of their bright futures. With dinner consumed, the young, happy couple held hands as they walked out of the dining room, descending to the street level where Casey's beloved sports car was parked. There, sitting under a streetlight, top down and ready to rumble, Casey started the engine and listened for its primary growl. He then shoved in the clutch, popping out into nighttime traffic, past the White House on the way to their nighttime drive up rock Creek Parkway. Above their heads stars shone brightly as they picked out the few constellations they knew. Leah Anne, with her new-found scientific interest in things above, quickly related to Casey her understanding that Earthlings could see approximately 6000 stars without the use of scientific magnifying instruments. Though he found this interesting, Casey, now that the drive was underway, had already switched his focus to non-scientific, non-photographic, non-newsworthy matters. With these thoughts in mind he drove for awhile, then parked at a few of their favorite places, as both prepared for tonight and their futures. Above, all was serene as the alien mother ship continued its relentless passage towards Earth, the little blue water world.

CHAPTER 2

MESSAGE INCOMING

*B*eep, *beep, beep*… The historic message broadcast by President Obama beamed around Earth to all of its mesmerized inhabitants and then out it zoomed into the starlit night. Most importantly, the message was specifically broadcast towards the incoming alien spacecraft. This was possible since Earth's scientists had already calculated the direction of the traveling spacecraft towards Earth from Fomalhaut, its home star. The same scientists had also discovered the radio frequency used when the Redexians beamed their prior transmission to Earth. The alien spacecraft was still almost a light year away, a vast distance in Earth's civilization's normal traveling experience. Far away, but closing fast. And since it was clear we Earthlings had little, if any, control over this situation, the best choice was to wait patiently, collective breath held as the historic events unfolded.

Likewise, ever since Dr. James Westermonne, leg of lamb in hand, had decoded the incoming alien message announcing the returning alien visitation to Earth, our lead scientists had diligently studied the Fomalhaut star system hoping that it might shed some light on what Earthlings might expect. It turned out that Fomalhaut was actually part of a three star trinary system in which each of the three stars orbited one another. The primary star, Fomalhaut, was described as being a white dwarf star with approximately twice the mass of our home star, the sun. Fomalhaut's central core burned hydrogen almost 80% faster than our sun, producing much higher thermal temperatures. In cosmic terms this meant that Fomalhaut would only last for another billion years or so before it was expected to blow itself to smithereens. Earthlings could expect a more leisurely 5 to 10 billion years before the sun's big final explosion. The second star in the Fomalhaut star system was an orange-red dwarf star a bit smaller than our own sun. The third remaining star was a mere red dwarf, flirting around the other two, always seeking acceptance. This detailed scientific expertise regarding the Fomalhaut system was obtained using Earth's sophisticated orbiting astronomy instruments, such as the Hubble Telescope, the Cassini telescope, the Spitzer Space Telescope, and Earth-based telescopes such as the Atacama Large Millimeter Array. But long before these incredible machines were developed, early unsophisticated Earthmen had looked skyward and observed these stars for centuries. Fomalhaut, it turns out, was part of the well-known constellation Pisces described in some of astronomy's first written records as the Southern Fish. Only more recently had more well-informed scientists learned that Fomalhaut was part of the 16 star Castor Moving Group, with Fomalhaut being the brightest and most visible star in the group.

Obviously, even Earthlings with intelligence levels only slightly above a starfish soon realized that living beings don't exist on stars. Better look for life on planets orbiting stars or on their captive moons. And so smart science researchers, using well-thought-out techniques such as watching the wobble of a home star or the slight dimming of light caused by a shadow cast from a passing planet over the star surface, determined that there were six known planets in the Southern Fish triple star system. Two of those planets were clearly circling Fomalhaut, each within what was referred to as the "habitable zone." This pleasant little area was a zone where liquid water could exist on the surface of a planet and where temperatures could range between a life-supporting zone between 50 degrees below zero Fahrenheit and 125 degrees above zero Fahrenheit. Yep, you could almost go for a snowmobile ride in the winter or sunbathing at the local pleasant beach in the summer. Time for a vacation? Don't forget to pack the sunscreen and your insulated jammies. In a place never seen by human eyes or searched by human instruments, rotating happily around its home star Fomalhaut, circled a planet not too unlike Earth. It was perhaps

2/3 as massive with solid, distinct land masses interspersed with areas of liquid water, all enveloped within a denser atmosphere that allowed for less light to reach the planet's surface than Earth. Gravity was less intense, and the atmospheric pressure was also lower. Earthlings would soon learn that the alien locals referred to their planet in their prevailing worldwide language as Redex, a planet whose inhabitants, we would soon learn, had, according to their historic records, been "civilized" for more than 50,000 years. In rough terms this was more than 40,000 years before "civilization" took root on Earth. No mud huts on Redex, very few condos, and not a golf course in sight. That's refreshing!

Evolving up the tree of life, just like on Earth and on millions of other habitable planets throughout the universe, Redexians' ancestors started life as mere bacteria swimming around in mud slime. Over their centuries, evolution transformed them into what they considered to be an intelligent life form capable of mastering their environment. Further industrial development led quite naturally to exploration of the space throughout the Redexian solar system. This was an endeavor they had devoted much time and resources to in an ever-expanding movement outward in the Milky Way. They had been space faring now for over 2500 years. So while Earthlings thought they were hot stuff regarding their current state of space expertise, in comparison we were still riding donkeys without a saddle. Well, everyone has to start somewhere.

Redexians had discovered, long ago, that they were not alone in the universe or even in their home galaxy. They found a slew of neighbors within 15,000 light years of their home planet. This fact of life was critically important for the Redexians to understand. Others were out there, with as much or more talent and technology. Some of those others also exploring space might decide that planet Redex had resources they wanted badly enough to conquer their more backward neighbors. This knowledge had taught the Redexians that they needed to move off world to create a zone of relative safety. Moving outward from their home world quickly was better than slowly. Aggressively was better than passively. It was this continuing exploration process that had led to the Redexians' initial visit to Roswell, New Mexico, in July, 1947, a process that led them to explore in all directions from their home planet. Their current achievable goal was to explore everywhere within 50 light years from Redex to find new habitable planets from which they could watch, defend, and protect their home world.

On the bridge of the approaching alien mother ship, the captain was informed by his first officer that an incoming message had been received from those strange life forms on the little blue water world to which they were headed. The incoming message was duly deciphered and reviewed by the captain. He decided to defer a response until he determined where to "park" his mothership in orbit in this intriguing solar system.

The mother ship was moderate by their standards, being about the size and tonnage of three modern-day Earth nuclear aircraft carriers and staffed by a crew just in excess of 3000 crew members. It was a spaceship designed for lengthy interstellar voyages . By necessity, their ship needed to be self-sustaining, with all the resources on board to provide for life and leisure. Each voyage could be expected to last between10 to 50 Redexian years—not many places available to stop for gas or catch a quick lunch along the way. Given this, their spaceships were designed with multiple methods of power generation. Each method utilized different power production techniques in case one system or method failed. When their spaceship was near a planet, the mother ship utilized a fusion power system, which generated enormous quantities of power by fusing atoms of hydrogen into helium. This power source was self- sustaining as long as there was an adequate supply of hydrogen atoms available to crush into submission. And that, it turned out, wasn't very tough since hydrogen is the most available element in the universe. The technology to build containment structures while crushing this hydrogen together, the other hand, was incredibly complicated. But over time the Redexians had solved those problems. This meant that on Earth, MIT students would need an educational upgrade, and hot shot students attending Harvard better put in some overtime. This stuff was darn difficult to learn. Once beyond the local departing star system, the mother ship would unfurl massive solar sails to capture as much of the outgoing stellar particles and stellar winds as possible. These sails could also reflect laser beams shot from the mother ship's engine room. This form of power could triple the speed of the traveling spacecraft. Lastly, when the ship was in the vast interstellar no man's land where the next available star was located on average 3.5 light years away, it would switch over to gravity propulsion.

These innumerable regions of space were pervasive, cold, dark, locked in a vacuum, and had to be crossed time and again to get anywhere "out there" on extended explorations. And while interstellar space was often referred to as empty, it turned out there was gravity all over the place, attracting stuff big and small in varying degrees. It was the same gravity as "discovered" on Earth when Sir Isaac Newton got bopped on the head by a falling apple, with an emphasis on "falling" rather than "floating." Gravity, it turns out, is present everywhere, from the smallest moon, planet, local star, and star cluster to the entire galaxy. And with galaxies estimated to number over 100 billion throughout the universe, each containing 100 billion or more stars, that's a bunch of gravity. Gravity acts as a coalescing force throughout the universe, creating stars and galaxies, and, if harnessed, could enable explorers to move about quite nicely. The Redexians had learned how to do just that. Their fourth generation GS IV gravity drive system moved them around pretty darn quick. (The Redexian terminology for units, measurements, elements, distances, planets, moons and spaceship systems have all been translated from their Newee language into English for ease of use herein.) So when the Redexians left a star system behind or approached another, it was time to engage their starship gravity drive system. Move it out, rawhide!

The Redexians also learned that ordinary matter that makes stuff like planets, stars, asteroids, comets, dust, gas, and all those things that can be seen and examined only comprised less than 5% of matter. Also bubbling around space, both holding it all together while at the same time pushing everything apart, were vast quantities of dark matter and dark energy. Dark, because these forces cannot be seen directly and because no one on Earth at least really knows what they are yet. And so the Redexians' starship also sucked in what it needed from space and blew out its reactive power through its graviton GS IV system to quick make headway past the backyard playground of the Redex solar system.

Traveling at near full speed at 40% of the speed of light, or almost 70,000 miles per second, the Redexian spacecraft was quickly closing in on Earth's solar system. Anyone on Earth want to race? Line up your Ferraris, Buggattis, Bentley Blowers, and Tesla S at the local racetrack. Or load up a Saturn V rocket or Russian Megalift rocket on the launch pad and let her rip. That might get Earthlings moving at 27,500 miles per hour. Or slingshot your satellite or spaceship around a planet or two for a gravity assist to get up to 50,000 miles per hour. Clearly there was no real challenge from Earth regarding speed of travel. The Redexians, in comparison, might think they are hot stuff, but on other star systems, maybe those guys were working on or had achieved folding "space-time" and just hopping across vast distances at multiple times the speed of light. Warp speed, as termed in *Star Trek* parlance. Just one leap here and another there and boom, you've arrived at almost the same time you left. Now that's the real future of space travel.

This information about speed and distance was communicated to one another aboard their mother ship using a language the Redexians had developed over centuries, which was a conglomeration of audible sounds, nasal clicks, humming, and hand and ear movements. It was kind of like a full body ballet conveying reams of information to the intended recipient. It was a language that in modified form progressed from oral language to writing, first as pictograms and later as individual words or phrases. It was the language taught universally on Redex by parents to their offspring, and it was known in their parlance as "Newee." A standardized, simplified version of Newee had become the "go to" language throughout the Redexian zone of influence, similar to how Greek and then Latin, French, German, Spanish, and English had become, one at a time, Earth's primary method of international communication. Even relatively unsophisticated life forms, such as Earthlings in general and Dr. James Westermone in specific, could, with practice, learn to understand and decipher the intended meaning of messages communicated in Newee, even if the nuances were sometimes beyond their comprehension.

On board the mother ship, Captain Oulah IV called a meeting of his senior staff to review his preliminary navigation plan. Based upon the information supplied by the science officer, he intended to choose an orbiting location for the mother ship from among the multiple planets and their moons that could serve as a safe first staging area. Three planets and their accompanying moons presented different pluses and minuses as potential safe locations. Captain Oulah intended to choose a location relatively near Earth but not so close that the local inhabitants could pose any threat. Sure, he realized, Redexian technology and defensive abilities were thought to be far superior to anything Earthlings could muster, but why take a chance? Maybe Earthlings would find something strange or new to throw at them if they felt threatened. Better to stand clear and stay parked out of range from any interference with their plans.

With safety in mind, the merits of the planets known by the locals as Mars, Jupiter, and Saturn were analyzed at length. Mars was felt to be too close to Earth for comfort as an initial staging location, and Jupiter was too gaseous. But Saturn, with its many encircling rings and 53 orbiting moons, looked just right. In due time and after due deliberation the captain selected Saturn's moon, Titan, the most Earthlike place in this solar system. Titan orbited Saturn at around 750,000 miles from its surface, completing each full transit in 16 Earth days. Titan had both hard land surfaces and lakes containing liquid methane, which might prove useful. The temperature on Titan's surface, while cold, was sufficient for their purposes. Its thick clouds had created an atmosphere that was suitable and would shield any of their surface activities from prying Earth view. Once he decided upon Titan, the captain summoned his navigator. "Chief, prepare to insert our ship in a synchronous orbit around Titan at 5000 miles from the surface," he ordered.

"Aye, Captain," the navigator politely responded. "I will make it so," he added, his ears flapping in studied submission. His red eyes were averted towards the deck in passive submission. The decision made, Captain

Oulah IV returned to his neatly arranged quarters and logged into his private computer system to review his written orders. He had now expertly guided his ship and crew to a point in space almost 24 light years from Redex, although it must be noted that his starting point for this voyage was a planet previously colonized by the Redexians 5 light years from Earth's solar system. Just like other captains from Redex before him, he had guided his exploratory spacecraft one careful move at a time. Be smart, don't overextend. Keep your supply lines and communication intact. But even a relatively small distance away, like 5 light years, made quickly sending a message back to the nearby colony's governor impossible. Any message to the nearby governor would take 5 years to be received and another 5 years to return. Similarly, a message to Redex would take 24 years to get there and 24 more years before any response could be returned. To deal with this unavoidable fact, the Redexians had developed a system of substations and governors who each had the authority to direct actions on behalf of the home world. And where that communication was far off, ship captains like Oulah had been granted explicit discretion within the parameters of their written orders for their missions to proceed as they thought most prudent. The captain's written orders, which he now reviewed for the umpteenth time, set forth in formal Newee, the following:

1. Make contact with political leaders on planet Earth capable of making and enforcing worldwide decisions;
2. Secure the immediate return of their earlier Redexian brother explorers in whatever condition they presently exist;
3. Find and place 3 observation satellites in secure locations in Earth's solar system;
4. Find and place multiple bases and embassies on planet Earth;
5. Determine whether enlisting Earth's population as a trustworthy ally for the Redexian Federation is feasible, or whether enslavement or, as a last resort, destruction of Earth's human population is most beneficial to Redex's long term needs.

Captain Oulah understood that the prime directive was to safeguard Redex and its people. This had been the foundation of his stellar career, the reason why he got up in the morning. Pondering this, he looked forward into the fixed reflective surface on the wall above his desk and studied himself. *Handsome devil*, he thought, *the kind of captain who can make monumental decisions*. Perhaps someday the textbooks of Redex would make mention of his name, honoring him for his accomplishments. Perhaps his name would be associated with the anticipated new outposts and colonies he would establish. Perhaps he could even be the instrument for learning something useful from those life forms inhabiting the little blue water world. While that was doubtful, it could happen. Maybe he would find native medical remedies, useful plants or flowers, edible food substances, or useful DNA that they could harvest. Maybe he could even (squeeze your big red eyes closed and hold you nostrils) crossbreed a few Earthlings with a few well-compensated Redexian volunteers and see what they could get as a hybrid. And if that were too nuts, there was always test tubes, cloning, and grafts. Hold on, slow down, there's plenty of time before making that wild jump into the unknown. How gross!

CHAPTER 3

RETRIEVAL

Early Monday morning, following Leah Anne's delightful dinner with Casey, she dialed the *Washington Post's* phone number and asked to be connected with its editor-in-chief, Mr. Charles Evenridge. Together they arranged a prompt Wednesday morning meeting. Arriving five minutes early on Wednesday morning for their appointment, both Leah Anne and Casey had dressed in their snappy professional clothing. Ms. Billingsley greeted them cordially and then ushered them into the editor-in-chief's presence. The editor was sporting a jaunty blue bow tie, a blue blazer, and dark blue reading glasses offset with hand painted flowers, an apparent Georgetown affectation.

"Well, I'm pleased to see you both. What brings you to my office,?" he said, tongue kind of in cheek, knowing that well-written news stories about the Roswell alien event with corroborating photographs could give the *Post* a hefty circulation boost.

Leah Anne leaned forward in her comfortable brown leather chair, her face lit up with a cheery smile, and with her eyes directed towards Mr. Evenridge stated, "I've spent quite a bit of time thinking about your generous offer of employment. I have discussed the offer with my friend, Casey Foster, since he will also be involved. Given the importance of this Roswell story, I have decided to accept your offer. I have a feeling that we all have a great deal to learn and a corresponding great deal to inform the paper's readership about this unfolding historic event. Please let me assure you that I will give this opportunity all of my professional attention. I will work diligently with Casey Foster and you to provide factual and entertaining news on all that transpires regarding Roswell. Thank you for this chance to be part of something important." Casey, listening intently without interrupting, contentedly nodding his head in agreement, just like a pleasant bobble head doll.

"Welcome aboard, Ms. Bailey, on behalf of the *Washington Post's* entire professional staff. It's always nice to welcome bright, young, talented people who can assist our newspaper in its continuing quest to be a worldwide leader in presenting the news to the public. Your credentials, background, training, and exposure on the ground to the Roswell story make you just the kind of professional we want on our team. Please feel free to call upon me any time you have questions concerning your job or the Roswell story." Mr. Evenridge then turned his gaze to Casey Foster and asked, "And what brings you along, Casey?"

"Two things, Mr. Evenridge. First, I wanted to hear Leah Anne accept your offer to work here at the paper. And secondly, we have something we wish to bring to your direct attention. It just so happens that when Leah Anne, Lone Wolf, and I uncovered the additional hidden pieces of the crashed spaceship outside Roswell and forwarded the photographs to the *Post*, we realized that the government would soon take us into custody. I immediately reburied a few crash items a short distance away so that they would be protected as indispensable firsthand physical evidence. As you know, we were apprehended and taken away. Luckily, and unbeknownst to us, at about the same time, Lone Wolf's grandson, Tecote, observed the government operatives closing in and take us away. He was smart and wily enough to scramble down to the location where I hid the materials and collect them. These materials included a plastic-like notebook binder containing a number of circular metal discs each within its own plastic cover. Tecote grabbed the binder, raced away from our location, and again reburied the binder near Bison Wells. To this day, I don't believe anyone has informed our government officials regarding these important additional materials. We thought it best to bring this to your attention directly so that you could make a determination concerning how this should be handled."

"That certainly is interesting information," responded Mr. Evenridge. "I will meet with our legal department to develop a plan of action. My initial reaction is that we will need to turn these materials over to the government. However, if done correctly, we may be able to parlay this into a position where the *Post* remains the continuing prime news source outlet. Your quick thinking in the field may once again turn out to serve the *Post* very well. I thank you both again," he beamed. "I will get back to you once a course of action is planned. In the meantime, my congratulations in advance to both you and Leah Anne for what I suspect will be your insightful news coverage."

With that said, all hands were presented for shaking. Mr. Evenridge then escorted his employees to his office door. Ms. Billingsley, always at the ready, clicked her heels together like Dorothy before escorting the editor's guests to Leah Anne's new pristine office space on the 5th floor of the *Washington Post* building. All, it appears, had been arranged in advance. It seemed that Mr. Evenridge knew that Leah Anne would be unable to turn down the challenge of this prime story. What else was Leah Anne to work on, drug applications and labeling frauds? Hell, this was big time!

Arriving at her new spacious office, Leah Anne was introduced to Kelly Oliveri, her new, bright red haired, whip smart, and attentive secretary. *It's nice to be on this payroll*, Leah Anne thought to herself. "See you later Casey," she said. "I've got work to do." Then a quick polite hug, wink, and kiss on the Kepi' were administered as Casey pivoted on his heels and walked out the door to the photo lab.

Upstairs, from his 10th floor office suite, Charles Evenridge asked Ms. Billingsley to get Bob Williston, general counsel of the *Post*'s legal department, on the phone. As Bob picked up the phone he was greeted by his boss. "Hey Bob," he asked jokingly, "are the legal beagles under control today?"

"You bet; they're all eating from their bowls on command and heeling when ordered. I think I've got all of them barking at their assigned tasks. Now, how can I be of assistance today?"

"We have an interesting new wrinkle in the Roswell story. Can you come up to my office so we can discuss this matter face-to-face?"

"I'll be there in a few minutes. Would you like me to bring along a legal beagle in training? I can bring one that's housebroken."

"No, I don't think that will be necessary. I'll see you in a few minutes."

With that Bob swiveled in his brown leatherback judge's chair towards his important files, which he kept under lock and key. Inserting the key, he turned the lock and rolled out the files marked "highly sensitive." There before him were the alphabetically filed papers relating to the Roswell event. He gathered the files up and placed them upon his well-polished desk. First, he reviewed his handwritten file status notes. Then he reviewed the legal memorandums that cataloged each step undertaken by the *Post*. He knew the hallmark of a competent professional attorney was preparation, preparation, and preparation. He would not attend a meeting with his boss without having the facts already known carefully reviewed. Once he had accomplished this, he grabbed the important parts of the file, tucked them under his arm, and began his march to the upper sanctum of the *Post*.

Bob Williston arrived at Charles' 10th floor suite and was cordially greeted by Ms. Billingsley. Without further ado she escorted Bob into the office and seated him in front of the editor's desk.

"What's happening now?" asked attorney Williston.

"Well," said the editor, "I just had a follow-up meeting with Casey Foster and Leah Anne Bailey. You may be pleased to note that the *Washington Post* just hired Ms. Bailey to work with us full-time on the Roswell story as a special science reporter/editor. During my meeting with them I was surprised to learn that there are apparently additional Roswell crash artifacts that were not turned over to the government. It appears that the most interesting find is a plastic binder containing a series of metallic discs. I'm wondering whether we need to inform the government about this additional crash debris. Secondly, should the *Post* turn these additional crash pieces over to the government for analysis? But thirdly, from the *Post*'s perspective, if we do turn these additional pieces over, can we secure an ongoing commitment from the government that our newspaper will remain as the primary source for release of new information in exchange? I suggest that you contact the same outside legal counsel used on this matter earlier to coordinate this with the government. What do you think, Bob?"

"One never knows for sure, but each new piece of crash debris may provide critical new information. And I agree that these items may need to be turned over. With your approval I will contact attorney Kalnikoff, whom we used the last time on the Roswell matter, and schedule a prompt meeting. After hearing his views, I will present you with a plan of proposed action for your review and approval. How does that sound to you?" asked Bob.

"I like that plan. Let me know what you learn." With that said Charles Evenridge stood up, circled his desk, shook Bob's hand, and walked him out of his office. Bob nodded to Ms. Billingsley on his way downstairs to his general counsel's office.

Arriving at his office, Bob sat at his large mahogany desk, looked out his window at the sprawling Washington morning traffic, and buzzed his longtime legal secretary, Renée. " Renée, do me a favor, please get outside legal counsel Charles Darwin Kalnikoff on the telephone. You may remember that he's with the law firm of Olson, Frank, and Sweeta. Let me know once you have them on the line. Thank you."

Within a few minutes, the ever-efficient Renée had attorney Kalnikoff holding for her boss.

"Hi Bob, any aliens taking you out to dinner tonight?" Charles smirked as they connected.

"Funny you should ask, Charlie, because that's exactly why I'm calling you. It seems that our intrepid group of newshounds at the *Post* have some additional Roswell artifacts that we have not yet been turned over to the government. I'm hoping you'll be able to assist us in retrieving these materials and turning the items over to the government. In exchange for the *Post*'s cooperation, it would like the continuing right to act as the primary source of news dissemination regarding this entire Roswell alien matter. Can you help?"

"Bob," responded Charles while his fingers almost tangibly danced across his calculator figuring future billable hours, "that's what I'm here for. I'll be happy to do anything I can do to assist. How about my stopping by your office tomorrow morning so we can come up with a preliminary battle plan? If you have the time after we finish our discussions let's have lunch at my club so you can bring me up to speed on what's current at the paper. How does that sound to you?"

"That's great. How about eleven?"

"Eleven's fine; I'll see you then. In the meantime, I'll review how we handled this situation the last time."

Once the phone call was complete, attorney Kalnikoff, without missing a beat, asked Renée to connect him with the United States Secretary of Defense, Ramsey Kalnikoff. While most mortals might find access to the United States Secretary of Defense impossible to obtain, a first son's access was usually immediate when the Secretary was in town. So it was, that 10 minutes after placing the call, the Secretary of Defense was connected with his son. Sure is nice to know people in the Capitol. Even better to be related.

"Hey, Dad," Charles quipped, "any Chinese sneaking across our borders undetected today? How about those miserable Russians or nasty Iranians? Are they making any threats today? And are those pricks up on the Hill trying to cut your defense budget again?"

"Wow," Ramsey responded after listening with half an ear. "Thanks for the heavy vote of confidence. I'm sure if there's any problem I can't solve, I can always call upon you for some suggestions. Now what the fuck do you want that's so pressing to call me during business hours?"

"I called because I have a new Roswell alien issue that I need to talk to you about privately. How about if I drop by the house for dinner with you and mom later this week?"

"Call your mom and work out the details. So while your billing the crap out of your poor unsuspecting client, I'll get back to real work defending American interests. See you soon son. Love you," he responded, meaning it, then hung up without further ado.

Charles, holding up his end of the bargain, dutifully called his mother and together scheduled dinner for Wednesday at 8 PM. No military time for good old mom. *Home cooking*, he thought, *yum*!

At the appointed time and place the Kalnikoff family sat down for a quiet dinner at home. Just like the good old days. Then Mom, like many other moms, began with her opening salvo: "Where's this new girlfriend you've been talking about? Don't you think it's time that Dad and I had a chance to meet her? It seems to me that you're old enough and established enough to put all this dating behind you and get married."

"I didn't realize that I'd be here tonight for dinner and grilling at the same time," Charles said quietly. "Of course, as I've told you both before, I've been dating Sue Pyledriver for quite some time. But it hasn't gotten far enough along to decide whether this will be permanent or not. What if I arrange for all of us to have dinner together next month so that you can meet Sue? I can't imagine that you won't like her. I think she's pretty special." Closing the door on that subject, Charles turned towards his father and, without saluting, explained the situation to his dad, including the retrieval of the discs and the *Post*'s demands.

"What a delightful subject to raise here at the dinner table. And to think that your generous client will turn over all of this perhaps critical security material just to keep informing the public about a newsworthy subject. How civic minded. But in any case, we need these materials, and I don't really care which news outlet gets first crack, especially within the confines of our home, if it's your client. I will check with the White House NSA staff tomorrow and give you a formal reply at your office. Of course, we won't put any of this in writing. How messy. Now let's complete our dinner while Mom continues to interrogate you concerning this girlfriend of yours. Hopefully she can at least read and write and knows which fork to use when it's time for the salad."

"Trust me, Dad, one look, one conversation, and you'll like Sue just fine," said Charles.

The next morning, as promised, Ramsey dialed up his son's law office. Charles picked up the receiver and asked, "Do we have permission to proceed as discussed, Dad?"

"Yes, it's a go. I'll have the government assist in picking up the additional materials to take into custody. Please advise your client that sensitive matters that affect national security may not be published without prior government approval. The government will appoint a censor to review all articles and photographs prior to their publication. Have your team available at your office tomorrow morning at 9 AM. I will make arrangements to have them picked up for their transfer out to Roswell. Copy?"

"That sounds fine to me, with the exception of a censor. As I'm sure you may have read at some point, the US Constitution permits and encourages freedom of speech. And nothing would be as worthy of designation in that category as news confirmation of an alien presence on Earth, including a return trip. However, for the time being, my client will accept these terms and work with the United States government as you have outlined. For your planning purposes, I understand the *Washington Post* will be sending Casey Foster and Leah Anne Bailey to Roswell. Once there, we will also need to will pick up Lone Wolf's grandson, Tecote, who's located on the Mescalero Apache reservation. These three individuals know where to find the materials we discussed. Let me formally thank you for your assistance on this matter, sir."

"OK, son, cut the shit. Let's move this forward. Remember you owe me big time. I'll call it in when I really need it. *Capisce*?"

"Absolutely," responded Charles. He thanked his dad, hung up the phone, bit his teeth like a race horse all doped up and ready for the "Run for the Roses" at the Kentucky Derby, then dialed up the *Washington Post* and asked to speak to Robert Williston, general counsel. "Bob, I'm pleased to inform you," he puffed, "that following a series of meetings and phone calls to the proper authorities I have obtained continuing permission at the highest levels of the national government for the *Washington Post* to continue as the primary news source on the Roswell story. In return, you will turn over to the government all new materials about Roswell. I have made arrangements for the government to pick up Casey Foster and Leah Anne Bailey at my offices tomorrow morning. Can you please make arrangements for them to be here at my law office 9 AM?"

"Home run; you're a miracle worker. Thanks, Charles, that's great news. I'll have everyone available tomorrow morning at your offices. I knew I could count on you!" Robert knew his editor would be thrilled with the enhanced lead press source confirmed. That should help to sell a shit pile of papers with their tag alongside advertising revenues. Perhaps even some news awards might accrue to the *Post* if their reporting was up to snuff.

Casey and Leah Anne were notified of the decision and began planning their trip. Each packed a small suitcase and presented themselves at Charles Darwin Kalnikoff's office the next morning. This time, instead of hiding from government agents, they were swept up in a protective web of assistance. Leading the government task force was none other than their prior pursuer, Jon Boy. He greeted them formally in their attorney's office and then led the way downstairs and out into heavy Washington morning traffic. Waiting at the curb, blocking morning rush hour traffic, two black, armored government GMC SUVs with a security detail were ready for action. In went the passengers and out went the SUVs. A short ride later everyone was discharged without incident at the CIA's private air center.

Up into the air lumbered the CIA's transport plane, cleared through the military transportation system for the flight to Roswell. Since the government now deemed this an important mission, the transport plane was shadowed by two Air Force jets. At this stage, Casey and Leah Anne had become necessary members of the world's preparation for its returning alien visitors. Military and secret service security teams were assigned to protect them. A far different situation than before. Leah Anne no longer needed to worry that being scared would lead her to peeing down her professional, well-dressed leg. Five hours after leaving the congested nation's capital, the military aircraft set down at the site of the prior Roswell Air Force base. Disembarking from the aircraft, Jon Boy was met by General Sealls, the base's commanding officer. Tagging along at his side, wearing an honorary Air Force insignia on his shirt, was none other than Tecote. He had already been picked up along with his friendly, tail wagging, beloved Muffy the mutt. It appeared that Muffy was also sporting an Air Force in insignia on her doggie collar. How spiffy.

General Sealls' remarks were brief. "I have assigned two Blackhawk stealth helicopters and a crew of eight armed Marines to accompany you. I don't suspect that you'll run into any resistance, but it always pays to be prepared." With that, Jon Boy thanked the general and herded his three human passengers and one dog to the waiting Blackhawk helicopters.

Once everyone was on board, the stealth helicopters churned up their rotor blades, hovered low over the ground, and then sped off towards the barely visible horizon. Two stops were planned on this expedition. The first would be to retrieve the non-controversial metallic crash debris pieces hidden away by Casey Foster. Those items were located near the point where Casey, Leah Anne, Lone Wolf, and Tecote had camped the night prior to their being picked up by military forces. Having exact coordinates stored in the onboard computer from the earlier mission made short work of locating a landing area and disgorging the landing party. Casey then led the way down the canyon towards the spot where he had buried the crash debris. Four Marines, automatic weapons at the ready, went along in case any saboteurs would try to intervene in the process. Nothing un-usual occurred, and Casey made short work of recovering those items. A grizzled Marine sergeant produced a metallic security case to store the recovered alien crash materials, which were deposited inside, carefully locked, and handcuffed to his wrist. Casey, of course, photographed the Blackhawk helicopters, the accompanying military personnel, the attend-ing Pentagon personnel, and Leah Anne and himself. *Certainly a little self puffing won't hurt our careers*, he thought. *It's good to be a household celebrity.* Casey also photographed the site where the materials had been reburied as well as the pieces themselves once they were uncovered. These photos were quickly loaded into his laptop computer, and, with a stroke of the keyboard with a powerful satellite uplink, the materials were forward instantly to the *Washington Post's* photo lab in Washington, DC. Nice to be prepared.

Having accomplished their first task, Jon Boy, with Tecote's assistance, directed the attack helicopters to Bison Wells. Upon arriving, the team debarked, and Tecote led the way back to the site where he had reburied the plastic-like binder with its enclosed circular metal discs. The military authorities had taken the precaution of sending a hazardous materials experts along on the expedition. It seems that there was some concern as to whether or not the binder might be radioactive, contain alien bacteria, be booby trapped, contain explosive materials, or otherwise present a serious hazard. Each of the personnel with the exception of Tecote and one armed Marine stayed stationed at the canyon floor. Tecote, with his escort in tow, carefully labored up the side of the canyon wall until they reached the high point where he had reburied the binder behind some protruding boulders. No one would have found this location without Tecote's guidance. At Tecote's direction the hazmat expert carefully dug down to the covered binder and brought it out into the daylight. A quick glance disclosed no immediate danger and the binder, along with its enclosed metal discs, was carried down to the awaiting expeditionary force. From a safe distance Casey carefully photographed the plastic binder with its two sizes of internally-stored metal discs. Again, as was his practice, these photographs were immediately loaded into his laptop computer and transmitted to the *Post*'s photo lab for further processing. The military hazard expert loaded the binder into an additional metal container, which was locked and handcuffed to a second Marine for the helicopter ride back to the Roswell Air Force base.

The recovered metallic spacecraft debris proved interesting and further confirmation of the July 2, 1947, alien spacecraft crash. But the metallic pieces alone held no great significance now that the government had mostly reconstructed the craft. However, the binder and its enclosed metal discs were of a completely different magnitude of importance. Speculation ran high among the retrieval party concerning what the metal discs were designed for and whether each might contain information that could be extracted. From a purely preliminary visual inspection, the discs appeared similar to 21st century DVDs or CDs. The two different sizes might relate to different types of recording equipment or formatting. They speculated that the discs might be manuals describing the operation of the spaceship's operating systems, documentation of the intended objectives of the alien visitors to Roswell, or perhaps even something akin to a galactic encyclopedia. Obviously, great care would be necessary to decipher the contents of the discs. Casey Foster speculated that these discs were probably utilized at or near the bridge of the crashed alien spacecraft. Since the US government had painstakingly reconstructed the downed spacecraft, it was possible scientific experts could learn the location where these discs were utilized and, in so doing, learn how to decode and decipher their contents.

Once the materials were secured, everyone boarded the two stealth helicopters and they darted low over the surface of the Roswell desert just as the sun started to descend over the horizon. Arriving at the Roswell air base, the helicopters one by one squatted on their landing pads. General Sealls was present to greet the retrieval team and take possession of the recovered materials. It was his job to make certain that these new items received the appropriate scientific attention. He had expert scientists on hand to begin the process.

Casey Foster, Leah Anne, and Tecote were escorted inside the facility and treated like important guests. This time there were no automatic weapons pointed in their direction, no handcuffs behind their backs, no interrogation, and no direct or implied threats. General Sealls shook hands all around and thanked each member of the recovery team for doing their patriotic duty to America. Dinner was scheduled for 19:30 hours, or 7:30 PM by ordinary civilian time. Eating, drinking, storytelling, and laughing were the order of business. General Sealls, a lifetime military man, gladly participated in the celebration, knowing that the best cause for optimism was to maintain a strong defense. How effective that defense would be against an alien species with much more advanced technology was unknown. Still, it was better to be as prepared as possible than to not be prepared at all. When the dinner was complete the guests were each escorted to their accommodations, where they would remain until tomorrow morning's flight back to Washington.

Leah Anne had been careful to take thorough notes throughout the trip. She had also asked Casey to provide her with copies of the photographs he had taken. Now, alone in her quarters and with the expertise she had gained from years of hard work in Washington, step-by-step she prepared a detailed outline for the first of many articles that the *Washington Post* would publish under her byline. She hoped her articles would help educate the public about what was happening and what to expect. It was a complex and daunting task. With a pencil clenched between her teeth for later editing, Leah Anne tapped out on her laptop keyboard the first outline and draft opening paragraphs of her news article. A sparkle in her eyes and a smile upon her red lips were the outward signs that this was the work she was meant to perform. This was what all of her education and training were meant to lead her towards. She wanted to be the vessel through which Earth's people would learn about the opportunities and risks ahead. Where, she wondered, would this take her? Where would the story lead? What would they learn? How would to story unfold? All of these and a multitude of other questions were floating around inside her head. *Yep*, she thought to herself, *I'm on the right track now. I'll finish this part of my task and then go looking for Casey to share a few nighttime laughs.*

Two hours later, Leah Anne stood before Casey's door, a smile on her face and a raincoat wrapped loosely around her. She gently tapped the wooden door with her knuckles. Casey peered through the keyhole and then opened the door to admit her.

"Nice to see you. What's up?" he asked. Leah Anne stepped through the door and pushed it closed until she heard it click behind her. Then, with a strange, devilish smile, she dropped her raincoat to the floor, leaving her stark naked. Casey's eyes moved slowly from Leah Anne's face downward. *Dessert has arrived*, he thought. He barely had time to internally say "yippee" before Leah Anne jumped into his open arms. *It's good to be working at the* Washington Post *and on a road trip*, both thought simultaneously. *Let the good times roll!*

CHAPTER 4

COMMITTEE MEETINGS

As the alien mother ship traveled on its relentless journey towards Earth's solar system, Earth's leaders continued their preparations. The Group of 8, as they had been named, consisted of the main power nations of Earth. This group consisted of the United States, Russia, China, Germany, France, Israel, India, and a United Nations representative. They moved forward with planned committee meetings to produce action papers on a variety of important subjects such as diplomacy, communications, security, site selection, and public preparation. Each committee was tasked with preparing a preliminary written report on its appointed subject for presentation to the Group of 8 within 20 days. Once the reports were finalized they would be placed into action. Time to get organized, Earth.

The Group of 8 selected London as the location for the committee meetings, and so the committee personnel began to arrive one delegation member at a time. Time to hunker down for the real work that lay ahead. Black limousines and secure SUV convoys brought representatives from Heathrow airport into the heart of London. Some members settled into their lodgings at the Mayfair Hotel, while others choose the Grosvenor House. Later arrivals were ferried to the Kensington Hotel. A few later arrivals stayed at the Dorchester Hotel, and the remainder were split between the Savoy Hotel and the Haymarket Hotel. Rooms and meeting areas had been set aside for their use, paid for by their various government sponsors. In short, those present intended to work hard and play hard at government expense while living pretty high on the hog. While the formal meetings were to start on the coming Monday, all groups and delegations were in

London by Sunday noon for a pre-meeting get-together. This preliminary shindig was sponsored by the British government and would be led by Sir Mark Justin Lyall Grant, the British permanent representative to the United Nations. Naturally, based upon his background and standing as one of the British aristocracy, he arranged for the preliminary get-together to be held at the exemplary Claridge Hotel in the heart of London's Mayfair district. British tradition demanded that important events should be kicked off with High Tea at The Claridge, for which it was famous. Sir Grant would play host while the hotel staff served the committee members delicately-formed scones, attended with appropriate jellies and jams, topped with dollops of clotted cream, little wedge-shaped finger sandwiches, and tiny luxury desserts, all accompanied by appropriately British steaming Earl Grey tea with a side of organic milk for the sophisticated. High Tea would wind down with an assortment of quality cigars made available for those who wanted to indulge themselves further while preparing to hear Sir Grant's opening remarks.

"Gentlemen and ladies," began Sir Grant, "it is with great pleasure that I welcome you to our beloved London, where we are tasked to prepare committee reports for our Group of 8 concerning our expected extra terrestrial visitors. We here on our quiet British Isles have been welcoming foreign visitors and dignitaries for over 1000 years. This experience has made us uniquely ready for this special task. Everything that we have accomplished as a human civilization on our home world will be on display. Therefore, your committee work must be undertaken diligently, carefully, and with resolve. I know that each of you will put forth your best efforts. History has taught us that when we work together great things can be accomplished. This is one of those times. We must put aside our special interests and plan for our worldwide future, hand in hand with one another. It is a time of great expectations and risks. There are a plethora of exciting possibilities. If we work together and stand united, this will become a watershed moment in Earth's history. But if we fail to stand together, surely we will fall separately, one at a time. One of our illustrious former world leader, President Franklin D. Roosevelt, once told his nation, 'We have nothing to fear but fear itself.' Our situation is somewhat similar. While we need to take precautions, we also have a great opportunity to learn more about our universe. So we are here to meet, plan, and prepare committee reports to provide our Group of 8 leaders within the next 20 days. Those reports, we hope, when acted upon, will move all of us safely forward into the future. I know that with your best professional efforts we will succeed.

"Tomorrow morning at 9 AM," Sir Grant continued, "each of our committees will initiate its work. I have arranged for each of the committees to have a secure location to meet. I also have appointed a committee chairman to facilitate each group. Let me take a moment of your time to announce where and how we will proceed. First, I have arranged for Sir Peter John Westmacott, British Ambassador to the United States, to act as chairman of the diplomacy team, meeting at Clarence House here in London. Sir Westmacott is here with us today. After tea he will be pleased to meet with those members of the Diplomacy Committee present to coordinate your first meeting. Secondly, I have arranged for Sir George Young, leader of our British House of Commons and Lord Privy Seal, to act as chairman of the Communications Committee, with meetings at Llwynywermod House in Wales. Similarly, Sir Young is also present with us to meet with the Communications Committee to coordinate the initial meeting. Thirdly, I have arranged for Lord Strathclyde, British leader of the House of Lords and Chancellor of the Duchy of Lancaster, to act as chairman of the of the Site Selection Committee, which will meet at Anmer Hall in Norfolk on the Sandringham estate in Norfolk. Likewise, Lord Strathclyde is here to coordinate the first meeting of the Site Selection Committee. Fourthly, I have arranged for Mr. Phillip Hammond, British Secretary of State for Defense, to meet with the Defense Committee. He is here today for his first meeting with committee members to make arrangements for tomorrow's meeting. And finally, I have made arrangements for Mr. Jeremy Hunt, our British Secretary of State for Culture and Media, to act as chairman of our Public Preparedness Committee. The Public Preparedness meetings will be held at Kensington Palace here in London.

"Now, gentlemen and ladies, it is time for all of us to launch into our sacred endeavors. I wish all of you the best of luck. Hear, hear, I say. God save the Queen!" Concluding his remarks, Sir Grant returned to his chair at the head of the table while his guests completed their tea and enjoyed their fine imported cigars. Tomorrow, work would begin in earnest.

At 9 AM sharp the committees were each gaveled to order by their pre-selected committee chairman. Sir Peter Westmacott addressed the Diplomacy Committee at the Clarence House in London proper. Around the polished mahogany conference table sat an interesting accumulation of experts in international diplomacy. Many knew each other from prior professional postings. The committee members immersed themselves in protocol matters as they discussed the level of contact to be expected from their alien visitors. It was apparent to all that the Redexian leaders would not be present on the mother ship or any shuttle craft. Rather, Earth could expect the aliens to be led by their starship commanders, perhaps regional governors and science officers. Therefore, the Diplomacy Committee members would plan for meetings between ambassador-level personnel, military leaders with diplomatic experience, and relevant science experts. High level national Earth leaders could be made available later, if needed. The committee also explored the topics which they felt might be the subject of discussion. The unusual aspect to this diplomacy planning was that there was no agenda. There was no "problem" that needed to be resolved, no known treaties that need to be prepared, and no pending issue concerning trade, duties, or taxation. In short, there was no agenda yet, and the parties would have to start from scratch once they met face to ugly, bulging face with the aliens. There was perhaps one exception of merit. How would Earth inform the returning aliens that their two earlier alien "visitors" were deceased? Worse still were the questions of whether proper medical attention had been provided and whether their remains had been preserved with proper honors and formalities. How would they explain that both aliens had died with one body frozen and the other more or less pickled? The committee members felt the best approach to this knotty issue would be that they had been totally unaware of the proper medical treatment to administer and the standards for handling remains of their distinguished foreign visitors. Accordingly, Earth had done its best and had eventually preserved the remains in two different formats until they could be collected by their comrades. These shortcomings would be explained to their visitors in a most solemn manner, while at the same time asking for understanding and forgiveness.

The committee further discussed the tone that should be used in any talks with the new alien arrivals. All present acknowledged that the anticipated visitors would in fact have far superior technological abilities than the host planet, Earth. This dictated that the chosen diplomats present themselves as being polite, discrete, helpful, and welcoming. They hoped to establish a case for mutual recognition, honoring each species' traditions and offering to engage in a peaceful exchange of ideas and knowledge. They had no idea what the aliens had in mind or whether they could do anything about the aliens' plans for Earth, whatever they might be.

Other diplomatic problems included choosing a site for the initial meetings, the language for communication, the level of diplomatic interaction, whether these initial meetings would be formal or informal, whether or not to serve food and or drink, the matter of dress code, and the level of politeness and formality, such as whether touching such as shaking of hands would be proper. As a collective group, the committee discussed the history of interactions at the diplomatic level between new civilizations. Coming to mind immediately were those instances when Europeans met for the first time with the native populations of the New World. In those situations, the Europeans considered themselves to be far superior and the native populations to be grossly inferior. Europeans in that instance decided to slaughter the native population and steal as much of their treasure as possible. Not a good omen. Perhaps the interstellar traveling alien visitors would be more generous. Well, they were probably more socially advanced. Or maybe they would feel the same about Earthlings as Europeans felt about the New World's native inhabitants.

The diplomats also understood that they would need to make arrangements for tight security during the meetings. The visiting aliens must be protected at all costs from any physical dangers. Injuries to visiting aliens might result in deadly retaliations. So the committee continued its deliberations, each member providing his or her thoughts and together generating outlines for proposed plans of action. There was no exact precedent to follow. There was no history of similar contacts. Instead, it was a blank slate on which they hoped to write a safe chapter of first interactions between different species from different worlds. And so, day by day, Sir Peter Westmacott led his committee members in discussing the important issues before them. They worked diligently to develop a proposed diplomatic overview to be shared with the Group of 8. The 20 day deadline would approach quickly. Better finish.

Starting also at 9 AM, Sir George Young gaveled his Communications Committee to order at the Llwynywrmod House in Wales. He told the Communication Committee that there seemed to be two major decisions before them. The first would be the language in which Earth would communicate with the approaching alien visitors. The second would be how best to decipher the incoming radio transmissions and, later, the more difficult face-to-face communication. As to the first matter of selecting a language to be used by Earthlings, he solicited suggestions from the assembled committee members.

One of the French delegation members rose first and spoke eloquently that French, in his opinion, was the most sophisticated and melodious language on Earth. He felt that using French would imply a level of high intellect to the approaching visitors. Next, Helmet Schmidt from Germany rose to suggest the use of German as an inspiring and forceful language. He mentioned how German had, throughout the ages, been the language of science and history; it would serve their purposes well. The Russian committee member Nikita Smirnoff thought that Russian might be best since the language spanned all of Europe and further west to the Pacific coast. The Chinese delegate Ling Song Chow impressed upon the committee that Mandarin Chinese was the most widely used language on Earth. She further indicated that its written characters were a thing of beauty to behold. Neither the Israeli or Indian delegates attempted to garner support for their home languages. Both these delegates realized the chances for their languages success were limited at best and might be scorned at worst.

After listening intently to these presentations, Sir George Young lightly tapped his gavel for order and stood to address the committee. "A number of committee members have made a solid case for the use of their home language for a means of communication. However, let me note for this committee a few important considerations. English serves as the most common first or secondary language throughout the globe. English has become today's primary language of science and history. English is the language that we utilized to broadcast our first formal communication to our incoming alien visitors. English is the language that the alien visitors will hear upon their return to Roswell, New Mexico, to retrieve their unfortunately now deceased 'brothers in exploration.' Given all of these factors, I suggest that we choose English as our primary language of communication. However, as a matter of fairness I will now hand out blank slips of paper to each of our 15 committee members. I asked that each of you write down the language which you think we should use for our communication with the aliens. Once these slips are returned I will tabulate the responses and advise you all of the results. Then we can continue in this fashion until we make our decision."

Once all committee members had spoken in favor of their local language, the actual votes indicated a nearly unanimous decision to utilize English as the language of communication with the aliens. After a little more discussion and cajoling, English became the official choice of the committee for communicating with the aliens. If present, even William Shakespeare, whoever he really was, would have been proud of this decision to use English. A truly universal language.

The much trickier issue was how to accurately decipher the incoming radio transmissions and communicate face-to-face with the alien visitors. Dr. James Westermonne, as the American committee representative, stood to address the committee. "As I am sure you are all aware, I was the first to decipher the incoming alien radio messages. To accomplish this I utilized a series of specialized algorithms that I invented, which I then ran through the Chicago University super computer. After many trials and quite a few errors I produced a reasonable translation of the aliens' incoming message. With our combined language expertise funneled through the worlds' major super computers, I anticipate that we can together invent a fairly decent methodology for decoding alien messages. I also suspect that a species far enough advanced to travel among the stars will have researched and solved foreign language translation issues as well. Perhaps our visitors have already learned to speak one of our languages. In that case, I suspect they have developed something like a universal translator. Furthermore, I expect that by now our returning visitors will be monitoring our radio and television broadcasts. I feel confident that they will know how to communicate with us. For our part I suggest that we as a committee start work on what I will refer to as an English/alien cross dictionary with usage guidelines. Of course, the more communications we receive from our alien visitors the better we may become at this task. Repetition is everything in decoding communications. *Nu?"*

Next, the Israeli committee member rose to address the group. "We," he said, "have made it a national prerogative to be able to receive, record, and decipher messages from everywhere around the world. For us to survive as a nation we have had to develop skill in the art of languages; not only spoken language, but written language and code transmissions as well. I, for one, concur with Dr. Westermone that we should all work together to develop our best cross dictionary and usage guidelines for our anticipated visitors. And we will need to train a few individuals to act as our expert interpreters for direct communication with the aliens."

The other committee members all took a shot at providing input and suggestions. After a while it seemed clear that on this committee everyone was more or less on the same page. English would be the primary language for transmitting information to the aliens, and they would all work together to establish a cross dictionary, develop guidelines for decoding incoming messages, and train interpreters.

Situated in Anmer Hall on the grounds of the Sandringham Estate in Norfolk, Lord Strathclyde called to order his committee on Site Selection. While his committee members arrived dressed informally, Lord Strathclyde was more comfortable in addressing his committee members in formal attire. Perhaps centuries of service to King and Court had bred in him a sense of formality. Style, language, and presentation were matters of great importance to him. Standing at attention in front of his committee, Lord Strathclyde picked up his morning sherry glass and tapped it gently with his solid sterling serving spoon. "It is a great pleasure of mine," he said, "to address this august committee concerning selection of a site at which to greet our incoming alien guests. I would like for us to review possible off-world and then on-world locations for our meetings. As to the first of these matters, off-world locations, I would like to hear first the comments of the Russian delegates, Chinese delegates, and American delegates, since they are in fact our major space-faring nations. Mr. Yankelovich, could you tell us please your views concerning possible off-world locations for a meeting with the aliens?"

Mr. Yankelovich stood before the committee proudly displaying upon his lapel both his aircraft flying wing designation and his Soviet lapel pin indicating a person involved in their cosmonaut program. "Well, gentlemen," he said with his Russian accent, "realistically speaking we have only two off-world locations to consider as meeting sites. One would be the International Space Station, or ISS, and the second would be on Earth's moon. As to the later, although we have had many satellites mapping the moon and a few manned moon landings in the early 1970s, Earth does not presently have a permanent base on the moon. Furthermore, there is no likelihood of having one available within the next months. So if we are to consider any off-world location it would need to be the International Space Station." Everyone present concurred without the need for extended discussion. The moon was a no-go.

Mr. Omer Hoe, a long time executive at America's NASA, a computer expert of some note, and, when not working, an expert golfer except for his wicked golf slice, gained the attention of Sir Strathclyde. With a slight patrician nod from the chair he began to address the committee. "While many of us are all greatly impressed with the ISS, I think we must consider this site location in relation to the sophistication of the approaching alien visitors. These aliens were sufficiently technologically advanced to fly a spacecraft to our planet in 1947 when we were developing first generation jet aircraft. Now the aliens have progressed to piloting their mother ship 24 light years from their home world to our solar system—quite an enormous accomplishment. Now let's compare that impartially to the ISS. The ISS is, in fact, a cobbled-together series of pieces and parts that has no formal space to hold meetings, no artificial gravity to hold participants in place, no proper bathroom facilities—which would certainly get my attention after a long trip—and is entirely lacking any reasonable food or beverage serving facilities. In short, it's not up to snuff. I am afraid that any attempted meeting on the International Space Station will only highlight our backward ways."

Looking about the conference room, Lord Strathclyde could see the near unanimous nodding of heads, signifying this group's understanding that the International Space Station was not impressive enough to use as a meeting location. "Well then, I take it we are all agreed that we will need Earth locations for our meetings," he said. It was easy to see a universal agreement to that statement from the committee. Therefore, he launched into his second level of inquiry by asking, "In that case, ladies and gentlemen, where would you suggest as meeting locations here on planet Earth?"

Various world capitals and historically significant locations were suggested one at a time. Other locations of incredible scenic beauty were brought to the table for discussion. There was some feeling that a location at an important port city might be a great choice since two thirds of the Earth's surface was water. Finally, all present seem to agree that Roswell, New Mexico, would be one of the locations that the aliens would want to visit first to pick up their dead brother explorers.

The committee members also discussed issues of gravity, air pressure, disease, microbes, and security. From a social perspective they considered communication, food, drink, and entertainment issues. All present eventually leaned towards an initial meeting in Roswell, with follow-up diplomatic meetings to occur in one or more well-developed world capitals such as Washington, DC, London, Moscow, or Beijing. Almost as an afterthought one of the committee members volunteered that perhaps the alien visitors would have some suggestions concerning where any meetings should take place. Lord Strathclyde didn't like the idea that the alien visitors might want to choose a location for meetings. *How rude*, he thought. *We would be the hosts, after all. Don't hosts get to choose where and when to meet?*

At 9 AM sharp on Monday morning, Mr. Philip Hammond, British Secretary of State for Defense, called to order his committee on defense at the Sandringham House in Norfolk. His committee, unlike the others, was comprised mostly of high ranking military officers and secret service operatives such as the CIA, Mossad, KGB, and Chinese undercover services. These folks knew that talk alone could be insufficient to win the day. Rather, these officers controlled enough military might and security data to formulate both defensive and offensive postures. On the whole, this group could be termed the Hawks of Earth. They might hold the answer to Earth's survival if the aliens turned out to be hostile. But civilians were necessary to remind these military hawks that it was always easier to unleash the winds of war than to rein them in for peaceful purposes. Addressing his crowd of militarily-dressed and heavily decorated personnel, Mr. Hammond started the discussion by saying, "We have been requested to provide the Group of 8 with Earth's defense and security analysis. Each of you has expertise regarding how your nation provides a proper and effective defense for its people. Uniting together as one Earth defensive force, we should have formidable assets available to defend our planet's interests. Nevertheless, in reviewing our defensive assets and combined military might, we must remember that it is more likely than not to be greatly inferior to that of our visitors. I mention that since it is apparent that their technology is far superior to ours. We must proceed with caution. Now I would like to hear your professional military opinions about Earth's defense situation."

General Chow Ling Wu of the People's Republic of China gained the chair's attention. "For we Chinese," he began, "with over 1.3 billion people to defend and a vast landscape to protect, we have made the matter of national security paramount. We also have a long history of other nations and people attempting to attack and control our people and revise our borders. Thus, we have been required to develop over time many different strategies for projecting our power and using military force. Here today we have representatives of the world's major naval, air, land, and nuclear military resources. We would be a formidable combined military force against any invading attackers. Nevertheless, having said that, an alien society that is 500, 1000, or 3000 years more advanced technologically might be sufficiently well-armed to scoff at our feeble military resources. So I strongly concur with Mr. Hammond's recommendation that we discuss this matter carefully and proceed with caution. If we try to project our combined military might against the aliens unsuccessfully, we may suffer grave and irreparable retaliation. We have nowhere else to go. We are bound to Earth."

In turn, each of the Defense Committee members blustered for a moment regarding their military wherewithal and then withdrew into a position of caution. Eventually, it came to pass that the Defense Committee developed a worldwide defense plan as well as a worldwide "hideout plan" to disperse and hide as much of their assets, materials, and people for a long-term rear guard resistance. In this instance the vast manpower resources of Earth's 7 billion people meant we could hide and fight for a long time.

Mr. Jeremy Hunt, the British Secretary of State for Media, hunkered down at Kensington Palace in London with the Public Preparedness Committee. It was the job of this committee to provide information to the world's population on how to be prepared for the alien visit but in terms that would not result in public rioting or civil disobedience. As Mr. Hunt looked out upon his committee members he noticed that they were in large part informally attired. These were not people bound by military tradition or diplomatic corps procedures. Rather, it was a collection of media stars who displayed the temperament necessary to connect with the masses. These were the folks who would be seen on the television nightly news reports, addressing the public regarding major national and international matters. They prepared articles for newspapers and news magazines that gathered the world's attention. In short, media personalities had learned over time how to sell, diet remedies to obese people, and vehicles of all makes and models to a world population hungry for consumption. Now their task would be to both inform the public as well as keep them from any detrimental outbursts. There would be a fine line between what the public wanted to know and what they would be allowed to know. So the Public Preparedness Committee needed to search for ways to look good, sound good, and project strength when in fact, as far as they knew, they might be merely tools in their visitors' tool chest. The committee started to meet and talk, meet and talk, quibble, argue, and prevaricate endlessly while seeking answers. This went on for days. Only as the time to finalize a report began to run out did they scribble down a proposed message for the public. This made Mr. Hunt's job regarding public preparation through media presentations quite difficult. *Well, someone had to chair this committee*, thought Mr. Hunt. *So it might as well be me. Boy, I feel lucky now!*

The days passed, and the committees met on a continuing basis to formulate outlines and plans. Discussions were generally polite. Outlines, points of contention, details for discussion, and the draft reports were circulated among each committee for review and discussion. Slowly, one by one, the committees prepared final reports. Each report was signed and delivered to the Group of 8 for further review. Onward, Mother Earth. Get your act together before it's too late.

CHAPTER 5

BYLINE, LEAH ANNE BAILEY

Imagine resting in a dark, quiet, peaceful place with drifting clouds composed of thin, wispy, slow-moving puffs of moisture passing overhead without rhyme or reason. Then, far in the distance, a subtle beeping noise appears. Ignore it and continue drifting from one wisp to another, clutching ever tighter to the soft, light yellow blanket that surrounds you. Then again, closer and more insistent, another soft beeping noise, and then another. Forget it. Ignore it. Hold tight, roll to the side, perhaps give a small sigh, drift on. Again: closer, more insistent, louder. The beeping is now a buzzing, then a ring. A ringing that won't leave, growing ever louder and insisting on grabbing your attention. Suddenly, one unhappy, slowly focusing blue blinker pops open, and Leah Anne gazed halfheartedly at the softly lit alarm clock on her nightstand.

" Hello, IVEE, what time is it?" Leah Anne Bailey inquired.

"Good morning, the time is 6:45 AM," responded IVEE.

"Hello, IVEE, what date is it?"

" Today is Monday, November 15, 2015."

Well, Leah Anne thought to herself, *this speech recognition software has some practical uses. But it still doesn't solve the problem of waking you from a sound sleep. Crap! It's my first day of work at the* Washington Post*! I better get up and get moving!* With that, Leah Anne tossed her blanket aside, slipped her feet onto the solid hardwood floor, and began shuffling over to the bathroom in her one bedroom walkup apartment.

While twisting on the hot water faucet in the shower, Leah Anne leaned over and glanced into the mirror above the sink. Staring back was a reflection of her bright blue eyes, freckled face, and long, wavy red hair. Is this the face, she wondered, that would soon launch a series of well-thought out news articles in the *Washington Post* regarding the Roswell alien event? Perhaps the beginning of an answer to that question would start to appear later today. A quick splash of soothing water, a bit of Dial soap lather, followed by an even quicker shake like a chocolate Labrador retriever after hauling in a downed duck, a robust toweling, and Leah Anne trotted into her working lady, walk-in closet. *Time for some professional dress attire*, she thought to herself as she grabbed a dark blue suit with matching accessories. Off the rack came a pair a sensible walking shoes. Then an application of a thin coat of makeup prior to encircling her neck with a thin string of faux pearls. Now she was ready for a wakeful glance at the clock, which confirmed it was time to get moving to the subway station. Dancing light-footed through the kitchen and passing by the refrigerator, she grabbed a container of strawberry yogurt and its nearby companion, a pleasingly crisp Macintosh apple. Both were snatched up and placed in Leah Anne's folding brown leather attaché case as she sauntered towards her front door. Out the door, down the steps, and into the opening morning daylight.

Leah Anne was surrounded by familiar sounds coming from the nearby National Zoo. She was quite fond of her peaceful neighborhood, nestled in Woodley by the National Zoo and Rock Creek Park. When she was in the mood and had the time she loved to go for a bike ride or a jog in the park. When she wasn't working out, there were plenty of nearby shops, boutiques, and restaurants within walking distance for plain old fun. But today was different. Today was the first day at her new job. She did not want to arrive late for work. Two blocks away, at the corner of Connecticut Avenue and Woodley Road, was the entrance to the Washington Metro subway system, sometimes referred to locally as the Underground. Leah Anne considered herself a connoisseur of the Metro system, having studied it carefully. On most weekdays she could count herself as one of the

750,000 or so local citizens whizzing around underground in an effort to avoid the crowded, congested, and noisy daily automobile traffic overhead. Down the 34 concrete steps, through the revolving gate. Leah Anne swiped her monthly Metro system card and moved towards the red line transit platform. A quick glance to the overhead information center showed in both English and Spanish that the next train would be arriving shortly. The crowd pressed forward in anticipation towards red line subway car. The doors popped open on arrival, exactly on schedule, and in flowed Washington's working masses. Swaying effortlessly along underground in the cavernous concrete tunnel, one could see the well-lit tracks and the upcoming DuPont Circle station. Stopping as planned, the doors slid open again; a few passengers departed, and many more, traveling towards central Washington DC, crammed their way on board. Some three minutes later Leah Anne's Metro subway car arrived at her destination at Farragut North Station, where she and another 50 or so passengers stepped out upon the welcoming exit platform. For those not familiar with the Washington Metro system, it was actually a thing of beauty as well as a marvel of engineering and architecture. Glance at the vaulted lighted ceiling. Nice, really nice. Leah Anne climbed up the neatly-scrubbed tile stairs leading to the Metro station exit into the heart of downtown DC proper.

Above ground, many well-dressed, briefcase-carrying professionals from all over the world descended each weekday morning to make a difference and earn their daily bread. Today would be the start of a new adventure for Leah Anne, an adventure that she had been preparing for since her first day of kindergarten at suburban Hubbard Woods school in Winnetka. This preparation had continued throughout her education and early employment years. Now the time had arrived to step up and show herself, as well as the world, what she could bring to the table. She started walking east on 6th Street. Passing one of the many newsstands, she grabbed and paid for a copy of that morning's *Washington Post*. She continued walking until she turned left on 15th Street NW, where after a quick half block later she arrived at the front entryway of the imposing *Washington Post* office building. Just like a tourist on their first trip to the capital, Leah Anne pulled out her smart phone and clicked off a few photos of the entrance. She even took a selfie. Then to even her own amazement she buttonholed another incoming *Post* employee and politely asked to have her photograph taken on the front steps of the building. A big bright smile, a turn to the right and then left, hands on hips, briefcase clutched in hand, and Leah Anne was captured with time, date, and place on her smart phone. Later in the day these photos were posted to her personal Facebook page. Life, it seemed, was good for those willing to grab hold and pull for all they were worth.

Up the stairs, into the lobby, and pressing forward with all deliberate speed, Leah Anne arrived at her brand new office. There to greet her stood the equally well dressed Ms. Kelly Oliveri, her ready-to-please secretary. Both hoped for a long run of decisive, attention-grabbing news stories.

This "Roswell thing," as Leah Anne referred to it, should have long legs and a gripping story of major significance. All she had to do was to find her voice and meticulously grind that story into the public's collective consciousness. Leah Anne would use her new voice at the *Post*, a daily newspaper noted worldwide for its exceptional editorial depth and international news, to grab some attention. The newspaper had a reputation for being one of the most recognized, well-respected, trusted media platforms in any kind of journalism. It was the type of journalism where its reporters contributed on an ongoing basis to the world's knowledge of unfolding newsworthy stories. The Roswell thing certainly fit within this category. She intended to work hard, think outside the box, and produce a string of fascinating articles to prepare her public for the upcoming alien get-together.

Just as a marathon starts with the first stride, Leah Anne began her quest by settling in at her desk and reviewing her meticulously-prepared Roswell notes. She had decided that her first article would chronicle the recent steps taken to secure the additional Roswell crash materials not previously turned over to the government authorities. Coupled with her news articles, she planned to include a handful of selected photographs taken by Casey Foster. The photographs would add to her story and at the same time create, through their nonverbal images, questions in the readers' minds concerning what the photographs revealed about the alien visitors. Where were they from? Why were they returning to Earth? How advanced a species were they? Are we going to be OK? Where are we ranked now on the food chart? You know, the simple little questions that enquiring minds wanted to know about.

So Leah Anne reviewed the notes of the recent trip to Roswell and Bison Wells. Then she reviewed the photo images taken by Casey on the trip. Suddenly her first outline for the article appeared in her mind, then on her laptop screen. Before long words, phrases, sentences, and paragraphs started arranging themselves inside her head. The time had arrived to write her first news article. Draft number one, then draft number two, and so on was written until the process produced a satisfactory article with accompanying photographs. Then with her secretary, Kelly Oliveri's, assistance, a polished product was at last ready to submit to her editor for final review before publication. This process was both exciting and terrifying at the same time. Plus, the new reality of having to complete a project for publication by a specific date produced a fair share of anxiety. *Shove off and see where you emerge*, thought Leah Anne. Her first article was ready for editorial review:

"Alien Return Visit to Roswell"
Byline: Leah Anne Bailey, *Washington Post*

As this is my first appearance on the pages of the *Washington Post*, I thought I would provide my readers with a short account of my background and intentions for my weekly news articles concerning the Roswell alien story. I have had the great good fortune to work in the Washington metropolitan area for the last several years performing science studies and research for the federal government. Along the way I've had the further good fortune to work professionally with Casey Foster, one of the *Washington Post's* outstanding young photojournalists. Together Casey Foster and I had the opportunity to travel to Roswell, New Mexico, on several occasions to collect materials from an alien spacecraft that crashed in that location in July, 1947. While this crash was denied by the government for many years, I feel confident that by now most of you have been made aware of the actual facts via President Obama's recent televised broadcast confirming the true nature of the crash and the returning aliens. The truth has finally seen the light of day. Recently I have had the further good fortune to have been offered a news position at the *Washington Post* to report on this story as it unfolds. It is a story that I find to be captivating, exciting, and eminently newsworthy. I hope my articles will make you all feel the same way about this subject as I do. I pledge to you my best continuing efforts to bring this story to you on a timely basis and as accurately as possible. You, as my reading audience, are invited to provide me with your thoughts, suggestions, and even criticisms, if any, at my professional twitter and Facebook pages, which will be noted at the end of this article. Here is wishing all of us the best!

It is written in the Book of Genesis, Chapter 1, "In the beginning God created the heaven and the Earth. And the Earth was without form, and void; and darkness was upon the face of the deep. And the spirit of God moved upon the face of the waters. And God said, Let there be light: and there was light."

So it was since the beginning of time on Earth that man has looked upward to the stars and heavens to see the light and has asked questions of himself regarding the nature of the universe. To assist in this holy quest for knowledge, man developed instruments of science to gaze ever farther into the cosmos. Throughout the centuries, many have asked: are we alone in the universe? Many have asked whether life exists solely on Earth or elsewhere in the heavens. To help answer these philosophical and scientific questions, man built newer, more powerful instruments, such as the telescope. In more modern times man has blasted his instruments skyward, unleashed by rocket power on artificial man-made satellites. The time has arrived for man to explore more fully our little corner of the Milky Way and the extended universe. Each discovery has shed more light upon the creation of the universe and man's place in the cosmos. Based upon these new exploratory tools, scientists concluded that the universe is approximately 13.8 billion years old. Earth is merely a newcomer, clocking in at an age of approximately 4.5 billion years. Man, on the other hand, has existed for a mere blink of time, perhaps give or take 1 million years.

Throughout our written history man has been fascinated by the heavens above, cataloging the passage of the moon and location of the stars. Man was also interested enough to name numerous constellations after favored animals and gods. Numerous art presentations depict the moon, stars, and other planets, icy comets and asteroids. More recently, man has depicted what can best be described as "visitors" from far away locations arriving at Earth in their spacecraft, referred to in the 20th century as "flying saucers." This fascination with supposed alien visitors has led many nations to conduct research on this phenomena. Many nations used to categorically deny the existence of alien visitors, but what else would you expect?. Why would a government confirm that little green men were here and we could do nothing about it? Only one government official, Governor Brown of California, didn't hide from this issue. He said, "Yep, there's aliens out there." This "truth" left him open to being referred to publically as "Governor Moonbeam," not a great calling card for election to higher office. So he was stymied forever to serve as the governor of California. Perhaps the better answer from almost all politicians seemed to have been, " I don't know about aliens; I haven't seen any proof. If I do, you'll be among the first to know."

But for those of you who followed this subject matter more intelligently, clearly the most well-known and documented alien episode was the July, 1947, crash of an extraterrestrial vessel with two alien pilots near Roswell, New Mexico. This incident was investigated, researched, and denied by the United States government. Now we have learned that while the government denied the truth of this subject publically, privately it was reconstructing the crashed alien spaceship while its lead scientists investigated the circumstances of this event. Finally, when no doubt could still remain, the President of the United States, in conjunction with leaders, announced to the public worldwide that an extra solar spacecraft had indeed crashed near Roswell. Aliens, it seemed, from planets circling other far away stars, are real. They have visited Earth before, and they're coming back! No more denials; no more cover-ups. Aliens from other planets, way out there, past our homey solar system, should now be considered a fact. Now we all know man is not alone in the heavens. We know life exists in other locations throughout the cosmos. Yes, we here on Earth have begun a new chapter in our understanding of the beauty and fullness of the universe. Further confirmation of this enlightening notion that other species inhabit our corner of the universe will soon be displayed before us. This alien species, here at least once before, is returning to Earth.

Recently, Casey Foster and I returned to Roswell, New Mexico, along with a US government security contingent to retrieve additional artifacts from the crashed alien spacecraft that had been stored for protection in the desert outside of Bison Wells, New Mexico. Arriving via government stealth helicopters and led by Lone Wolf's grandson, Tecote, from the Mescalero Apache Tribe, Casey photographed and then we turned over to the government three additional crash debris materials. The most interesting new item was a plastic-like binder containing 15 thin metal discs. A perfunctory visual examination of these metal discs led me to believe that they appear similar to DVD or CD discs. These metal discs are presently being studied by a consortium of worldwide scientific experts to determine their content and use. I am led to wonder whether these discs might contain alien music, history texts, spaceship operating manuals, an *Encyclopedia Galactica*, cookbooks, or an alien Bible. Well, your guess is as good as mine! But think of the wonders we may learn if we are smart enough to figure this out.

Please note the awe-inspiring color photographs with this article, which were taken by Casey Foster. His photographs enhance and help explain what is happening. I am excited by the opportunity to bring this story to the *Washington Post's* readership. What an exciting time for all of us to explore this incredible series of events. Together, I hope to discover many new and startling facts. I hope we learn to see our planet Earth and all of its inhabitants in a new light, perhaps even united in a common cause. I pledge to all of you to continue my best efforts to keep you informed and advised. If any of you wish, you may reach me at my business Facebook page, LABailey@WashingtonPost.com, or my business Twitter account at @LABailey. Finally, next week I will be publishing my second article regarding the recent meetings in England of the newly-established committees providing research reports on a variety of subjects to the Group of 8 world leaders.

One week later, Leah Anne's second article was finalized for editorial review and publication as follows:

"Group of 8 Committees Status in England"
Byline: Leah Anne Bailey, *Washington Post*

Last week, Casey Foster and I traveled to London to attend the preliminary meeting of the Group of 8 committees hosted by Sir Mark Justin Lyall Grant, the British permanent representative to the United Nations. This meeting was held at the Claridge Hotel in the heart of London's Mayfair district. Sir Grant challenged each of the committee members to give their best efforts to diligently, carefully, and with resolve provide thoughtful written reports on their respective assignments regarding the upcoming alien visit. Sir Peter John Westmacott was assigned as acting Chairman of the Diplomacy Committee with meetings to be held at the Clarence House in London. This committee was formulated to staff and train a specialized diplomatic corps to meet with the alien representatives. This group planned the subject matter that Earth hoped to review with our alien guests. Foremost among the members of this committee was Mr. Jacob "R.T." Witwenova, a Russian-born Israeli trained by Mossad who serves as a roving ambassador to various trouble spots around the globe such as Iran, Libya, Afghanistan, Somalia, Crimea, and the Ukraine, these last two being part of his next posting as the special ambassador to Prime Minister Netanyahu. R.T.'s talents include his disposition, familiarity with several languages, bright mind, and special social skills all of which make him a natural when the going gets tough. So "R.T." as he is known, a shortcut for his nickname, "red truck," which he acquired because of his passion for racing red trucks and fire engines, is the frontrunner for the initial ambassador to the incoming aliens. He hopes that the aliens are familiar with the sentiment, "don't shoot the messenger."

Sir George Young was delegated as chairman of the Communication Committee, which met in Wales. This committee was established to make suggestions concerning the language in which communications will be delivered to the incoming alien guests. Further, the committee was tasked to develop better means for deciphering incoming communications from the alien. And finally, the Communications Committee made recommendations concerning training interpreters to learn the alien language with the initial group to mostly be composed of diplomats.

Lord Strathclyde was appointed chairman of the Site Selection Committee, with meetings arranged for Anmer Hall in Norfolk. This committee's task was to review off-world as well as on Earth locations for meetings with the aliens. A number of sites were discussed and a few were selected for these historic meetings.

Mr. Philip Hammond was designated as chairman of the Defense Committee, with meetings to be held at Sandringham House in Norfolk. This committee planned Earth's integrated worldwide defense, should that become necessary. Unlike the other committees, it was staffed by high ranking military officers and components of worldwide security agencies such as the CIA, Mossad, KGB, and the Chinese national security forces. By its very nature this is the most secretive of the committees, and its reports will not be made available to the public. One member in particular gained attention as a consensus maker. Colonel Chole Anh Sing, a member of the Chinese delegation, is particularly well versed in inter-government military maneuvers and deployable assets. Though she is low key in presentations, she has a startling overall knowledge of current top of the line military equipment. Her tendency to be always moving forward has earned her the nickname " Chloe on the go-ie." Colonel Sing's approach is to present all of the facts without making value judgments. No bombast, no swaggering, no condescending glances—each country's capabilities were presented equally well. The Colonel's stock grew with each meeting, and she is well placed to be the "go to" military advisor for evaluation and worldwide response to the alien presence.

Lastly, Mr. Jeremy Hunt was appointed as chairman of the Earth's Public Preparedness Committee, with meetings to be held at Kensington Palace in London. This committee prepared a plan to educate Earth's national governments and their citizens regarding what can be expected with the return of the alien guests. The intent is to provide sufficient information to Earth's inhabitants about what could be anticipated when the alien spacecraft lands at Roswell.

I attended the initial committee "high tea" as an invited news observer and subsequently was granted further permission to attend meetings of the five committees. Now I am pleased to report my thoughts. This is one of the only instances in recorded history where a "home" population has been granted advanced notice of an incoming "alien" appearance on their land. This leads me to be hopeful that the returning aliens may have peaceful motives for their visit. Why else would they let us know of their expected arrival, thus permitting us time to prepare? I, for one, believe that this interchange between species will be a positive experience for all of us. Just imagine what we may learn about the cosmos and its varied inhabitants. Just imagine the potential for new explorations, the potential for new discoveries that could be made available to us on Earth. The potential upside is stupendous.

Having alluded to the positive, I am quite confident that Earth's leaders, through the committees I just enumerated, will review a variety of responses available to pursue. I have faith that this may turn out well. I will be continuing to report on this news story on a weekly basis. I will share with you as much information as becomes available. The attached photographs were again taken by Casey Foster, photojournalist at the *Washington Post*. God speed to us all.

Once again, with Kelly Oliveri's professional assistance, the second proposed article was reviewed, proofed, packaged, and forwarded on to the editorial staff before publication. Leah Anne breathed a sigh of relief as confidence in her reporting skills grew one paragraph at a time. A readership for her Roswell articles was forming, as shown by the increasing daily public mail responses sent to the *Post*. *Yikes*, she thought, *what will I do for my third article, due to be published next Friday? These deadlines are a bitch!* Various ideas rolled around in her suddenly overburdened brain. *Make a list, check it twice; should I write something naughty or nice? I guess I'll roll this around tonight and decide in the morning.*

On a more personal level, Leah Anne was enjoying her news reporting trips with Casey Foster. It seemed that their work time together joined seamlessly with their off hours playtime. Tonight seemed like a great time to get together with Casey while she planned something more special on their next trip. She needed to decide if this was going to turn into a more permanent personal relationship. If the answer was yes, Leah Anne would make sure that Casey thought he had made the decision. Duh! And one more item of importance occurred to Leah Anne: she would communicate to Casey that there would be no private photographs of her or them in any of their private moments taken for any purported purpose, ever or else!

CHAPTER 6

ORBITING TITAN

Captain Oulah IV sat quietly at his command station reviewing the mother ship's present operation. Surrounding him on the bridge were his senior officers, carefully monitoring all spacecraft functions, including the status of the crew. With a wave of his hand Captain Oulah signaled his second-in-command to his side.

"Have we performed any recent calculations concerning our expected arrival at the moon circling our target planet in this solar system?" he asked.

"Yes Captain, I have just confirmed with the navigation officer that we can anticipate arriving at our target moon in 10.683 days using our normal protocols for travel in a developed star system. These protocols will be continuous travel at a solar system speed of 20% of the speed of light, approximating 37,000 miles per second, 2.2 million miles per minute, 133,000,000 miles per hour, rounding out to 3.2 billion miles in a 24 hour Earth day. Therefore, the mother ship plans on covering in excess of 32 billion miles of mostly empty interstellar space in the next 10 days.

That's moving along at a pretty good clip, especially when compared to a present-day fast moving rockets launched from Earth. At best, you could expect an Earth-launched rocket ship to speed along even, with a gravity assist, at approximately 50,000 mph. Traveling along continuously at that speed, an Earth rocket could cover 1.2 million miles in a day, 120,000,000 miles in 100 days, 1.2 billion miles in 1000 days, and a similar 32 billion miles in 30,000 days, which converts into a travel time of 82 years. Traveling in space at today's Earth speeds means you better hope that no one's in a real hurry. Dinner's getting cold. Missed training camp. Girlfriend's very old and wrinkly."

Continuing, the second-in-command added, "Of course, Captain, we can modify this time frame within reason based upon your specific orders. Is our present speed suitable for your needs?"

"Yes," replied the captain, "we have no need for any greater speed or earlier arrival. In addition, advise our science department to conduct an updated standard scan of each of the planets in this solar system. I also want a complete analysis of the various radio transmissions from Earth, including a breakdown of their major cities and languages. Furthermore, I want to receive recommendations for the permanent placement of three satellites in various stable orbits to continue monitoring all aspects of this solar system and surrounding space. Most importantly, I want you to coordinate sending three separate shuttlecrafts with crews to orbit, map, and land on three possible targets. The first target is the moon we are orbiting, known as Titan. The next target is the fourth planet from the host star, known to the locals as Mars. Send the final shuttlecraft to the blue water world's moon to search for placement of potential permanent bases. The shuttle craft commanders should be ready within 15 days. As we have discussed, our prime mission is to establish a permanent outpost in this solar system to keep tabs on this quadrant of space. It is imperative that we locate appropriate sites prior to our formal meetings with Earth's leaders. Schedule a meeting with the three mission commanders later today to review their objectives. Understood?"

"Aye, Captain," responded the second-in-command." I will make it so."

"Now it's time," the captain continued, "to transmit an updated message to Earth. Bring over the communications officer so that we can review the message."

When the communication officer arrived, the captain continued, "Well, gentlemen, I have analyzed the radio broadcast message received from Earth regarding their welcoming us to a peaceful meeting on their home world. In response, I have prepared a proposed transmission and would like your thoughts before sending it along." With that Captain Oulah read from the screen before him his proposed message:

This will acknowledge receipt of your prior transmitted message inviting us to a peaceful meeting on your planet. Be advised that we Redexians will be arriving at the sixth planet from your sun (Saturn) in 10 days. At that time, we will insert our mother ship into orbit around one of its moons, which you call Titan. Once a satisfactory orbit is achieved, we will send a shuttlecraft back to your planet to take immediate possession of our two prior visiting brother explorers near Roswell. We will send specific instructions regarding the exact location for the meeting and the method for you to confirm the exact location by beamed signal. Further, please consider this as an invitation to bring back four of your Earth citizens for a temporary visit to our mother ship. This will assist in preparations for our formal return to your planet. These four visitors should include two from the site of the recent Earth emergency radio transmission sent to us and two others of your choice. You may expect that our shuttlecraft will arrive at the designated location near Roswell in 20 days. Advise receipt of this message. Further information will be provided, as necessary.

Signed, Captain Oulah IV of the United Redexian Frontier

"Well, asked the captain, "what do you think of the message?"

"Excellent," they both responded. "Right on point. Sure to get their attention."

"When would you like to transmit the message, Captain?" asked the communication officer?"

"Send the message now. Then log a copy into our permanent database and forward a third copy to our closest subsystem governor. Make sure you advise me as soon as we receive a response."

"At once," responded the communications officer as he turned and headed back to his communication station.

Captain Oulah planned to secure this quadrant of space, install the three planned observation satellites, place permanent substations on habitable planets or moons, and make contact with the home world political leaders. The critical part of his mission would to be to determine whether the local population could be turned into reliable allies as opposed to being subjugated or eliminated. He felt comfortable that time, superior technology, and prior Redexian strategies in similar situations would allow him to complete his objectives. Well, comfortably only if his officers and crew functioned to the best of their abilities with a common objective and dedication to the final result. So far so good. He would continue to monitor the situation closely.

"Second-in-command," said the captain, "arrange a meeting with the three shuttle commanding officers to meet with us in the bridge center's conference room in one hour. At that time I will review our objectives with them."

The ship's second-in-command snapped off a salute and, said, "As you wish, Captain." He then pivoted smartly and returned to his duty station. In front of him at his command station was a marvel of advanced Redexian technology. A bevy of screens provided instant information concerning the ship's location, speed, armaments, engine room status, and crew disposition. Further displays provided 3D imaging of the solar system being entered with projections of the various sizes of all of the stars, planets, and their moons. A central computer system, easily accessible by audio command, was available for more detailed information. The second-in-command had learned early in his professional career that close monitoring of all ship systems was essential. Mistakes, though inevitable, must be kept to a minimum and corrected at once. One overriding principle had been drilled into his head, along with each of the other serving officers. This was the principle that you were on your own for years at a time. There was no place to stop for repairs, no one close by to ask for help, and no place within close reach to refuel. Dangers lurked everywhere, such as extreme temperatures, high radiation levels, and a lack of normal supportive gravity. Included within the risk factors were the psychological issues pressing upon the entire crew as a result of being locked inside the mother ship for extended periods of time. Communication with their home world became more infrequent. Contact with family, friends, and colleagues became rare, if not impossible. In short, they were all marooned, by choice, on this long range adventure with no place to go but forward. So second-in-command Weooh VII pressed forward to complete his duties as flawlessly as possible.

One hour later all the requested shuttle commanders had assembled in the bridge conference room for consultation. Second-in-command, Weooh VII opened the meeting by reporting on the ship's status. All ship's systems were operational and the ship's crew was performing in the expected manner. Everything was in place to continue this voyage as planned. Captain Oulah stood at the front of the conference room table and addressed the attendees.

"Gentlemen, we have traveled a far distance in pursuit of our peoples' desire for enhanced security for Redex from potential outside threats. Now we are on the verge of entering this new solar system, where we will complete the next portion of our assigned task. Each of you three commanders will pilot a crewed shuttlecraft to a selected location for intensive observation, mapping, and analysis of the potential for establishing a large observation base in this solar system. Each of you will also deploy one of the three satellites that we have brought along, which will collect and then broadcast continuous data concerning this solar system and other nearby solar systems. These satellites will scan for signs of life on other planets in these nearby star systems within the habitable zone. When your site analysis is complete and the satellites are positioned, I will review the data with each of you and then choose a location to establish a permanent observation base staffed by approximately 1500 Redexians. Nothing will deter us from these tasks."

Striding around the conference table, Captain Oulah IV touched his forehead to each of the other commanders' heads. At the same time he reached out his hand, and each member present touched palms in a ritual signal of unity. This is what they had all come so far to accomplish. This is what was necessary for their home world's security. After a moment of silence, Captain Oulah said, "Each of you will prepare a detailed plan of your proposed shuttle site examination outlining crew members to be taken, studies to be performed, projected length of time to accomplish your mission, and projected materials and costs. I will expect each of you to provide me with a written report within 48 hours."

Now, for the surreal portion of his official duties, Captain Oulah formulated his official report to transmit back to Governor Elaouhe III, located on the planet Anexia. This is where they had started this interstellar journey from a planet circling the nearest star to this sun in the Alpha Centauri system. Alpha Centuri was also a trinary star system composed of three stars each circling each other in a complicated dance dictated by gravity. The closest star to Earth's sun was called Proxima Centauri, still a formidable 4.24 light years away. But there, tucked in the habitable zone circling its small red star 110 million miles away, was a planet as yet unknown to Earthlings. It was almost twice the size of Earth and richly covered in life forms, although none had evolved yet into intelligent beings. Sending a report seemed surreal to Captain Oulah because even traveling by radio transmission at the speed of light to Governor Elaouhe at 186,000 miles per second, it would take almost 4 years to reach its intended audience. Thus, presuming Governor Elaouhe was still alive, on the top of his game, and responded promptly, the captain could expect to receive a reply in no sooner than 8 years. So while protocol demanded that intermediate messages be sent up the chain of command, it was obvious to Captain Oulah, like all Redexian space explorers before him, that he would need to proceed using his best judgment based upon his traveling orders. That's the way it had been done and would continue until such time as someone could invent a quicker means of communication. Nevertheless, Captain Oulah complied by sending the required message:

Greetings, Honorable Governor Elaouhe:

I am pleased to inform you that our mother ship has almost reached its target solar system, which includes the small blue water world where we have previously located signs of intelligent life. Please be advised that our further observations and analysis confirms that the local life forms have reached an industrial age with early-stage space exploration. We are presently evaluating sites within this solar system for creation of our permanent observation stations. We will also deploy three satellites in elliptical orbits around the subject star at regular intervals to serve as a part of our early warning system. I anticipate initial formal contact with the local world species in approximately 30 days. I will advise you concerning the prospects for recruiting dependable allies or, in the alternative, subjugating the planet and its resources for our needs and benefits. Please note that all systems on our mother ship remain active and functioning. Please further note that the officers and crew are all performing at the highest level for which they have been trained. I plan to have sufficient data within 60 days to begin the process of creating a permanent observation base to be staffed by approximately 1500 of our citizens. I will also be reviewing other close-by star systems for further examination once this project is complete. Please note that we have located so far an additional 50 such star systems within 16 light years of this solar system. A few such stars have planets within the habitable zone and look promising. Presently, I favor Barnard's star at 5.963 light years from this star, Sirius at 8.5 light years, or Procyon at 11.402 light years, each of which are within range of this mission. I will send the exact coordinates of these additional stars to you shortly. Wishing you continued success. Further messages will be sent as necessary. Please advise as to any suggested course of action.

Yours humbly, Captain Oulah IV of the United Redexian Frontier

Captain Oulah completed his tasks on the bridge and returned to his private quarters. He concluded that all systems on board the mother ship were operating to his satisfaction and that his obedient staff was carefully implementing his plan for this solar system. All was progressing as desired; now he could afford some private time to do as he pleased. On board his mother ship he was as majestic as any king who had ever ruled over a nation within the Milky Way. He had at his fingertips incredible technology, resources, and a dedicated crew available to serve any of his needs.

Setting aside his captain's uniform, he changed into his favorite powder blue lounging attire. He exchanged his military boots for fluffy green slippers. Addressing the speech recognition computer system within his quarters, he called up scenes from his favorite location. Instantly, each of the interior walls in his main sitting area turned into full scale viewing screens projecting lifelike images that surrounded him completely. It was as if he was living inside a 3D hologram. To his left he could see long plains stretching out before him, reaching to the distant, rolling green hills. Above, where the ceiling tiles had been moments before, he viewed an afternoon sky presently showing the three stars in his home world, the Fomalhaut trinary system. Lastly, to his right he could see a deep blue pool surrounded by stark white rocks, where the water was artificially warmed to a tantalizing temperature in which he could float at his leisure. Slowly, minute by minute, he let his pressing duties slip away and entered into a realm of quiet, contemplative meditation. His huge, complicated brain, floating in his enlarged head, wound down. He had earned a break. Captain Oulah's intellect and powers of concentration were legendary. They had allowed him to rise one step at a time through a society that rewarded brightness and hard work. At each step of the process he had excelled beyond expectations. He had accumulated great honors, buffered by outward humility towards his peers, who were proud to consider him a friend. His superiors were quite pleased to have someone with such talent under their command. He was one of a few dozen Redexians who had been provided with a Class 1 starship to command in order to extend and protect their empire. And in this special traveling environment he had earned the privilege to act and be treated like a king. It was an honor he had appreciated. So he enjoyed his privileges within the limits of rational behavioral. *Time to stand down*, he thought. *Relax for a while.*

Pressing the intercom button, Captain Oulah ordered up a pitcher of spiced alcoholic drinks accompanied by small, dissolvable, multi-flavored cubes. Within minutes his order was delivered by the young female serving twins on his personal staff. Both Enu and Renu had been serving with the captain as his personal serving staff for the last three years. They were happy and content to participate in this fascinating voyage of exploration with continuing access to the captain. The fact that they were decidedly younger than the captain and considered to be exceedingly attractive by Redexian standards was well known throughout the mother ship. No one begrudged the captain's personal right to enjoy his free time.

Once they arrived together carrying the requested snack, the captain, not unexpectedly, invited them both to stay and join him in some "quiet time." In unison they turned toward their captain, ears wiggling, eyes slightly downcast, and all fingers slightly trembling with anticipation. The captain turned and moved towards his private library table, opening its front metallic drawer to remove three identical crystal necklaces containing small carved stone pendants. Each of these pendants displayed identical symbols engraved in two rows of five symbols each. It was a pendant that every Redexian would recognize but not every Redexian was allowed to wear; it needed to be earned. Here and now the necklaces with their pendants were available to all three of these travelers. So, as was their custom, each serving girl quietly approached the captain while he placed the necklace over their smooth, silver gray, somewhat shiny, bald, multi-ridged heads. With great formality, Enu took possession of the remaining necklace and ceremoniously draped it over the captain's head while complimenting him on his handsome good looks. Well, what else could she say? After placing the necklace on the captain's neck, whistling and snorting noises could be heard as they were emitted from the two serving girls' well-spaced nostrils.

Having completed the first part of the ritualistic ceremony, Captain Oulah returned to the library table and removed a strange mechanical contraption. It was composed of three black leather half helmets, all connected by long black expandable cords running to a central computer outlet, which was plugged into the wall next to the outside viewing screen. The serving girls were each handed one of the half helmets, and all three then placed their helmets simultaneously upon their heads. They seated themselves on the floor around the serving pitcher with the multi-flavored cubes. Renu daintily poured the spiced alcoholic drink into a decorated, silver-engraved bowl situated in their midst. With a flip of the controlling switch by Captain Oulah, all were now connected into a virtual reality 3D network, infused with soft background tones that heightened all bodily sensitivity. Each of the three willing participants could see and feel everything available to his or her companions. Time for some romping, out of this world, soak it all in fun. The captain remembered to turn on the full color, zillion pixel hologram recording device for later private playback. During the next two hours the participants took turns lapping the liquid from the serving bowl with their long, pointed, purple- blue spotted tongues. Since the Redexians had evolved to a state where they had no teeth, all consumables needed to be liquid. No meat eaters on Redex. More like large hummingbirds lapping down high sugar content alcoholic flower nectar. Yum. Therefore, one at a time, flavored cubes were placed in the serving bowl to dissolve and enhance the drink mixture. After a period of warm-up stretching maneuvers, the participants each started making various cooing sounds. Then they moved closer together and began their physical activities by touching all three of their heads together directly over the serving bowl. Within a short period of time the captain, Enu, and Renu began to slide one against another and entangle themselves in all sorts of contortionist positions. If an outside observer had been present, it would certainly appear that everybody was having a jolly good time. This activity continued until all the drink and flavor cubes had been consumed. Each participant's senses were tingling. With a joint shudder all three collapsed atop each other in a heap. Their helmets were then disengaged from the computer system. Deep sleep with pleasant dreams enveloped the captain's quarters. Woe be unto any crew member who attempted entry into these quarters until invited by the captain. During the next 24 hours, variations of the same conduct occurred several more times in various combinations of the three participants. Each reenactment was better than the one before. Each participant was more than willing to have at it again. Then, at exactly 24 hours after their mutual entertainment began, the captain's quarters faded to black, just like the outside surroundings. Oulah, Enu, and Renu blended into the new dark environment with their red eyes deepening into a dark ruby color. On their home world the dense atmosphere required more sensitive eyes to filter and sharpen the dim light. So over time evolution had favored large, dark red, sensitive eyes. These eyes, when exposed to almost total darkness, turned to ruby red automatically to enhance their ability to see. This change signaled that together time was over. The captain stood and walked slowly to each of the serving girls, retrieving their necklaces with dangling pendants. He removed his own necklace and returned all three to the library table to reside therein until the next encounter. Each participated in a quick shower together to remove all remaining "quiet time" residue. Then after toweling and dressing, Captain Oulah politely walked Enu and Renu to the entrance to his quarters, where they all touched heads before the twin girls departed. No mention would be made of their encounter. Redexians liked privacy. Only the 3D tape remained for the captain's later viewing pleasure.

Twenty minutes later the captain appeared unannounced on the bridge of the mother ship, dressed immaculately in his full military uniform. He was ready again to supervise the action. Surveying all about him, he calmly ordered each at their various stations to report. The captain was back in full control. Nine more days until the Redexian mother ship would be inserted into orbit around Titan. The plan moved relentlessly forward. There would be no foul ups during his watch. Ourah! Redexian Frontier forever!

CHAPTER 7

WHAT'S UP, EARTH?

Leah Anne Bailey was settling into her exciting new job, and it was a pleasure for her to arrive at work each day and continue her research and writing. She would research, study, learn, interview people familiar with the story, and prepare her readership for the unfolding monumental visit. Then, as she sat quietly at her desk looking out the window at the busy downtown Washington scene, in strode Charles Evenridge.

"To what do I owe the pleasure of your visit?" Leah Anne asked.

" Let me tell you about the telephone call I just received from US Secretary of Defense Ramsey Kalnikoff," he responded. "It seems, Ms. Bailey, that our national defense listening stations and SETI just received another incoming message from our alien visitors. We have been advised of a few interesting new facts. First of all, our aliens refer to themselves as Redexians, from the planet Redex, which circles their star Fomalhaut. Secondly, the Redexians plan on returning to Earth for a preliminary visit by shuttlecraft in approximately 20 days. At that time, they plan on retrieving what they refer to as their two brothers in exploration. They have also extended an offer to take four Earth guests back on their shuttlecraft when they return to their mother ship. What I'm sure will be of great interest to you is that the Redexians have invited two people who were present at the time the recent emergency message was beamed from Roswell to their mother ship as part of the four chosen Earthlings."

After a pause Evenridge continued, "Secretary Kalnikoff and I have come to the conclusion that you and Casey Foster should be chosen as those two participants. I realize that this incredible offer raises many issues.

What I suggest is that you and Casey discuss this matter tonight and meet with me tomorrow morning in my office."

"Is this for real?" Leah Anne gasped. "You mean Casey and I have been invited to take a trip to the alien mother ship?"

"I know it sounds crazy, but that's what happened. So while you and Casey talk this over, I'll get more details regarding what's involved. In the meantime, try to picture the incredible events that you could see and report on during your journey. Obviously no one from Earth has ever done anything like this before. Oh, and the *Post* pays overtime on all off-world reporting," Evenridge added with a wink as he closed the door behind him.

Leah Anne sat at her desk, flabbergasted. Her bright blue eyes looked like dinner platters, like a grouper looked just after being pulled from deep down in the water. The part of her brain that was still functioning, albeit slowly, was trying to process the information. Most of her brain just sat there jiggling around, trying to get a few neurons to bounce messages back and forth. *What the hell is going on?* she wondered. *Breathe, breathe again, breathe more deeply, look out the window, stand up and walk around. See if your feet can actually move your body from place to place. Try to make sense of this last discussion. Crap, it sounds like I've just been invited on a space trip to meet with a bunch of aliens. Should I go? Why not? Whoa, what a story this would make! But the most critical questions, what do I wear and what do I pack?*

Leah Anne glanced at her office telephone and considered dialing up Casey for a quick conversation. Nope, this required a face to face meeting, not a less personal office telephone call. Popping to her feet, she scrambled out her office door, informing Kelly on the way out that she'd be returning in a bit. Then she trundled down the steps towards Casey's normal hang out in the photo lab. Upon arriving she immediately checked the sign in sheet and found that Casey was entrenched in photo lab number six with his buddy, Kerry Ryan, the photo geek. Diligently, like any seasoned employee familiar with Washington culture, she scribbled her name on the entry line in a fashion that made any later reader unsure who had actually obtained entry. Deniability was an art form in Washington. Leah Anne knocked on the door and, without waiting, opened it and walked inside. Sure enough, turning around to see her stood Casey with his hands full of draft photographic prints.

"Well," he said, playing to his small audience, "what brings you to my little part of the world during work hours? Do you miss me that much? Looking for a little kissing? Perhaps a snuggle or a hug? Maybe something more exciting and a little more dangerous right here in the photo lab? You know the door locks, right?"

"Casey," sighed Leah Anne, "quit thinking with your dick for a minute and pay attention. This is important."

"Sorry, I'll behave. Tell me what's happening."

"I know this will sound crazy but I just had a visit from our editor-in-chief. He informed me that a new message has been received from the aliens. They will be returning to Roswell in approximately 20 days. But the incredible part is that the Redexians have invited four Earthlings to travel back to their mother ship. And guess what? You and I have been invited, since we were present when the emergency signal was transmitted from Roswell into space. Mr. Evenridge would like to meet with us tomorrow in his office to discuss this in detail. He would like us to quickly make a decision about going on this incredible trip. I'm leaning towards accepting the invitation. What a once in a lifetime opportunity. What do you think?"

Kerry Ryan just stared at his two friends with a blank look. Maybe this was just another test for the office geek, a chance to suck him in on another prank. Did aliens *really* want to visit and take his buddies into space for a visit?

"Well, enjoy your conversation," Kerry said as he took his leave. "I've got real work to do."

Casey just stared across the photo lab at Leah Anne without speaking. Was this for real? But Leah Anne rarely made jokes about anything of this significance. He felt frozen. Could it be true? Were they really invited up to the alien mother ship as guests? Would they make it back alive? If it was true, and if it could be done, did he have the balls to accept and go?

After a moment of silence, he said, "Why not? You only live once. We will never have another opportunity like this. Think of the photo opportunities. Think about being the first humans to really interact with and report on an alien species. So I'm game if you are."

"Well, how about joining me after work today? We'll take the subway to my apartment, bring some takeout food home, and talk about this."

"OK, you're on. I'll pick you up at 6. at your office and we'll head out to your place." A hug, a kiss, and a shrug were mutually implanted before Leah Anne dreamily departed the photo lab.

Following a mostly uneventful evening talking, frolicking, and soul-searching, Casey Foster and Leah Anne Bailey arrived the next morning in Evenridge's office. They were greeted respectfully and introduced to Secretary of Defense Ramsey Kalnikoff.

"Good morning, Casey and Leah Anne," said the editor. "I'm sure you both had much to consider regarding your invitation to visit the Redexians' mother ship as their guests. I have invited Secretary of Defense Kalnikoff to join us so that he can also give us his perspective. But before he begins, have you been able to reach at least a preliminary decision on whether you would be interested in moving forward on this grand adventure?"

Casey Foster faced his boss and the Secretary of Defense and responded, "Obviously both Leah Anne and myself have no expertise in matters of this nature. Perhaps no one here on Earth has encountered a situation quite like this before. But, after discussing this matter last evening, we concluded that someone will need to attend and report on this preliminary get-together. We have been chosen, among others, by the Redexians, and we both agree to go as long as we can go together. But we do have one other condition. We want permission to continue our reporting duties for the *Washington Post* while we prepare and go on this mission. If that's acceptable, we'd like to hear the Secretary's thoughts about what this would entail."

"Mr. Foster, Ms. Bailey, I am pleased to make your acquaintance. Your editor provided me some background information concerning you both yesterday. So last night I had our combined national security services perform a thorough investigation of all of your records to determine if you are acceptable candidates for this unprecedented meeting. I am pleased to inform you that you are both cleared to move forward, with our thanks and gratitude. Mr. Evenridge may have also told you that Earth may select two additional candidates to send to the Redexian mother ship. In helping you to make this decision you may wish to know on a confidential basis that the Group of 8 has also selected Mr. Jacob R. T. Witwenova, a Russian-born Israeli diplomat, and Colonel Chloe Anh Sing, a member of the Chinese military establishment, as the other two international candidates. Both are extremely well qualified for this assignment. You will have a chance to meet them soon.

"As to what risks are involved on this mission, we frankly don't know. To the best of our knowledge there has never been any interactions by an Earthling with an alien species before. Therefore, each of you needs to understand that we don't know what might happen, and therefore we cannot guarantee your safety, either when you're on the ship or during your return—if you are allowed to return at all. But my experience and the experience of others familiar with similar situations leads me to believe that the open nature of this invitation signals a likely favorable outcome. While others may agree or disagree with this assessment, only you two, along with the other two volunteers, can make the ultimate decision. Despite the risks, let me assure you that as a combined Earth project, all of us will do everything within our power to prepare you, assist you, and try our best to assure your complete safety."

"As to the *Washington Post*,", added Charles Evenridge, "you have our blessing and backing to report this event at every stage of the way. We will supply equipment to transmit your materials from space back to Earth. We hope the Redexians will permit this to happen. This is something we will inquire about before you leave. So, are you still willing to go?"

"I'm game," said Casey.

"Count me in," said Leah Anne.

"Thank you both very much," said Secretary Kalnikoff. "Now that we are all agreed that you are traveling to the Redexian mother ship, the next step includes getting you both prepared for what might happen. As of this moment I have arranged for each of you to have a high level security detail. They are in the building and will meet with you once this meeting is complete. You should be aware that your security detail will be with you 24 hours a day from this moment until you depart Earth. In addition, I have also made arrangements for each of you to attend the CIA's special two week training course at the Dulles Discovery Office in Chantilly, Virginia. This will be an intensive course in communication skills, information technology, project management, weapons training, observation skills, observation reporting, diplomacy, and specialized language training. Being residents here in Washington, DC, you may have heard this CIA training facility referred to as "The Farm". Please remember that everything that happens during your training sessions will remain totally confidential. Therefore, you will both be asked to sign the appropriate confidentiality documents. After your acceptance of these terms you will be entered into the formal records of your thankful government as special agents.

"I further understand," continued Secretary Kalnikoff, "that the Israeli security agency Mossad will be preparing a specialized five day course to be presented to you both in the Negev. An emphasis of that program will be specialized language skills and detailed documenting and transmission of sensitive information. Of course, all training will be at the government's expense. You will also both be compensated for your time by the CIA beginning today. This is in addition to whatever the *Washington Post* is presently paying you as employees. Please note that your security details will transport you to the CIA training facility this coming Monday. In the meantime, please go about your normal activities and personal affairs. I look forward to speaking with you both again once your training is underway. Mr. Evenridge, do you have anything to add prior to me introducing Casey and Leah Anne to their security details?"

"Just briefly," Evenridge responded. "Please accept the gratitude of the *Washington Post* for your dedicated service. We will support you in every way possible. And finally, I will have Robert Williston of our legal department prepare appropriate paperwork for your signatures."

Each of the four attendees stood, shook hands, looked solemn, and silently asked in the privacy of their own heads, *Where in the hell is this going*? Secretary Kalnikoff then escorted the two new soon-to-be special agents out the door and into the highly-trained hands of their individual security details. Casey and Leah Anne were each immediately fitted with a small hidden electronic transmitter, given a small lapel pin to be worn at all times, and a codename. Casey became Nikon, like the camera, and Leah Anne became Shakespeare, like the writer. The Redexians were codenamed Flappers.

With these formalities concluded, Leah Anne returned to her office, tailed by her new security detail. Leah Anne noticed her security team scan the hallways, doors, lavatories, and every passing person, as if there might suddenly be an assassin or terrorist lurking nearby. *Really*, she thought, *no one even knows about my new employment as a CIA spook, and I'm already being treated like an endangered government official*. She took a deep breath, glanced out the window, and then started banging away on her computer, beginning next week's new article.

"People of Earth Prepare for Alien Visit"
Byline: Leah Anne Bailey, *Washington Post*

Here on Earth, how is the public preparing for the imminent return of alien visitors? These alien visitors represent a species of intelligent be-ings from a planet they call Redex, orbiting its home star Fomalhaut, a star that exists within the Milky Way galaxy at a vast distance of ap-proximately 24 light years from our sun. So, what do the people of Earth think about this?

My research leads me to believe that Earthlings can be lumped into three approximately equal categories. The first category hasn't re-ceived much news, if any, about this historic event and wouldn't re-ally care one way or the other if it had. This includes people such as natives living in the Amazon rain forest, comprising some 2.1 million acres located in Brazil, Peru, Colombia, Venezuela, Ecuador, Bolivia, and French Guyana. It's a huge tract of land with the most biodiversity on our planet, containing some 390 billion individual trees. It is an area in South America which humans first settled almost 11,000 years ago and which is inhabited by millions of insect species, birds, mammals, amphibians, reptiles, and fish all living happily throughout the centuries with little outside human contact. For those humans present, such as the indigenous tribes of Quipous, Manaus, and Elem, their days are spent eking out a living fraught with rituals and traditions. Aliens from other planets roaming around their jungles looking for grubs to eat are the least of their worries. There's plenty of bugs to go around.

Farther north in Alaska, the largest state in our nation, there exists some 750,000 people, many of whom live intentionally in remote areas trying to avoid contact with other people. Similarly, concern about arriving aliens is not high on their list and won't be unless the aliens interfere with their hunting or fishing rights. And as far as being eaten alive, bears are the real danger faced by many. That's why those good folks carry real firearms when they move about. Aliens from Redex may not even like the taste of humans. Go figure. So Alaskans in general are not too interested or concerned.

Across the globe in Northern China there are some 23 million people who, along with their ancestors before them, carved out an existence for over 3000 years in an equally harsh environment. Most of these people are still unaware of any approaching aliens. They are much more concerned with local weather conditions as well as agricultural resources. Their Russian buddies in Siberia, extending from the Ural Mountains to the far Pacific, are also living in this nearly frozen northern climate. For them, the last major event that got their attention was the building of the Trans-Siberian Railroad in the early 1900s.

How about the level of concern about aliens for the local population in the Central African region? This large zone, straddling the equator and drained by the Congo River system, once served as the cradle of human life. It has a hot, wet climate wafting through the western Rift Valley with over 80 inches of rain per year. Aliens are definitely not a topic for discussion among the local Bantu tribes as well as the few merchants one might find in Burundi and Rwanda. So in this reporter's opinion, about 1/3 of Earth's population has little awareness or concern of the incoming aliens. Daily life is just taken one day at a time seeking sufficient food and shelter to get to the next day. Light years, ray guns, spaceships, and little aliens who want to eat your face off are just not on their agendas.

The second major category is comprised of those Earth citizens who have received news of the aliens returning visit and are unhappy about their prospects. Some of these folks include those whom I will lump together in the context of doomsday preppers. These anxious people are convinced that humans will end up as a major portion of the aliens food supply. We will be treated, according to them, merely as a local livestock resource. These aliens, according to the preppers, are also here to denude the planet of all our natural resources and various life forms. How all of these materials will be transported to some far off location for the aliens' benefits hasn't been explained yet. But rest assured the preppers are out there digging in, stashing survival supplies, and preparing to hold out for as long as it takes. Oh, and rest assured these guys are also concerned about nuclear war, global warming, and the coming economic collapse of the world's major economies. Get your guns, food supplies, and dig in. Pronto!

There is also a wide variety of upset religious leaders and conservative preachers with receptive flocks. For many of these folks, the arrival of "dangerous aliens" is a just punishment from God for our collective misbehavior. The devil will be upon us. Our transgressions will be severely punished. We will be wiped out just as in Noah's time of the great flood, never to reappear upon the Earth's surface. These stalwart, learned, highly respected religious authorities, be they Christians, Muslim, Hindus, Jews, or Buddhists, rally their parishioners with wailing, hair pulling, and voluminous tears while preaching for repentance and hope for redemption. Promises, in a variety of languages, are pledged to the Almighty that we humans can and will do better. They promise that our fellow man will be treated henceforth with respect, admiration, nay even love. They promise that there will be no more blaspheming, no more taking of God's name in vain, no more murder, adultery, theft, fraud, or even spitting on the sidewalk. We will be good, very good. So God, please give us a break and deliver us from these evil, non- believing, heathen, devil-like, aliens. In support of these doomsday preachings there are many who have taken to the streets of the world's cities, placards in hand, proclaiming that the end is near. They demand that our governments unite before doomsday arrives. And just in case, let us all arm ourselves to the teeth and prepare for the last hurrah. Oh, and by the way, lest we forget, abortion, gay tolerance, and gun control may be practiced by these evil-doing aliens. Stop them now before it's too late. Amen, brothers.

Thirdly, there exists, thankfully, a large group, to which I and perhaps you belong. This group is made up of those of us Earth citizens who view this alien arrival as an opportunity. This event, in my humble opinion, confirms the majesty of our universe and the diversity of the life that exists throughout the cosmos. Soon we will meet with another advanced intelligent species and open a new chapter in our collective understanding of the universe.

I, for one, am optimistic that no species travels across the galaxy for dozens of years just to wreak havoc upon another intelligent species. Why bother? We are no threat to them. I believe that some marvels will soon be shared with us. What can they tell us? What can we learn?

What new science and technology will be made available that perhaps we can comprehend? I suspect that I, along with all of you, will know some of the answers to most of these questions within the next few months. I pledge to you, my readership, that I will continue to provide you with all of the information and facts as they become available.

Thus, I am thrilled to be able to disclose to you my future involvement. Recently, Casey Foster and I had the opportunity to meet with US Secretary of Defense Ramsey Kalnikoff. He informed us that the Redexians will soon send a shuttlecraft to Roswell, New Mexico, to retrieve their prior deceased brother explorers for return to the mother ship. And Casey and I have been invited to return with the aliens to visit the Redexian mother ship. Our purpose is to help prepare for the formal meeting between the representatives of Earth and Redex. Casey Foster and I have accepted this offer. I will keep you, my readers, advised. Good luck and God speed to us all.

Having finished the draft news article for the coming Friday, Leah Anne hit the communication buzzer on her desk to signal Kelly Oliveri. Responding to the intercom, Kelly asked," What can I do for you?"

"Well, Kelly, I just finished the first draft of the upcoming article for this Friday's paper. I would appreciate it if you would come in, print out the draft, and proofread it for me. Please make any corrections you think necessary and leave it on my desk. I'll be leaving in a few minutes but would like to review your comments and suggestions first thing tomorrow morning. Once reviewed I will give it back to you for any final corrections before we send it off to the editor's desk for publication. Does that meet with your time schedule?"

"Sure, I'll take care of it. Have a nice evening, and I'll see you in the morning," responded Kelly."

Leah Anne then picked up her telephone receiver and dialed Casey in the photo lab. Once he picked up the telephone Leah Anne asked, "Are you ready to take me home and out to dinner?"

"That depends, does dinner include a follow up sleep over?" he asked.

"If your dinner manners are acceptable, I'll consider a sleep over. But you better treat me like a queen."

"OK, you're on; I'll pick you up in a few minutes. Be ready. Oh, and make sure you bring along your security detail. I think we can have some fun watching them protect us from evil villains," Casey said with a laugh.

CHAPTER EIGHT

SITE SELECTION

The Group of 8 designated President Barack Obama as the leader responsible for communicating with the Redexians. So, following consultations with the other leaders, he finalized Earth's next message for transmission into deep space:

This will acknowledge receipt of your recent message regarding your arrival in our solar system. Congratulations. Please be advised that we are making arrangements to receive your shuttlecraft at Roswell, New Mexico. Please let us know when you wish us to signal the exact location for your shuttlecraft to land. We will assist in the return of your prior honorable Redexian brother explorers. We regret to advise you that both pilots died from injuries sustained in the spaceship crash, which occurred in July, 1947. Please accept our sincere condolences for your loss. Pursuant to your kind offer, we will have four volunteers ready to return with the shuttlecraft to your mother ship. Please advise the length of time for the trip from Earth to your mother ship orbiting at Titan. Please advise what supplies, such as food, atmosphere, and protective clothing we need to supply to our visitors. All of us on Earth look forward to this peaceful meeting between our two civilizations.

Signed, President Barack Obama, Chairman, Group of 8

This message was delivered to NASA, SETI, and the Pentagon for simultaneous transmission to the incoming Redexian spacecraft. In a matter of minutes, the message was broadcast into deep space directed towards Saturn on the radio frequency used on the prior exchanges. These two Milky Way galaxy members were taking the first baby steps towards developing an intergalactic conversation. So far, all was polite, straightforward, and peaceful. Neither party appeared to be dictating terms to the other or signaling hostility. Rather, it was more like an open house. Come on down, it's time for dinner and drinks. Say hello. We'll be happy to show you around. Anything else we can do for you?

Nevertheless, the Redexians were holding most of the cards. Essentially their requirements could be met without the Earthlings' assistance. But, as they had learned as an ever-expanding space traveling species, cooperation could be beneficial. Merely imposing their will by naked force caused friction and possible future reprisals. Captain Oulah preferred to avoid conflict. That was Redex's written policy. Make friends where possible; make allies when possible. The cosmos held enough potential enemies for Redex without their actions creating new ones. He would try to seek cooperation in winning new friends, but he would resort to overwhelming force if necessary.

As the new message from Earth arrived, the captain, was on the starship bridge. He was observing the navigator entering the coordinates for insertion of the spacecraft into orbit around Titan at a distance of 500 km from the moon's surface. From this vantage point the captain and his crew were treated to a spectacular view of Saturn, with its multiple icy rings. Below, as the clouds moved past, they could see Titan's surface with its solid rocky surfaces interlaced with lakes and rivers of liquid methane. So nice to have something to view after years in the open, dark void of interstellar space. It was a pleasure to just look around and admire the wonders of nature.

In short order, the navigator confirmed that a stable orbit had been achieved around Titan. Each passing loop took 90 minutes to complete. It was nice to be "parked" after such a long haul. With a wave of his hand the captain signaled his second-in-command, Weooh to join him. "Make arrangements for the three shuttle commanders scheduled to explore for a permanent observation base to meet with us in an hour in the ready room. At that time I will review their proposed plans for action. When we are done with that task I want us to also meet with the commander and crew of the fourth shuttlecraft that will be traveling to Earth to pick up our brother explorers."

"As you wish, sir. I will see to it," said the second-in-command. "Let me also extend my congratulations to you for our safe arrival and insertion into orbit in this solar system. I am also confident that you will make sure that our mission is accomplished with great success. As always, I stand ready to serve you to the best of my abilities. Please let me know if there's anything else I can do to assist at this time."

"Thank you, Weooh; I would expect no less. I'll see you and the first group in one hour."

Just like clockwork, the shuttle commanders presented themselves to their captain in the starship ready room at the appointed hour. The captain circled his shuttle commanders for an informal inspection to confirm their readiness for their upcoming mission. "Fellow Redexians, I am pleased to note that all is in readiness for the next stage of this critical operation. Tomorrow morning each of you will pilot your shuttlecraft to your designated target. There you will first insert one of our satellites in the proper pre-selected long term elliptical orbit. Then you will continue to observe, record, and map appropriate locations to establish permanent observation bases in this solar system. We need detailed information concerning each of your target sites. As you are each aware, shortly I will order another shuttlecraft back to Earth to retrieve our earlier honorable brother explorers to our care. We will also pick up and transport back to our starship four guests from Earth. All of this is in preparation for our first official visit with Earth's political leaders. It is imperative that each of you perform at the highest level in providing detailed information regarding site selection for a permanent observation base. The primary observation base will be designed to support approximately 1500 fellow citizens to monitor activities on Earth and act as an early warning system for any other alien species entering this sector.

"You are ordered to complete your examinations within 10 days and report back to me with your primary proposed site selection and two alternatives. I expect detailed maps, photographs, topographical information, mineral lists, environmental problems, and potential dangers to be included in your written reports. Remember to keep in mind that we will be transporting voluminous materials and personnel to establish such a permanent base. Therefore, we will need a good access point with an appropriate landing area. Finally, keep in mind that this is a long-term project and that the selected area will need to have extensive infrastructure and manufacturing potential. Do not fail in your assigned tasks. Do any of you commanders have any questions?"

One shuttle commander looked his captain straight into his deep red eyes, slowly nodded his bulging, wrinkled head, wiggled his ears in standard regulation etiquette, and asked, "Captain will you want to visit the proposed permanent observation base sites before traveling to Earth?"

"That is indeed a good question. Yes, before I make my presentation to Earth's leaders I will indeed visit the top selected sites. Keep that in mind throughout your preparations. If you have further questions prior to departure direct them to our second-in-command. Dismissed."

The following morning at 7 AM, standard Redexian time, each of the shuttle commanders piloted their shuttlecrafts away from the mother ship towards their targets. All maneuvers were still scheduled based upon the use of standard Redexian time, a practice long employed by all of their travelers that made them feel bonded to their home world. Naturally, their official timing devices displayed other time zones and always included the more primitive local time utilized by the native species; it made the natives feel more comfortable with their Redexian guests. So as soon as the shuttlecrafts departed into the night sky, each crafts journey's was monitored closely from the ship's bridge. As little as possible would be left to chance. 2500 years of trial and error in interstellar exploration in their ever-expanding zone of protection had created solid guidelines for action. Nature, in its various forms in their quadrant of the Milky Way, had confirmed repeatedly that there were predators and prey. There were survivors and also numerous extinct species. There were those who enjoyed the bounty that they found or developed, and there were the less successful who lost or were deprived of the resources that they had once called their own. Years upon years of education and natural selection taught the Redexians that winning was much better than losing. It was a game they enjoyed playing while refining the rules and objectives. So, as the three shuttlecrafts departed on their missions, Captain Oulah ordered the bridge communication station opened. With great solemnity he transmitted to each of his commanders' shuttles a simple, time-honored message. "Gentleman," he said, "*Shalom*; may peace be upon you."

In unison, they responded," *Shalom Aleichem.*"

As Shuttlecraft One departed the mother ship, its commander had a twinkle in his deep red eyes. What a joy to be at the controls of his shuttlecraft again and away from the mother ship, a joy created as a response to years of routine residency on board their traveling mother ship. He gleefully maneuvered the shuttlecraft towards Saturn to deploy the observation satellite. Picking up speed, the shuttlecraft maneuvered towards the encircling rings. The sun reflected off the billions of ice fragments, each reflecting light like a prism of primary colors, broadcasting into the universe. The shuttle commander chose to dart between the gap located between the A and B rings, known on Earth as the Cassini Division. Shooting through the gap at 50,000 miles an hour, the shuttlecraft continued past 16 orbiting moons until it reached the farthest moon, Phobe, approximately 13,000,000 km from Saturn's surface. He deployed the satellite at a distance of 15,000 km above Phobe's surface so that it would remain in a synchronized orbit. Now the satellite would orbit its new home, Phobe, which would orbit Saturn, which would orbit the sun, which in turn would orbit the center of the Milky Way galaxy. The satellite would continuously scan the skies looking for relatively close stars with possible new habitable planets or, as a worst case scenario, incoming hostile intruders. It would look, listen, and observe in this quadrant of the Milky Way, then transmit any significant findings back to close proximity planetary substations and then on to Redex.

Shuttlecraft One completed the placement of its satellite and traversed back towards Titan. Slowly descending towards Titan's surface, the commander viewed one of the most Earth-like places in the solar system. It contained hundreds of miles of rocky surface interspersed with liquid methane lakes and rivers, kind of like landing at a giant floating gas station. From the shuttlecraft, Titan's surface appeared welcoming. Unfortunately, the data collected at the mother ship confirmed a surface temperature of around -289°F; not exactly favorable for sledding or ice skating. It was perhaps even too cold to cobble together a snowman. The commander's job was to search meticulously until the most favorable sites were thoroughly documented. The shuttlecraft's onboard computers hummed as terabytes of data were collected. For the analysis to be complete, rotating ground crews were dispatched from the shuttle with sophisticated gear to search the landscape for a suitable building site. Oh, and don't strike a match—igniting the methane lakes on the surface would result in what Americans might refer to as a spectacular 4th of July celebration. Kaboom!

Shuttlecraft Two dropped away from the mother ship and initiated its longer two day journey towards Mars. Slowly, hour by hour, the fourth planet from the sun grew in the bridge's viewing screen. It's bloody, rust-like appearance, the result of the decomposition of the iron rich minerals on its surface, came into sight. One day into the journey the outline of Mar's polar ice caps become visible, as did the appearance of mountain ranges and deep, long valleys. Some six hours prior to insertion into orbit the incredibly tall Martian mountain, Olympus Mons, some 27 km high, punctuated Mars' surface. Even more impressive, the shuttlecraft crew viewed a canyon system traversing approximately 1/5 of the distance around Mars at a depth as great as 10 km. In comparison, the Earth's Grand Canyon just got downgraded to a secondary ditch. Here on Mars, numerous channels, valleys, and gullies provided scientific evidence that liquid water once flowed across its surface. That liquid water might still be present seasonally upon the surface if one knew where to look. The shuttle's sensors also picked up signals of methane gas, a potential sign of life, in some as yet unknown capacity.

The commander of Shuttlecraft Two was impressed with the numerous potential sites for development of a permanent base on Mars' surface. The developable land available was similar to that of Earth, which, while twice the size of Mars, had 2/3 of its surface covered with water. At a distance of some 142,000,000 miles from the sun, Mars clearly resided within the habitable zone. It also had a thin atmosphere comprised of carbon dioxide, nitrogen, argon, and trace particles of oxygen, which could be exploited along with many useful minerals. The smaller mass of Mars also dictated a surface gravity approximately 2/3 less than was present on Earth. For the smaller, less physical Redexians, this might be prove quite pleasing.

The shuttlecraft circled Mars at an altitude of 15,000 km for the next 24 standard Redexian hours, mapping the planet's surface. When the data had been collected and analyzed, the shuttlecraft commander deployed the satellite in an elliptical orbit. He then selected a landing site near the Martian equator that looked promising. The large, flat location 10° north of the Martian equator, known on Earth as Oxia Palus, was selected as the primary landing site for exploration. Landing upon Mars' surface, the shuttlecraft crew made preparations to exit for their first exploratory trip. How nice to take a little walk on the surface of a potentially habitable planet after years of interplanetary space travel. How nice to take a drive in their 8 wheel drive, three speed rover after being cooped up for years. Traveling through interstellar space, while necessary, was nowhere near as fun as romping around the surface of a habitable planet. Picnic time, quick trip to the beach, perhaps a hike. Today's forecast: surface temperature 45 degrees Fahrenheit, low risk of dust storms. Nice!

Meanwhile, Shuttlecraft Three departed the mother ship on its three day journey to the Earth's moon. Reflecting the sun's light, the moon shone brightly alongside its startling blue benefactor planet, Earth. The two, both seen simultaneously through the shuttlecraft's viewing screens, were a welcoming sight. Even from a distance it was obvious that good things were happening at this outpost. The moon, held captive by Earth's gravity, was clearly in a synchronized orbit with Earth. One side was always facing the Earth's surface, while the other faced the darkness of space. Impact craters covered much of the surface, chronicling a long history of incoming space debris. Clearly, based upon the size of these craters, some impacts must have been monumental. Orbiting presently at a mere 250,000 miles from the Earth's surface, the moon's proximity would serve as a fantastic observation post. The downside of that equation was that even with Earth's presently limited space-roving abilities, the moon was already within their reach. This was documented by the numerous artificial satellites circling the moon as well as the leftover debris from prior Earthling landings scattered about the surface. *Can't these folks learn to pick up after themselves*? wondered the shuttlecraft commander. *Pigs, clean up*! The shuttlecraft first deployed its specialized satellite 15,000 km from the moon's surface. Then it was inserted into a scanning orbit around the moon at a distance of the mere 500 km from the moon's surface to locate an initial landing site. The onboard computers compiled data from their sensors, confirming a relatively extensive lunar water ice presence in the numerous shadowed craters at both the north and south poles of the moon. Picking a site near the moon's south pole, the shuttle commander directed his ship to a favorable landing zone in the Sea of Tranquility. Upon touchdown, the localized weather report showed a sub-freezing exterior, no atmosphere, and a significantly lower level of gravity than Earth due to the significantly lower mass of the moon. The shuttlecraft commander ordered a crew of two to suit up and explore the surface. Since the radiation from the sun was intense, each crew member required appropriate shielding materials in their spacesuits.

A few hours later the crew returned covered in a fine coat of moon dust. They entered through the isolation chamber, bringing aboard rock and surface debris for scientific evaluation. The rocks contained a variety of minerals that could be exploited for construction purposes. The dust had an unpleasant characteristic of adhering closely to their spacesuits, raising the possibility of contaminating the interior of the shuttlecraft. That is why the Redexians had long ago designed isolation chambers to clean off all incoming crew members and their equipment. Every three hours one exploration group returned to the shuttlecraft as another departed for the surface. The commander had developed a two day plan to document 50 square kilometers of surface area as potential permanent observation base sites.

Reviewing the preliminary information as it arrived from the three shuttlecrafts, Captain Oulah was pleased. There was sufficient time to send the fourth shuttlecraft to Earth to pick up their previous explorers and return with the four invited Earth guests. Then, after reviewing the compiled data and reports, he could select the best sites to establish permanent Redexian observation posts. Analyzing all of this material in conjunction with meeting the four Earth guests would prepare him for his important visit with Earth's political leaders. All was going well and proceeding as planned. Everything looked good for accomplishing his goals. Keep steady; keep moving forward. The captain decided to tour the complete interior of his mother ship. He wanted to see firsthand how his thousands of fellow Redexian crew members were getting along. He wanted to see firsthand the arrangements being made aboard the mother ship to transport, construct, and occupy permanent observation bases in this solar system. He wanted to meet with those individuals who would be sent to construct and colonize this new outpost. He also wanted to spend some quality time with the intended new colony governor to discuss his plans for deployment. In short, he wanted to see, hear, listen, and be prepared.

CHAPTER 9

INTELLIGENCE TRAINING

With only a few weeks remaining before the expected arrival of the Redexian shuttlecraft in Roswell, it was time to begin training the four selected Earth guests who would be returning to the alien mother ship. Casey Foster was picked up by his security detail and transported to the CIA training facility in Chantilly, Virginia. Likewise, Leah Anne Bailey's security team hustled her out of her apartment into their waiting van and hurried her off to the CIA training facility as well. Arriving together from the Washington consulate were the Israeli diplomatic agent Jacob Witwenova and Chinese military agent Chloe Anh Sing. Soon they were all assembled together at the massive wrought iron front gate of The Farm. Then a CIA team arrived to escort them to the intake center. A drive down a long, twisting gravel roadway, past numerous observation towers, led to a guard station surrounded by a heavily armed contingent. Each of the four occupants exited at the guard station and had their entry documents carefully screened. Fingerprints were taken and matched to prior records along with corroborating face photographs, which were checked against passports. Once cleared, the four were escorted by caravan to a secluded landing strip. Awaiting them on the tarmac sat a camouflaged Sikorsky helicopter with its rotor blades chopping the air. Each of the four special agents were silently escorted to the helicopter while a CIA security detail dismissed all other personnel who had arrived with the caravan.

Once all were aboard, the helicopter quickly gained altitude, turned east, and traveled on a circuitous route for another five minutes before landing in an open valley in the heavily-wooded Virginia countryside. As if out of nowhere, ten heavily armed CIA agents surrounded the helicopter, taking possession of the four somewhat bewildered "guests" arriving for training. They were escorted into the woods where a hidden passageway opened in the side of a hill. Cleverly placed inside the entryway was a steel, reinforced elevator door. Casey, Leah Anne, Jacob, and Chloe were ushered into the elevator, and the door closed solidly behind them. The inside of the elevator was totally empty, without even a keypad. The only visible enhancements were two small overhead halogen lights. After a short period of time a continuous white line appeared at the top of the elevator and slowly descended from the ceiling to the floor. To these four new agents inside the elevator it appeared as some sort of scanning procedure, kind of like those semi-intrusive full body scans at the airports. Leah Anne felt a little shiver of anticipation. *Be a big girl*, she told herself. Then, the elevator began a rapid descent downwards. With the absence of any numbers appearing to indicate levels or floors, the occupants could not discern how far down the elevator was actually traveling. It was all starting to feel pretty creepy. Eventually, the elevator slowed to a stop, and its doors opened to a darkened descending hallway. No one was present to guide them to their destination. They felt alone, without any control over their safety. That was indeed the intention of the CIA's training center in "welcoming" for these four very special agents. It was the first of many planned training sessions trying to simulate what it would be like traveling on an alien shuttlecraft to an alien mother ship beyond reach of anything that was even remotely familiar. There would be no one available to come to their rescue. There would be no one available to answer their questions. There may be no familiar food, drink, clothing, or social interactions. Rather, they each would be at the mercy of their hosts. Worst still, there were no similar prior experiences to draw upon in designing this training program. So buckle up, take a deep breath, and get ready for the ride.

Waiting patiently at the end of the hallway, standing at the front of the chosen classroom, was CIA special agent Judd Mayer. He had been serving as the CIA's agent in charge of specialized training for over ten years. A solid American citizen of Romanian extraction, raised by a military family, he embodied the spirit of a clandestine spy. Mayer had been born into a hard working family on the north side of Chicago, in a neighborhood called Rogers Park. Later he moved on with his family to receive his early schooling in a northern Chicago suburb, nestled cheek to jowl with Lake Michigan. It was a suburban community fueled by successful, competitive, upwardly mobile American families. All opportunities laid before Judd if he would only produce the effort to reach for the brass ring. After graduating from high school at New Trier he continued his college education at Michigan State, where he was exposed to ROTC training. The military training fit him like a tight but comfortable leather glove. Before long he applied for a transfer and was accepted at West Point Academy, where he excelled in rugged physical training as well as intelligence-gathering techniques. Graduating with honors, Judd, nicknamed by his classmates as "the Romanian horse thief," was assigned as a first lieutenant to an American tank division stationed in Frankfurt, Germany. It appeared that although he had a working knowledge of the German language, he spoke it haltingly and read it with great difficulty. But while this may have been a stumbling block for some new officers, his specialty for training subordinate troops and gathering intelligence became quickly apparent. First Lieutenant Mayer quickly advanced through the ranks to Captain, then Major, and before long he was promoted to Lieutenant Colonel. Not a bad start to a career of service for his beloved country. As an intelligence officer he trained a network of deep cover spies and recruited double agents to secure invaluable intelligence on their current cold war enemy the Bolshevik Russians. Eventually, Colonel Mayer came to the attention of the CIA as the number one military spymaster trainer in Europe. It seems the CIA was trying to develop an updated modern system of intelligence gathering in Europe. So Judd, now a full Colonel, was brought to The Farm along with a class of 15 other potential senior agents for testing. Judd's special skills were perfectly suited to the CIA's needs. He excelled at training other agents as opposed to acting as an embedded spy. Special Agent Mayer had a knack for grabbing your attention. He could force feed your mind by filling it, bit by bit, with the principles of quiet, effective intelligence gathering. Over the years he steadily moved up the ranks to become the CIA's go-to agent for special projects training. Shadowing his every move was his well trained hound, known simply as " The Small Colonel", a look alike, well trained Schnauzer. Where agent Mayer went his dog followed, sometimes with a clipboard in his mouth. A real dog gone helper. Woof, woof, woof.

As soon as US Secretary of Defense Kalnikoff was advised that the four Earthlings had been invited to the Redexian mother ship, he had contacted the CIA to arrange a specialized training program. Judd Mayer was the CIA's unanimous choice for the instructor. He could be jovial, engaging, and even delightful when he was in the mood. But he was also a hard taskmaster who expected full attention and the highest level of performance. He would instill in his charges his "get it done" attitude. And this project in particular required the best he had to give to these new special agents.

A few minutes after the elevator doors slid open the four new special agents made their way cautiously through the darkened hallway to their classroom. It was apparent that even during the short time they had spent together they had already started to bond as a unit. Safety in numbers coupled with cooperation always made humans feel more comfortable.

"Welcome to The Farm," said special training agent Judd Mayer, as the new recruits arrived in his classroom and were signaled to be seated. "I am CIA special training agent Judd Mayer, and I will be in charge of your intensive two week training course. Most of our new potential special agents are provided with an initial three-month course covering a generalized program of intelligence-gathering and spying. This is followed by an additional six months of specialized training depending upon which area they show the most potential in. You four special agents do not fit within this category. I understand that two of you, mainly Jacob Witwenova and Chloe Anh Sing, are already accomplished diplomatic and military intelligence officers. I've been apprised that Casey Foster and Leah Anne Bailey are total novices. Well, I don't really care. The situations that we expect you will be facing with the Redexians will be totally novel. We unfortunately don't have any background or experience with this type of situation. It's like we're all babies in the care of a hopefully paternal relative. Sometimes babies are coddled, and sometimes they are treated harshly with spankings. This training that you are about to begin will prepare you for any possibilities. Keep in mind that everything that is about to happen during your two-week stay at The Farm is a test. Nothing here is real. Nothing is as it seems. You have just stepped through the looking glass, like Alice in Wonderland. Your abilities to cope with these situations will prepare you for what comes next. Keep in mind that I am not your friend. I am not here to hold your hand and whisper sweet encouragements in your ear. I am here solely to train you. Now I will have you escorted to your living facilities, where you will be issued specialized gear and provided with your first meals. All additional training will occur here on the grounds of The Farm. Much of this training will occur underground. You will report back here in two hours, at which time your training will begin. Your attention to training will be essential to your survival and usefulness as an agent. There will be no questions at this time. Dismissed," he said and then swiveled on his heels in military fashion and departed with his silver gray hound close at his heels, obediently following behind.

Two hours later the four new special agents reassembled in the underground conference room wearing matching training gear. At the front of the classroom stood their training instructor, Judd Mayer. "We are now ready to begin your specialized 14 day training sessions," he said. "Normally, a new class of specialized agents numbers around 30, and we provide basic training and fitness courses. Because of the nature of your assignment I have developed a short course specifically for your interaction with the Redexian aliens. Agent Witwenova, I understand you have been assigned duties as the diplomatic officer in charge of communication and interpretation with the returning aliens. Your training will focus on language skills as well as multiple courses on pursuing diplomatic relations with an unknown entity. Flexibility will be the key to your training, along with preparing scrupulous notes on your interchanges. I understand that Agent Anh Sing is a military weapons and equipment specialist. Your training will focus upon learning as much as possible concerning the Redexian military arsenal and delivery systems. You will be trained to look for weaknesses in their systems, methods to disable these systems, or places to attack. Similarly, you will prepare extensive detailed analysis and records concerning your findings.

"Casey Foster and Leah Anne Bailey are the two new recruits. Chances are that neither of you know anything about spying or intelligence matters. While I will provide some information on these topics, your roles will be different. Casey Foster, as a professional photographer, will be trained to photograph and videotape, without drawing undue attention, every aspect of the shuttlecraft, the exterior and interior of the mother ship, and the officers on the Redexian spacecraft. I hope you will be able to take your regular professional photographic equipment along for the journey. In addition, you will be provided with specialized miniature photographic instruments to be used secretly, if possible. We will also provide a means for transmission of this documentation from space back to our headquarters. That way we hope to have information before you return. Finally, as to Agent Leah Anne Bailey, your assignment as a journalist is to collect information both on the shuttlecraft as well as the mother ship for publication in the *Washington Post*. I hope to provide sufficient training so that Leah Anne can gain access to places such as the bridge of the mother ship, the engine room facilities, and any weapons or military hardware areas. Leah Anne will also be taught to document and record as much information as possible.

"Normal training here at the CIA is for insertion of long term secret agents ferreting out intelligence to transmit back to headquarters for analysis. These agents also attempt to recruit local elements to act as double agents or local spies. Your situation is different. You won't be blending in and looking like or acting like Redexians. How could you? So you will act friendly, cooperative, and available as fellow galaxy members to inquire about all the new things you are experiencing. You will look, listen, learn, question, and record as much as possible for transmission back to Earth. Finally, our normal operations are always filled with plans for extraction of agents if things get out of control. This will not be available for any of you. You are on your own. We have little protection to offer you other than normal diplomatic protocol. Unfortunately, we also do not know whether the Redexians adhere to Earth's standards. Your safety is in your hands and your fellow agents' hands. Act accordingly. Any questions?" he asked? No one raised a hand or voiced any concerns. " OK, time to get started."

Casey was led by Judd to the CIA's well supplied photography department. An essential element of training for each agent was to learn the means to document their surreptitious assignments. Casey felt like a kid in a candy store, or like a computer geek set free at Microsoft. There were incredible gadgets, photographic equipment, and spy gear everywhere. This equipment ranged from very sophisticated digital cameras with incredibly large interchangeable lenses to tiny hidden cameras located in things such as cigarette cartons, lighters, eyeglass frames, attaché cases, the soles of shoes, fountain pens, and even packs of chewing gum. In short, the smaller the camera, the more nifty the device for hiding it. One camera system that Casey particularly liked took photographs in secret that resulted in a blurred image that was then run through specialized software so that the original image would appear magically before you in perfect condition. It was kind of like transmitting a message in code. In addition to all of the camera gadgets, there remained the issue of transmitting the photographic images back to Earth. One transmitter of normal size and regulation would be disclosed to the Redexians as a means of transmitting "normal images," uncontroversial in nature, back to Earth. That should not cause a problem. But the CIA had also prepared miniaturized transmitters to be hidden in Casey Foster's gear. These could be used in addition to or instead of the regular transmitter system. The coolest transmitter, as far as Casey was concerned, was built directly into one of his cameras. Take a shot, hit a button, and radio waves traveling at the speed of light sent the images home instantly. *How cool is that*? thought

Casey. So for the rest of the afternoon Casey was led from one camera and transmitter to the other and was asked to select three cameras and transmitters that appealed to him. He would receive more detailed instruction concerning their use and capacity once he chose them. It didn't get much better than that for a photographic geek. Boy, he wished Keary Ryan was with him to share this treat. His smile was almost a mile wide. He already loved being an interstellar spy in training.

Leah Anne Bailey was taken by Judd directly to the intelligence section. Her assignment would be to collect and document as much information on the shuttlecraft, mother ship, and Redexian officers as possible. Given her occupation as a news reporter, the focus of her training would be to conduct detailed interviews with as many crew members as possible regarding as many subjects as possible. More specifically, she was asked to collect information on how the shuttlecraft and the mother ship operated, the power sources used, and the Redexian purpose for returning to Earth. *Nothing to it*, she thought to herself. *I'll just ask, and they will tell me. I mean, I'm perfectly trustworthy, right*? So, in general, Leah Anne was to act kind of like a blonde dingbat reporter. How difficult could that be? Just poking around for fun to report for her *Washington Post* news readership. Just listen to what they tell her, wander around, talk to alien "people," look excited and interested, and collect and record all the information available.

Once Leah Anne collected the information she would prepare news articles for transmission from space for publication in the *Washington Post*. She would insert within each news article code words, which she would be required to memorize. The insertion of any such code word in the first or last paragraph of the article would signal the real status of events. It was supposed to be a failsafe method of describing what was really happening with the Redexians. These code words were not to be shared with her fellow Earthling agents. In effect, she would be transmitting a message within a message. Pretty clever for a backward culture. Yep, we cool!

Jacob Witwenova was escorted by Judd to the language department and immediately introduced to Dr. James Westermonne. Jacob would greet the incoming shuttlecraft crew and travel back to the mother ship as the designated diplomat from Earth. He needed to communicate with the Redexians in a favorable diplomatic manner. It would be a most delicate job without any known parameters regarding both the language and social interactions. He would have to learn on the fly and keep the interactions as even-keeled as possible. Dr. Westermonne, Earth's leading expert on the Redexian language, took Jacob aside and explained how he had been able to interpret the transmitted messages. He explained his methodology for developing interpretive software and the computer programs used for detailed analysis. A current copy of this software and a basic Redexian language primer and dictionary were provided to Jacob. Their job would be to spend enough time together so that Jacob could understand the basics of the Redexian language and communicate with the aliens. Repetition translated loosely into learning. So they began speaking to each other solely in the Redexian language Newee, without the nuances of flapping ears and wiggling fingers. It was close; certainly better than nothing. Westermonne explained that as more communications, either in written form or orally, arrived, the better they would become at deciphering the meanings.

In addition to the language training, the CIA had prepared a crash course for Jacob in diplomatic maneuvering. He would be taught diplomatic skills for interacting with either friendly or hostile emissaries. He would be taught observational skills to determine the level of social interaction needed, including such things as whether to touch the aliens, such as by shaking hands. He would learn such skills as where to look when speaking, how to enter and leave an audience chamber, and the appropriate level and tone of his voice during conversation. Drilled into the training was the need for continuous revamping of his diplomatic exchanges based upon his interactions. In all interactions he was taught to be willing and cooperative. Don't be threatening, obnoxious, overly forceful, or demanding. Earth was looking for an evenhanded, cooperative approach, a hoped-for meeting among equals, an interchange between two independent species that could be beneficial to both. Jacob hoped that he would be perceived as a friendly message bearer. He hoped that any ill will would not be taken out on him personally; he hoped they wouldn't kill the messenger. This, of course, was a well known hazard of being the lead diplomat. Sometimes the return message was to terminate the messenger to show your displeasure.

Chloe Anh Sing was brought by Judd directly to an assembly of leading worldwide military officers familiar with each others' military capabilities. Together they would review Earth's capacity for air, sea, land, and space military maneuvers. Her assignment would be to speak with the Redexian personnel to determine their intentions regarding Earth. As the military agent, Chloe was also to determine the level of sophistication of the aliens' military capabilities and any shortcomings or defects which Earthlings might attack, if needed. Included within her assignment was to determine whether or not any nuclear weapons, chemical agents, or biological agents could be effectively employed against the aliens as deterrents. Good luck with that!

For her technical training, Chloe met with various military hardware experts as well as specialists designing new and improved weapons systems. They explained to her what they were looking for so she could gather the necessary intelligence. Earth's military leaders wanted to know: what were the Redexian weapons systems? What means did they have to deploy these weapons? What was the magnitude of their force and the nature and extent of damages that could be expected? In short, find out what military potential the Redexians had and how best to defeat it.

For 10 days each of the four CIA special agents continued their individual training under Judd Mayer's watchful direction. Then, on the 11th, day all four were led to a mockup of the Redexian shuttlecraft complete with fully costumed miniature aliens. For the next eight hours they were left to their own devices as they sought to communicate with the alien shuttlecraft crew. It was slow going at first, with much gesturing and limited amounts of meaningful communication. Casey went about his task trying to communicate and quietly photographing everything in sight. Leah Anne used her best efforts to interview each of the alien crew members.

Jacob initiated a conversation with the shuttle commander exercising his diplomatic protocols while Chloe wandered about the small shuttlecraft examining the control panels while subtly looking for the power source. The hours spent on board the mockup proved useful for training purposes. As expected, their skill set improved with repetition. At the completion of the 14 day training session it was apparent that all four agents had improved their understanding of the Redexian language and their individual assignments. Then, on the last day of training, Judd Mayer thanked the new agents for their attendance. He provided each with a small lapel pin denoting their graduation from this specialized CIA training. They were told that they could not wear those pins. And they were also informed that their names would not be recorded at the CIA or elsewhere showing them to be CIA agents. As in, hey, you don't really exist when it comes to the CIA. And if you are somehow found out, we will not provide a way out or acknowledge your status. This was intentionally a one way street. You help us, period. Together, Judd Mayer and his dog The Colonel said goodbye and sent the newly trained agents on their way with a strange parting order to "Bite their faces off."

The four graduates were then flown to Israel to complete their last five days of training. Once on the ground, a Mossad special task force escorted them to an isolated outpost which was the Israeli Negev desert training center. Striding forward, they were met by IDF Major Scott Nathan. Short, stocky, devoid of most of the hair on his head, round faced and austere, he addressed the assembled agents.

"We have a limited amount of time to allot to each of you during your remaining training. My job will be to facilitate this training so that you can have the best possible outcome during this unusual alien encounter. We will spend most of our time working on language skills, mental toughness, survival skills within the context of a closed environment, and, most importantly, documenting whatever it is you may learn. Everything that you come in contact with may be totally different from your normal experiences. To the extent that any of this new information can be transmitted from space, so much the better. So keep your eyes and ears open, be attentive, and soak in as much information as possible. Be a sponge, a blotter. Anything that you can learn will expand our understanding of this alien species. Also, try to keep in mind that as guests aboard their craft you will also be observed, tested, and questioned. Undoubtedly these Redexians are just as interested in us Earthlings as a species as we are interested in them. You should expect them to be probing each of you for information." Major Nathan left out the part that they may also be probed physically. Why insert an extra layer of anxiety? Instead Scott merely said, "Try to find an ally or a weak link. Try to extract information regarding the Redexians' weaknesses. Keep your wits about you, act as pleasant as possible, and divulge as little as possible."

The final phase of the Mossad training focused on the interaction between the four agents. They developed a methodology for passing information between them. This they practiced until smooth interactions became second nature. Recording and transmitting information was practiced using each of the available devices. Code words were developed as well as code gestures. The trainees were now as well prepared for their mission as was possible. It was time to wait and reflect. The next step would be to meet the incoming alien shuttlecraft in Roswell, New Mexico, and move forward as guests on the Redexian mother ship.

Unseen by the four agents, the Mossad hierarchy had different concerns than the mere preparation of the four agents to meet aliens. These guys and their forefathers had been fighting for their very existence for a long time. Israel, in its historical context, was surrounded by a vast horde of people who wished it did not exist. But Israel had no intention of evaporating into the hot mist of extinct civilizations. So, to this leadership group, these four "soldiers" were clearly expendable, if necessary. But they did have great value. Perhaps they could be used as a delivery system for a destructive attack on the Redexians. Unknowingly, each could be injected with a deadly virus and sent along by shuttlecraft to the mother ship to infect the entire alien crew. Or one or more of the special agents could silently be recruited to poison the mother ship's food, air, or, better yet, water supplies. This might, in fact, be the only opportunity to carry out such an attack. But the consequences of failure were grave. The Redexians might survive and decided to decimate Earth. Or success now might lead to a later returning Redexian force to obliterate the planet. Cooler heads in Mossad prevailed for now. They decided to wait and see what happened with the initial shuttlecraft meeting, and then wait longer until the full Redexian diplomatic presence arrived so they could see what it wanted. Wait and contemplate; then a decision could be made. Cooperate for now, try to destroy the Redexians later, if needed. Wait, evaluate, and prepare. Wait for now!

CHAPTER 10

BROTHER EXPLORERS RETURNED

The Redexian mother ship remained safely in orbit around Saturn's moon, Titan, collecting data from its three recently deployed satellites. Moving forward with his mission, Captain Oulah IV gathered the three returned shuttlecraft commanders in the bridge conference room to discuss their reports regarding locating sites for developing permanent observation bases in this solar system. The first presentation was made by the shuttle commander who had surveyed Titan. He indicated that Titan's rocky surface could serve as a permanent observation base whether above ground or more cleverly placed underground. However, the extremely cold surface temperatures at -289° would make living conditions far from ideal. On the other hand, the existence of vast quantities of liquid methane and other important minerals might make the surface of Titan an excellent location for a mineral substation. This location could be readily developed as a resource and fueling depot staffed with a minimum Redexian crew. Such a substation on Titan was well beyond the Earthling's current abilities for interference. His recommendation was to construct a small substation location at Ontario Lacus in Titan's eastern hemisphere near the south pole. It contained a nearby shallow lake filled with an extensive quantity of liquid hydrocarbons.

Next to report, the shuttle commander who had surveyed Earth's moon presented his findings. He indicated that his survey of the moon showed a location at Mare Nectaris, which contained sufficient water ice and various useable minerals, making it suitable for a permanent observation base. Its proximity to Earth provided an excellent staging point to observe Earth activities and beyond into the nearby regions of the Milky Way galaxy. Unfortunately, like Titan, there were serious drawbacks. They included the lack of any atmosphere, pesky surface dust, and widely varying temperatures between the dark side of the moon and the light side of the moon. Furthermore, even present Earth technology would place any permanent Redexian observation base within their reach. So while a base could certainly be established, it was not an optimal choice as a primary location.

Finally, the shuttle commander who had surveyed Mars presented his findings. He indicated that Mars was intriguing. It had a thin but sustainable atmosphere. It had a livable surface temperature range with seasons and thus was clearly located in this star's habitable zone. Its surface held numerous minerals worth mining with an emphasis on rich iron ore. Perhaps most importantly, it had vast quantities of water, both underground and in easily reachable permafrost layers close to the surface. Studies also showed various locations on Mars having actual running surface water during various seasons and weather conditions. In addition, Mars was close enough to Earth to make observation both readily available and yet far enough away that, in the near-term, Earthlings could not interfere with any Redexian plans. Most intriguingly, if the Redexians chose, it appeared that Mars could be terraformed over a reasonable period of time to raise its surface temperature sufficiently to develop both a breathable atmosphere and the growth of agreeable plant life. Given this situation, Mars could, within approximately five years, readily support an expanding colony of Redexians living comfortably on its surface. In the meantime, their present technology would allow a permanent observation base sustaining 1500 crewmembers in more than adequate living conditions. In short, Mars held great opportunity and little in the way of disadvantages for a permanent base. The commander strongly recommended a site in the Oxia Palus region due to its ease of access and nearby materials, which could be used for construction of the base.

Captain Oulah listened carefully, reviewed each of the three detailed reports, and told the shuttle commanders he would make his decision in due course. Following this meeting, the captain called together his second-in-command and the mother ship's communication officer. "Gentlemen," he said, "the time has come to send a shuttlecraft to Earth to pick up our brothers in exploration. We will then transport back to our mother ship four Earthlings for preliminary discussions. Therefore, you will transmit the following message to Earth:

"Gentlemen, please be advised that we are sending a Redexian shuttlecraft to Roswell for arrival in five of your Earth days. At this time, please engage the emergency signaling device retrieved from the crashed Redexian spacecraft by pressing its top red button once every six hours for the next five days. This will provide an exact location for our shuttlecraft to land. Upon arrival we will take immediate possession of our former 'brothers in exploration' for return to our mother ship. We will transport back to our spaceship four Earthlings for preliminary discussions. We have made arrangements for our crew's safety while on your planet. We have made further arrangements to transport the four selected Earth guests to our mother ship and maintain them safely while visiting. You will not need to make any arrangements for their care. Please extend your cooperation to our shuttle commander concerning his requests to visit other Earth locations during his visit. Your cooperation is anticipated.

"Signed, Captain Oulah IV of the United Redexian Frontier"

"As you wish," replied the communications officer. "I will transmit this message now on the same frequency utilized previously." With a nod towards the captain and the second-in-command, he was off to his station to comply.

"Second-in-command, please make arrangements for the Earth shuttlecraft commander to depart with his crew in two hours. I will want to speak with him just before he departs. Plan on attending the meeting," said the captain.

"Aye, Captain; where would you like to meet?" asked the second-in-command?

"The bridge conference room will serve us well."

A little less than an hour later Captain Oulah, the second-in-command, and the Earth shuttle commander Aounah III were all seated at the conference room table. "Commander," said the captain, "your mission will be to rendezvous at Roswell at the location of the transmitted emergency signal. You are to complete the following tasks. Pick up our heroic brothers in exploration and return them to the mother ship. Provide them with medical treatment, if possible. Request accompaniment of a senior ranking Earthling to tour Washington DC; London, England; Beijing, China; and Jerusalem, Israel, one of which will later serve as our primary embassy location. Then return to Roswell to conduct a survey of the adjacent area to locate a permanent recreational base for our rotating crewmembers. Lastly, return to the mother ship with the four selected Earthlings for preliminary discussions. Considering your travel time to and from Earth, I expect to have you back at our mother ship within 15 days. All transmissions back to our communication center must be sent in standard Redexian exploratory code. Good luck on your mission. Second-in-command, do you have anything to add?"

"Just a quick comment, sir. Commander Aounah, just as on our other similar missions, don't expect the local inhabitants to be as intelligent or thoughtful as our fellow crew members. Although their appearance may be repugnant, you will communicate with them politely. Be patient. Be pleasant. Try to be respectful. Good luck. We await your successful return," said the second-in-command.

"*Shalom*, and may peace be upon you," said the captain and second-in-command in unison.

"*Shalom Aleichem*," responded the shuttle commander, head bowed in respect, ears and fingers wiggling slightly with excitement.

With that, commander Aounah III was escorted to his waiting mid-sized shuttlecraft and departed with his well-trained crew for Roswell. It was a trip of approximately 225 million miles to be covered in under 5 days at an average Redexian mandated speed of 1.8 million miles per hour, quite astounding by current Earthling standards. It was a speed well beyond any current Earth technology, proposed Earth technology, or even scientifically available technology. Furthermore, had such a propulsion system been in a planning stage, the construction materials and methodology had not yet been discovered on Earth. So Earthlings would not be hopping around space from star system to star system at these kinds of speeds for quite some time. Earthlings were still shackled by horse and buggy technology as far as space travel was concerned. Better than nothing, but with a long way to go. Perhaps it was time to recognize that Earthlings were newcomers in a 4.5 billion year old Milky Way galaxy. A little like advanced breeding mammals in a 13.7 billion year old universe. Plenty of other star systems had evolved in the Milky way to support intelligent life as advanced as either Earth or Redex. So remember to keep your heads (of different sizes and complexities) up and look around. Hope to improve. As for Earthlings, they were apparently proud of their current stage of evolution just knowing how to use knives, forks, spoons, and table napkins. It's a start.

Back home on Earth, the Group of 8 received the action reports from each of their designated committees. The group also received the most recently translated Redexian communication indicating its shuttlecraft would return to Roswell in approximately 5 days. Given this situation, an emergency meeting was scheduled to review the five committees' reports and make decisions concerning each committee's proposals. The Group of 8 decided to hold its next meeting in Paris, to be led by President Barack Obama as the designated interim chairman. Once all had arrived at the Carlton Court Palace alongside the banks of the Seine river, Chairman Obama gaveled the meeting to order and issued his opening statement.

"Gentlemen, the time has arrived for the imminent return to Roswell of the extra solar aliens, who refer to themselves as Redexians. We have commissioned and now received action reports from each of our five designated committees, attended by representatives from each of our nations. These action reports have been circulated among us, and it is time to make some decisions regarding how we proceed. I will present a brief review of each committee report and ask for your input so the matter can be voted upon.

"First, with respect to the Diplomacy Committee, my understanding is that Mr. Jacob Witwenova of Israel has been nominated as our lead diplomat. He has extensive experience as the lead ambassador in a number of troubling locations. I further understand that he has undergone two weeks of specialized Redexian training at CIA headquarters as well as an additional five days of training by Mossad in the Negev. My recommendation is that we approve of Mr. Witwenova as our initial diplomatic ambassador with additional training to be scheduled for selected associate diplomats, one from each of our nations and another to be nominated by the United Nations. Please raise your hand if you are in favor of this proposal."

Without discussion, each voting member of the Group of 8 signaled their unanimous consent.

"Secondly," continued Chairman Obama, "with respect to the Communications Committee, the recommendation is that we develop as much expertise as possible in the Redexian language. We will also plan on communicating with them in English. I understand that Dr. James Westermonne has begun training our selected ambassador Jacob Witwenova in the Redexian language and has developed a preliminary cross dictionary of essential terms. I further understand that each of the four selected agents to return to the Redexian mother ship has also received some basic Redexian language training. My suggestion is that we again approve the committee's recommendation that we make our presentations in English while training our ambassadors to speak Redexian. In addition, I suggest that any meetings held with the Redexians in a host nation location be conducted secondarily in that nation's native language. Again, please raise your hand if you are in favor of this proposal."

With a somewhat vigorous nodding of heads, all voting members of the Group of 8 signaled their unanimous support again.

"Thirdly, as to site selection for our proposed meetings with the Redexians, our committee has recommended that we choose from among Roswell, New Mexico; Washington, DC; London, England; Jerusalem, Israel; Beijing, China; Moscow, Russia; Tokyo, Japan; Paris, France; and Berlin, Germany. Of course, we cannot control any choices that may be suggested by the alien visitors. We will just have to wait and see if they have any preferences. To facilitate this decision, I am now going to pass out voting slips with these choices and recommend that we choose the top four. All in favor of this suggestion for voting please raise your hand."

Again, with little discussion, the Group of 8 moved forward with this proposal. Five minutes later the balloting had been tabulated, with the top four choices selected being Roswell, Washington, London, and Beijing. The Group of 8, upon reflection, confirmed these four choices as proposed sites for future meetings with the aliens.

Chairman Obama, starting to feel the pleasant glow of cooperative momentum, moved directly forward to the issue of security. "Gentlemen, as you are aware, the visit of these aliens to Earth will garner tremendous interest among our local populations, raising vexing security issues. We cannot afford to have any incidents that could injure any visiting aliens. Again, I have reviewed and circulated among you the report from the security committee. It has recommended that each of our nations, as well as the UN, provide 20 of their most highly trained security officers to work as a combined task force. I recommend that this task force be led by one security officer each from China, Russia, and the United States. Meetings and coordination of this joint security force should take place in Germany with transportation to and from other sites facilitated by France."

Following a brief discussion, this proposal was again unanimously approved.

"Finally, we have some decisions to make with respect to public preparation, by which I mean how much we tell the citizens of our planet concerning our plans, the intentions of our alien visitors, and the locations for any meetings. The committee reports circulated among you recommend that we cautiously advise the public only to a limited extent and about nothing of major importance. I would like to first hear the views on this subject from the Group of 8 representatives from India and China, as our most populous nations."

Standing in place, Ms. Indira Ganuruh of India spoke eloquently in her high British accent to the assembled committee members. "We in India are members of the world's largest democracy. We endeavor to inform our citizens of all important matters and decisions to the best of our abilities. However, in a nation as diverse as India, some matters are carefully doled out in abbreviated form. We cannot afford our nation to have opinions getting out of control. Wide spread demonstrations, meetings, and protests are avoided wherever and whenever possible. This seems to us to be the correct course to take in informing our citizens about the Redexians. I recommend that all public communications be channeled through the Communications Committee and circulated among our Group of 8 for approval prior to public disclosure. Normal gossipy news publications of little substance should be tolerated."

Next, Mr. Wan So Ping of China rose to address the group, not in his native Mandarin but in what he considered to be more sophisticated French. Whoa, Mao would be mighty pissed by his choice of language if he was present. Perhaps a whap in the head with the *Little Red Book* would be in order. Perhaps a few years in a "retraining facility." "My dear fellow members," he began, "as you all know, China's ever-growing population is well in excess of 1.3 billion comrades and growing steadily. As such, we long ago recognized that communication of important nationwide information has to be disseminated through an official government news agency. Otherwise, the clamor of different opinions is potentially destructive. So we carefully dole out acceptable information to the public. Accordingly, I wholeheartedly concur with Ms. Ganuruh's suggestion that we present a united voice for public presentation of screened information. News that we consider to be inflammatory or defeating should be censored. And, of course, any such news presentation should be channeled through our Group of 8 for approval prior to publication."

"Thank you both," said Chairman Obama. "Now, unless there is further discussion, all in favor of the public preparation proposal please raise your hands."

Once again a unanimous vote confirmed the methodology suggested by the committee as amended by the Indian and Chinese delegates.

"It seems," said Chairman Obama, "that we have reached agreement on each of these committee proposals. Please keep in mind that these procedures need to be in place within five days. I now suggest that we adjourn this meeting. All in favor please say 'aye.' We are adjourned."

The Group of 8 members dispersed to the dining area. Now, drinking, dining, and self-serving yapping, their professional specialty, was in order. Those very same members who had recently been cooperating for their mutual survival now started haggling with each other concerning daily issues such as trade, treaties, international hot spots, and other nationalistic agendas. The unity that prevailed with respect to the outside threat from the Redexians disappeared like a puff of smoke from a campfire. Cooperation, present one minute, disappeared into the ether the next. Perhaps the incoming Redexians' actions would teach them that their special self-serving national interests could not continue to prevail in order for Earth to survive as an independent world.

Five days later, the midsize Redexian shuttlecraft appeared in the late afternoon sunlight hovering over the beacon focusing on the Roswell landing site. Without making a sound, the circular craft slowly lowered itself to its designated parking position. Its landing gear was lowered and its landing lights were turned off. A few minutes later, which seemed like an eternity to those on the ground waiting, an access ramp was lowered to ground level. Standing at the top of the ramp and surveying the surroundings stood one lone Redexian dressed in what appeared to be a military uniform. Behind him stood three other crew members in matching military uniforms and matching boots. Their leader walked forward and stopped approximately 10 paces from his greeting committee, composed of the hopefully well trained Jacob Witwenova, Earth's designated ambassador. Jacob signaled his welcome with a practiced bow, tilting slightly from the waist before slowly standing tall and raising his right arm in a gesture intended as a peaceful signal. Without hesitation the Redexian visitor reached downward, drew out his ray gun, aimed carefully at Jacob, pulled the trigger, and vaporized him without hesitation. Not even a cinder remained. The remaining members of the greeting committee were stunned and wordless with amazement, apprehension, and fear. The Redexian shuttle commander merely smiled benevolently as he lowered his discharged ray gun.

Jacob woke up from his dream drenched in sweat and screaming in Hebrew. *Well,* he thought, *the big meeting is still two days away, and already I'm an anxious mess. Time for some acid reflux medication. Where's my Nexium when I need it?* Rolling out of bed, he began a slow, wobbling walk to the shower where he stood rocking back and forth, letting the warm water soothe his limp body. *Let's hope the real meeting goes better,* he thought. *I'd hate to be the first Earthling in history to be vaporized by a visiting off-world alien. That's not the type of history book entry that I find appealing.*

Two days later, the real Redexian shuttlecraft appeared with flashing colored lights hovering over the prepared landing site at Roswell. Slowly lowering itself downward, the craft extended its landing gear for a soft touchdown. A few minutes later an access ramp was lowered to the ground presenting a view of four alien visitors ready to disembark. Each was dressed in matching military style clothing. The feature that stood out to all the Earthlings present was the visitors' large, bald, gray heads with deep set, enormous red eyes. Almost eerie. Similar to Jacob's dream, the lead Redexian casually moved forward and stopped approximately 10 paces in front of him. Ambassador Jacob Witwenova, with practiced grace, bowed gently from the waist, eyes focused upon his visitor, stood up slowly, smiled cautiously, and raised his right hand and arm in a hopefully universal gesture of peace and greeting. Thankfully, the shuttlecraft commander reciprocated with a slight nod of his bulging alien head, also raising his right arm and hand in a reciprocal gesture. Neither approached closer to the other for the next few seconds. It was rather like two boxers having entered the ring where both were sizing each other up before taking action.

Then Ambassador Witwenova, as the home court greeter, ventured to say a few well-practice sentences in something resembling Redexian syntax, roughly translated to mean, "Welcome to our world. Greetings from Earth. We are pleased that you have arrived for a peaceful interchange between our two respectful peoples. My name is Jacob Witwenova, and I am the Earth's ambassador for these preliminary meetings. I look forward to our exchanges and will assist you however I am able. Here on Earth people meeting for the first time generally shake hands as a show of trust and greeting. Please let me know whether this is acceptable." Having uttered his rehearsed remarks, Jacob nodded slightly and waited for a response. He really hoped the ray gun would not be produced, aimed at his head, and fired, burning him to a cinder.

The shuttle commander waited a few seconds and began his remarks in near perfect English. "My name is Aounah III," he responded. "I am here as the preliminary representative of our noble Redexian people. We have come to your planet in peace to explore a shared vision of mutual respect and common defense. Specifically, my orders are to secure the prompt return of our two beloved prior explorers for return to our mother ship. Further, I wish to discuss with you the visitation to a few of your Earth capitals. Finally, we would be pleased to return to our mother ship with four of your chosen Earthlings as our guests. This will assist in our mutual preparation for more formal discussions in the near future. With respect to your suggestion that we shake hands, I agree. Our social customs also generally permit meetings between new individuals to culminate with a gentle touching of heads. With your agreement I suggest that we move forward to middle ground and undertake these social gestures."

With that, shuttle commander Aounah III and Jacob Witwenova each stepped slowly towards middle ground, extended their right hands, and gently shook hands while cautiously touching heads, with the not too tall

Jacob leaning slightly forward. Multiple cameras took photographs and videos of the event to record this first meeting for posterity. The gesture went off without a hitch. After, both backed up a step and smiled at each other. Someplace in their different brains each thought the other was a bit repulsive looking. Luckily, both were smart enough to keep these thoughts to themselves.

Ambassador Witwenova then led Aounah and his three companions inside the Roswell air base receiving facility. Jacob quietly explained that, to their knowledge, the Redexian shuttlecraft visiting Earth in July, 1947, had become encircled in an intense lightning storm, causing it to break apart and crash in the desert outside Roswell. Once the authorities were notified, rescue crews had immediately been sent to the crash site to assist. Two pilots had been found at the scene. One was apparently already deceased, and the other pilot had appeared to be in grave physical condition. Attempts had been made by the available medical personnel to treat the injured pilot, but they had proven unsuccessful and the second pilot was declared deceased by the medical staff. Those present had been unfamiliar with the appropriate social protocols with respect to the deceased's remains. Accordingly, with all due respect, one of the bodies had been immersed in an available liquid preservative agent. The second pilot's remains had been placed in liquid nitrogen as a long-term conservation freezing agent. It had been hoped that should the pilot's remains be claimed in the future by their fellow citizens that these actions would be viewed as acceptable under these unusual conditions. Finally, Ambassador Witwenova tendered his gravest apologies on behalf of Earth should any missteps have taken place. He then offered to render any further assistance regarding transfer of the remains to Redexian control. Jacob awaited a response, holding his breath, for this, he knew, was a ticklish matter.

Shuttlecraft commander Aounah indicated he understood the extenuating circumstances. With a wave of his hand and a nod of his head he signaled his second crewmember, a medical officer, to come forward and take charge. Following the medical officer's directions, the first pilot was removed from the liquid holding tank and placed upon a metal table. A preliminary examination revealed that this Redexian pilot had suffered grave injuries at the time of the crash, which had led to his immediate death. The medical officer then attached a series of metallic leads to the deceased pilot's head and neck area and initiated electronic impulses. A second probe was then inserted in the pilot's mouth, and the medical officer uploaded the returning signals with as much of the pilot's stored memories as were available. Once this task was completed, the pilot's remains were placed into a silver metal container, resembling an Earth casket, for transference to the shuttlecraft and then back to the mother ship. Once aboard the mother ship, honorable Redexian ceremonies would take place as proscribed by custom for their deceased brother explorer.

Next, the Redexian medical officer supervised the removal of the second pilot's body from the nitrogen container and subsequent thawing. A thorough medical examination was followed by an extended surgical procedure and injections by the medical officer. Some minutes later, after consulting by radio telemetry with the mother ship's lead medical director, two further injections were administered and a brain stimulator was attached. Applying an external device, the medical officer administered an electric shock to the pilot's body. To the amazement of Ambassador Witwenova and the other Earthlings present, the "deceased" pilot came to life before them. He sat up, touched heads with the medical officer, and was given a beaker of fluid to ingest. Shortly thereafter, with a polite bow towards the Ambassador, the formerly deceased and now suddenly alive Redexian pilot was escorted back to the shuttlecraft. Now there's a doctor you want to have listed in your rolodex. Forget Medicare, Medicaid, and health insurance. Sign me up. I want some of that, whatever that turns out to be.

Commander Aounah then asked for access to the crash debris materials rescued from the 1947 incident. As a result, he was led to the reconstructed shuttlecraft. He thanked the Ambassador for the great care taken in restoring the spacecraft to the extent possible and with their limited available knowledge. Stepping forward, the third Redexian explained that he was an engineering specialist. He moved toward the reconstructed craft, opened an unseen recessed access door, reset a few dials, and inserted something that looked like an external battery pack. With a few further adjustments, a hidden access ramp slid from within the external body of the craft and touched down on the floor. The Redexian crew walked inside as the engineer approached the deck control panel. Again he opened a recessed access door, and before long the inert control panel came to life. Lights flashed, and the viewing screens became illuminated. What the engineer was really interested in obtaining was the flight recorder, internal computer databank, and the secretive black box. Before long each was in his possession for return to the mother ship.

So far, all had gone according to the Redexian plan. Everyone present seemed satisfied. No aggressive action had been taken by either side. That was a relief to all present. Aounah then suggested that they move to an area where they could discuss their remaining plans. Once suitably removed to the comfortable conference room, Aounah began, "Our captain has ordered me to evaluate four major Earth cities as possible embassy sites. In particular, he is interested in an examination of Washington, DC; London, England; Beijing, China; and Jerusalem, Israel. Can you make arrangements for those visits within the next three days?" he asked.

"Let me look into that," responded Ambassador Witwenova. "I hope to be able to provide you with an answer by early tomorrow morning. What time schedule are you interested in pursuing?"

"I have been ordered by my commanding officer to start the return trip back to the mother ship in three days' time. To speed up this examination process I suggest you may wish to accompany us on our shuttlecraft, since we can travel much faster. Is that acceptable?"

"Again," responded Jacob, "let me look into that and give you an answer tomorrow morning. In the meantime, would it be possible for us to serve you some refreshments?"

"Yes, that would be pleasant. But please be advised that we Redexians only intake liquid refreshment. Something on the order of a fruit drink would be acceptable."

"Of course," responded Jacob, "I will have servings of orange juice, apple juice, and lemonade brought immediately. You might wish to sample these drinks. I also understand that you have generously offered to take four of our Earth citizens back to your mother ship. We are concerned for the safety and comfort of our four Earth citizens during their travels with you. And while we are all excited by your generous offer to host these people, we don't want to be a burden. Will we need to make special arrangements for their atmosphere, clothing, food requirements, or other matters?"

Aounah responded, "This is a subject that we have dealt with on many prior occasions with other planet species. Please understand that, based upon data previously collected from your planet, we are well acquainted with your species' requirements for travel, atmosphere, food, and entertainment. All has been arranged. I would be happy for one of our staff to review this with your emissaries prior to departure. But let me assure you that all will be provided with a comfortable and interesting journey. If these four people are available, perhaps we can meet at this time."

"Thank you for your consideration, Commander," said Jacob. "It just so happens that I will be one of the emissaries to travel to your mother ship as a guest. Let me introduce at this time the other three guests whom we plan on bringing along with your approval. Please follow me."

Once they arrived at the adjoining conference room, the other three Earth guests lined up, bowed slowly, and nodded their heads in the direction of the shuttle commander. One by one they extended their right hands to shake and tilted their heads forward slightly to touch the Redexians. "First let me introduce Mr. Casey Foster. Mr. Foster is a professional photographer with one of our leading Earth newspapers, the *Washington Post*. Mr. Foster was also present at the time the emergency signal was sent back to planet Redex. Secondly, standing next to Mr. Foster is Leah Anne Bailey, a newspaper reporter with the *Washington Post* who was also present when the emergency signal was transmitted back to Redex. You may also find it interesting that Mr. Foster's grandfather, Mr. Newton Foster, was present in Roswell, New Mexico, when your shuttlecraft crashed in July, 1947. Finally, let me introduce you to Ms. Chloe Anh Sing, a citizen of China with knowledge in the area of mechanical systems. Each of us looks forward to this special occasion of traveling to your mother ship and meeting more of your fellow crew members."

"Thank you for that information," responded Aounah III. "With your permission we will plan on returning tomorrow morning at first light for your decision concerning our requested city visits. If approval is granted we will expect to depart later in the morning."

The formalities having been concluded, the four Earthlings and four Redexians sat around a dining table over the next couple of hours, some eating, Redexians drinking, and all attempting to communicate with one another. Minute by minute each group's peculiarities and habits began to become familiar to the others. Nothing too gross appeared. The Redexians were mildly appalled that the Earthlings were chewing and swallowing huge hunks of dead, rendered animal flesh. Pretty barbaric by their standards. As far as the Earthlings were concerned, watching the Redexians lapping up liquids from a bowl with their blue spotted tongues like a dog lapping up water from a doggy dish didn't appear too civilized either. Well, at least no one had been vaporized, shot, or harpooned yet. Tomorrow morning's second meeting would provide more clues on their mutual behavior and ability to get along together.

The next morning the eight members of this intergalactic get-together met for "breakfast" to review their plans. Ambassador Witwenova informed the group that permission had been secured to visit the cities requested by the Redexian guests. It was agreed that they would leave following breakfast to inspect Washington, DC, by midday and travel on to London to complete that inspection by nightfall. And so it was that these eight mixed species boarded the shuttlecraft and traveled from Roswell to the nation's capital in less than one hour. The trip was not announced to the public ahead of time to avoid the possibility of panic. Most of the

Redexians' goals for inspecting Washington were accomplished in a series of fly over figure eight maneuvers at relatively low altitude across the extended city complex. The shuttlecraft then touched down at three requested locations: Congressional Hill, the White House, and the National Zoo. Unannounced or otherwise, a silver alien craft landing at the White House caused a situation of some magnitude. Hundreds of tourist and locals alike whipped out their smart phones and video recorders to take photos and videos. Soon the internet was awash in shared viewing. More hits than the Academy Awards, and almost as much attention as a nude photo of Lady Gaga or Justin Bieber. Upward and onward. Two hours after arriving in DC, all eight were again aboard the shuttlecraft for a quick pop over to London. Arriving some 75 minutes after leaving the US capital, the shuttlecraft was hovering over the greater London metropolis. The shuttlecraft executed more figure eights and two landings. The first landing occurred on the well-manicured grounds behind Hampton Court Palace. The second landing took place at the Tower of London overlooking the Thames River. There were no meetings with any political figures at either site on the first day of this inspection trip. There were also no interviews for publication to Earth citizens. More photos and videos were snapped to share with whoever was interested, which was everyone.

Casey Foster was busy snapping photographs from morning until night to document the trip. This was permitted, and no attempt was made to restrict his access to subjects that he could photograph. It did remain to be seen whether of any of these photographs would eventually be cleared for publication to Earth's citizens. Similarly, Leah Anne Bailey continued her discussions with the Redexian crew about the operation of the shuttlecraft for her intended publication of future news articles in the *Washington Post*.

Day two of the trip found the eight galaxy travelers visiting both Beijing in the morning and later Jerusalem in the afternoon. The same routine occurred in Beijing, with low altitude surveillance followed by a touchdown near the Forbidden Palace for more specific documentation. The landing of the shuttlecraft caused a similar level of interest for the locals in Beijing as elsewhere. It seemed the world population who had been alerted about these aliens were captivated by the little silver guys and their technology. They were becoming like off-planet rock stars. You could expect T-shirts emblazoned with their images to go on sale soon.

The trip to Jerusalem was different. Commander Aounah requested and was granted an audience with the Prime Minister of Israel, Benjamin Netanyahu. This special two hour-long meeting was attended only by the Redexian commander, Ambassador Witwenova, and the Prime Minister. A short side trip by all three was made from the Prime Minister's office to the Wailing Wall in Jerusalem's Old City under tight security. Those local folks present when this threesome appeared at the Wall were quite astonished. There, standing nearby them at this sacred site, was an alien, the one they had been reading about. A creature from another planet, kind of small with a big head, different but not overly disturbing. And he must be relatively OK, or our Prime Minister would not be standing next to him. *Oy gevalt*! Maybe this weird looking visitor was just a very small Jew from very far away? No statement was issued following that extended meeting by any of the attendees concerning the subjects discussed. Was that kosher?

By early the next morning all eight travelers were back in Roswell. The shuttle commander then began his analysis of the adjacent areas to locate a site suitable for a substantial permanent recreation base. Once that task was completed preparations for the trip back to the Redexian mother ship were finalized. The four chosen Earthlings huddled together and talked about their options. Either get aboard, travel to the mother ship, and hopefully return alive in one piece soonish, or stay put on mother Earth. It was a decision not to be taken lightly. Their lives were at stake. However, so far all had gone well. They had been treated fairly and felt pretty comfortable with the aliens. Individually and together they decided that they would take a chance, based upon a pure leap of faith, and board the shuttlecraft for the trip to the mother ship. Someone from Earth had to be the first to sample life with aliens, so why not these four? They were informed that they could expect to return to Roswell in approximately 30 days with a full contingent of Redexian leadership . And so it was. With little outward fanfare but great expectation, those officials remaining at Roswell watched the Redexian shuttlecraft quickly vanish beyond Earth's viewing capabilities. A message was transmitted back to Earth from the shuttlecraft thanking those who had helped with this part of their journey and promising a return in 30 days for formal discussions. The Group of 8 and everyone else on Earth paying any attention wondered what would happen next.

CHAPTER 11

MOTHER SHIP

Shuttle craft commander Aounah III plotted a course from Earth back to the mother ship. The trip would include close flybys of Earth's moon, Mars, Jupiter, and Saturn. The four Earth guests were treated to spectacular sights of their journey through the viewing screens. Casey Foster snapped one photograph after another documenting a space flight never undertaken by humans. Leah Anne Bailey continued her interviews and note-taking for her anticipated first space byline. Jacob Witwenova practiced his diplomatic exchanges with the shuttlecraft commander, remaining three crew members, and the amazing Redexian crash survivor, who had spent the last 65 years frozen as solid as a block of ice. Chloe Anh Sing probed the shuttlecraft interior seeking clues as to its propulsion system and military capabilities. Together, these nine traveling explorers enjoyed a discovery flight of a lifetime. For those lucky Earth travelers, each new mile on the move set a new record for distance traveled beyond Earth. For those lucky Redexians, each new mile set a record for their exploratory travel within this solar system. All wore a look of contentment on their dissimilar but very happy faces.

The Redexians also made arrangements for their Earth visitors' comfort. The internal atmosphere of the shuttlecraft had been fine-tuned to a pleasing mixture of Earth and Redexian standards. Artificial gravity was simulated to approximate Earth gravity. Food, drink, clothing, and sufficient articles for daily living were provided. It was similar to a trip on an Earth luxury ocean liner. All prepaid, no sales tax, with entertainment provided along with pleasant traveling companions. Apparently, no Earthlings were probed, tortured, or eaten alive on the trip. The flyby of Earth's moon brought the shuttlecraft to within 15 miles of its heavily cratered surface. Commander Aounah III pointed out surface details of interest, including craters filled with significant amounts of water ice. He also pointed out landing sites in areas which could be readily developed with permanent bases.

Twelve hours later the shuttlecraft arrived at Mars, where it was inserted into a temporary elliptical orbit providing spectacular views of the Martian surface. Swooping down to 20 miles from the surface provided a close-up view of the solar system's highest planetary point, the dormant volcano Olympus Mons. For a further thrill, the commander hovered his shuttlecraft at 5000 feet above the solar system's largest canyon, crossing most of its 1500 miles in length, before swooping back up and out of the Martian limited gravity field. Cameras flashed, smiles appeared, conversation was intense, and all present enjoyed the show. Next in line was Jupiter, comprising some 300 times the mass of Earth, by far the largest of the solar system's planetary bodies. It slowly filled the shuttlecraft's view screens. Its features, including the Great Red Spot, a well documented storm system hundreds of years old and four times the size of the entire Earth, were breathtaking to view. The continuously swirling cloud system obscured anything distinguishable that lay underneath. Jupiter appeared as a boiling mass of circling clouds surrounded by its numerous close flybys of Jupiter's moons, Europa, and Callisto. These moons both looked promising for more intensive scrutiny. 24 hours later the shuttlecraft neared Saturn, the most visually spectacular planet in this solar system. This gas giant planet was known for its spectacular icy rings, each orbiting the planet at different speeds. Further enhancement of the Saturn system was provided by 18 distinguishable moons, with Titan serving as the most impressive.

So, after a leisurely tour of Saturn and its moons, the shuttle commander brought his craft and four earth guests to the docking berth of the Redexian mother ship. Its sheer size, larger than three Earth aircraft carriers placed end to end, seemed incomprehensible to the Earthlings, whose own spacecrafts resembled flying telephone booths. Yet here, orbiting Titan, appeared this massive craft obviously constructed in a space dock orbiting its home planet. Over 4000 feet in length, crewed by 3000 Redexian occupants, adding and subtracting crew members as a result of new births and expected deaths, this spaceship was on an exploratory mission scheduled to last for over 50 years. This was a vessel of enormous capabilities. The guest Earthlings were excited to roam about its interior spaces, meet the ship's officers, and talk informally with the ship's crew. Wow and double Wow!

Following the docking procedure, the four Earthlings were brought directly to the bridge to meet Captain Oulah IV and second-in-command Weooh VII for formal introductions. Addressing Ambassador Witwenova and the others, the captain expressed formal greetings from the Redexian Frontier. Ambassador Witwenova responded on behalf of all of Earth's people that the Redexians were welcome to visit our solar system for a peaceful interchange between equal galaxy members. These formal opening remarks were followed by the now ritualistic shaking of hands and touching of foreheads. It doesn't take long to teach new space dogs new space tricks.

"Our spacecraft is named Alliance 6," began the captain. "It's a part of our fleet sent out from Redex in search of new frontiers and allies. It has taken 50,000 years to develop our civilization to this point. More specifically, scientific developments allowed our people to begin exploration of our section of this galaxy almost 2500 years ago. This exploration has led us to find new exciting worlds. It led us to discover your star and planet Earth, circling in its habitable zone, almost 1200 years ago. Since it seemed interesting, we started collecting information about Earth. We have been continuing this effort ever since that time. Our first small exploratory satellite arrived in your solar system over 700 years ago. Not much of interest was happening. Later, more sophisticated satellites sent 200 years ago found your world in the early stages of industrial development with no signs of space exploration. By the time we sent a piloted shuttlecraft to more closely monitor your planet in July, 1947, we found a rapidly developing technological world engaged in a fierce battle for worldwide dominance. This was a troubling situation from our perspective. We have continued to monitor your planet ever since becoming aware of your first small steps into space exploration some 55 years ago. Now we have seen recent evidence that you have been able to land a few people on your moon. We observed that and sent pilotless satellites to examine other planets and moons in your solar system. We are also aware that your earliest satellites have finally reached the stage of exiting your solar system and entering interplanetary space. These are matters of great importance to Redexians. We want to know what is going on in our neighborhood. We congratulate you on these early efforts and anticipate your citizens' continued interest in further space exploration. It is only natural. 'Intelligent' species always seem to want more information, more answers, and to find out why things happen. Our observation is that intelligent species who survive long enough to achieve space technology have pushed outward from their home planets. We of the Redexian Frontier have moved far enough along to extend our reach in all space time directions to a distance of approximately 25 light years from Redex. We do this in part as pure scientific research. But we also do this to protect our home world. One of our first space efforts was to protect our world from annihilation from incoming asteroids, comets, and large space rocks. To do this we researched and documented all such known objects approaching our world. Later we used our technology to install defense mechanisms to deflect or destroy any such incoming objects. While we have not been totally successful, I am happy to report that no major destructive events from incoming space debris has occurred. Hopefully, our success in this area will continue. Hopefully, you on Earth will do likewise. Why let one wayward space rock destroy a whole civilization?

"Like you, our civilization was interested to learn whether or not we are the only life forms in the universe. We scanned our skies with our early telescopes and monitored our radio antennas looking for signs of life. We sent early exploration missions to our sister planets and their moons looking for signs of microscopic life. We thought we might even find some critters running about the surface of their worlds. At first, we did not have any success. But eventually, as our program of exploration became more sophisticated and our search area expanded, we did find proof of life. Life in all forms, shapes, and sizes. Life, we have found, is incredibly diverse and thrives in incredibly diverse environments. Some of these life forms we classify as plants, and others we classify as animals. A few of these diverse life forms we have classified as intelligent life forms, in varying degrees. Some are at an early stage of development and others, which we have found farther out in the Milky Way galaxy, appear to be even more highly advanced than our Redexian species.

"Our planet's recorded history includes major conflicts between our world's citizens at various stages of early development. Luckily, as our civilization matured, our world began to unite under a spirit of cooperation and mutual respect. Today our world no longer experiences major conflicts among our citizens. Unfortunately, as we searched through the universe, we found evidence of major devastating conflicts between life forms of various home worlds. This concerned us drastically. We do not want to be caught up in any such catastrophic conflict.

"As I am sure your scientists on Earth have now learned, our Milky Way galaxy alone has over 200 billion stars, many of which have habitable planets. The universe contains over 200 billion galaxies. So far our search for life has allowed us to make contact with and establish mutually beneficial relationships with some of these nearby intelligent species. We plan on continuing our efforts to push further out from Redex to create a mutually beneficial defensive arena.

"What really concerns us is the possibility that another far more advanced species will reach our home world with the intention to enslave or destroy us. This is a possibility that should also greatly concern your Earth population. So we can scan and look for any incoming dangers and would like your help in doing the same with us. To date, we have found no evidence of civilizations more advanced than ours within 200 light years of Redex. I hope we are correct in this determination. Therefore, we assume that any advanced intelligent species who might do us great harm must be based further than 200 light years from our home world.

"We Redexians are now able to explore our sector of this galaxy traveling at speeds approaching 45% of the speed of light. We endeavor to increase these abilities to a speed of 80% of the speed of light. I mention this because any interstellar travelers proceeding at less than light speed are unlikely to cause us a problem. That is because the simple arithmetic shows that any such species would have to travel for longer than 200 years at near light speed just to reach our world. Most likely any such journey would take many hundreds of years to accomplish, a long way to go looking for trouble. But our concern is that a very advanced civilization might find a practical way to travel great distances at speeds in excess of the speed of light. This, of course, is in direct conflict with the prevailing universal physics theory that nothing can travel faster than the speed of light. But we also know that the prevailing universal theory of physics recognizes that space time can and is warped based upon existing gravity fields. Some very advanced civilization may have already learned how to sufficiently warp space time to jump great distances instantaneously. To travel from one side of our Milky Way galaxy to the other, stretching in excess of 100,000 light years, a civilization would need such abilities. To travel to our nearest neighbor hood galaxy, Andromeda, which exists 2.5 million light years away, would require such abilities. To travel to the many millions and billions of other galaxies in the universe would again require traveling at speeds greatly beyond light speed.

"Some Redexians in our advanced scientific departments believe that super massive black holes that exist in the center of galaxies may, in fact, be portals to other locations within the universe. While our scientists have not yet cracked this problem, they are certainly devoting their time and energies to doing so. If other more advanced civilizations have achieved this level of expertise we may find ourselves in grave danger. So we have now arrived at your planet Earth to begin discussions concerning efforts to establish a mutually beneficial alliance. I suspect that there are many other matters that we can share with each other that would be both enlightening and helpful. I suspect that each of our worlds has specialized knowledge in energy, science, health, and matters of social interactions that would be interesting to learn and adopt. These are matters that we can explore, given time and the willingness on all of our parts to share constructively with one another. It is for this reason that we invited you four Earthlings to our mother ship in preparation for our more formal discussions with Earth's leaders when we return to your planet. We hope you will get to know us and start to trust us. So please feel free to move about our spaceship and ask questions of interest. We will do our best to respond. Do you have any questions that I can answer at this time?" concluded Captain Oulah IV.

"Thank you for that explanation," responded Ambassador Witwenova. "We are pleased to be here on your mother ship as guests. We look forward to getting to know you and your crew. While I'm sure we have many questions, I suggest we defer them until we've had an opportunity to tour your spaceship. But I do have one pressing question that you may be able to answer. Can you provide any quantification of the extent of life you have found within our galaxy?"

"That is a great question," responded the captain. "It's one that is asked on every world where we have found intelligent life. The answer appears that life is pervasive throughout our galaxy and the universe. Almost everywhere we have searched we have found evidence of life. Life is tenacious. Once it arrives, it seems to take hold and spread into every available nook and cranny. I would estimate that on average almost 30% of every solar system that we have examined has some form of life on its planets or circling moons. Furthermore, perhaps one out of every ten of these planets reveals life that has evolved into complex multi-cellular living creatures. From these, we have found evidence of intelligent life on another one out of every ten planets that we have examined. Given that the Milky Way galaxy has some 200 billion stars, I would conservatively estimate that there are thousands of worlds in our local galaxy that have developed complex, intelligent life forms. We continue to be amazed at what we find. I hope this answers your question."

"Yes, it does. I can see that we on Earth have much to learn," answered Ambassador Witwenova.

With that exchange, the four Earth guests were taken on a tour of the mother ship. The remaining Redexian officers adjourned to meet in the conference room on the bridge. Second-in-command Weooh VII, began the meeting by telling Captain Oulah that he was impressed with his positive presentation to the Earthlings. To that, the captain responded, "Well, the possibility of working as allies with these new creatures *does* exist. So I have presented the most favorable viewpoint from their perspective. Of course, I left out the possibility that our best solution might entail enslavement or destruction of their species. We won't know which way to proceed until we have more contact with them. Now, the reason I scheduled this meeting was to instruct each of my officers to keep a close eye on these Earthlings. Make sure you instruct each crew member to act in a positive manner. Also instruct each of our crew members that we wish to convey the impression that we are looking for allies in a mutually beneficial relationship."

A number of decks below, in an area assigned to the Earthlings as their crew quarters, a similar meeting was taking place. Military expert Chloe Anh Sing addressed the group, saying, "That was certainly an interesting opening statement. I strongly suggest that none of us take it too seriously. While being considered as mutually dependent allies has great appeal, I'm sure that it's not the only possible outcome. Do you think the Romans told their gladiators, 'You all gonna die, suckas?' Let's make sure that we keep to our assigned tasks. Let's make sure that we collect as much information as we can so that our world leaders have options. Casey, please stick to your assignment and photograph as much of the interior of the mother ship as possible, with an emphasis on the bridge and engine room. Leah Anne, please stick to your assignment and interview as many crew members as you can. Jacob, your assignment will be to continue developing diplomatic relations with the Redexian officers. Finally, each of us, myself in particular, will be looking for any weaknesses in their defense system. Move about and see what you can learn."

Casey Foster jumped up first like a school boy at recess, moving about the mother ship snapping photographs with a variety of cameras, including what he referred to as his spy gear. Take one photo here and another there. Throw in a few of the Redexian crew at work or play, add the bridge, engine room, crew quarters, and dining facilities, then keep going. *Boy, this is fun*, he thought. *Can't wait to see a few of these on the front page of the* Post. Aim, shoot, click, and on to the next.

On the second day aboard he noticed a rash on his abdomen and a slightly elevated temperature. Hour by hour Casey's symptoms worsened, along with his mounting anxiety. He was far from home, in space with no medical attention available from a good old Earthling. By the third day the rash had spread to his neck and his fever went higher. No panic yet, but he was getting really concerned. *What the hell is this*? he wondered. Soon Leah Anne started experiencing similar health issues. She had a sore throat and bloodshot eyes. She found that as she went about interviewing available Redexian crew members her note-taking was becoming erratic. *What the hell is this*? she wondered. Both Casey and Leah Anne reported these matters to Jacob Witwenova as their symptoms worsened. Jacob wondered whether these maladies were initiated on Earth or were contracted from the aliens. In any case, medical attention was necessary. And to worsen the situation, the Earth team did not have proper medical personnel present. Jacob was faced with a choice. Either wait and see whether one or the other improved or refer the medical matters to their Redexian hosts and ask for assistance. Each course of conduct had consequences. If these illnesses were intentionally carried with them from Earth, disclosure to their hosts might interrupt a CIA defensive plan not disclosed to them. If this were merely an Earth disease picked up in ordinary course, disclosure to their hosts might raise issues of the Redexians' physical security while visiting Earth. Then what would they choose to do? If, on the other hand, these were maladies picked up through contact with their hosts, their disclosure would alert them to the Earthlings' weaknesses.

Jacob concluded, after some careful analysis, that he really had no choice. Each of his fellow special agents would need to disclose their illnesses to their hosts and seek medical treatment. Each would need to place themselves in alien hands for medical care. The aliens were not surprised by this request. It was expected. What Jacob did not know was that there were intentional gaps in each of his agent's memories. In fact, shortly after each Earthling was ushered aboard the shuttlecraft for the trip back to the mother ship, each human was rendered, without their knowledge, instantly unconscious. While in that unconscious state each of the four Earth agents was scanned, examined, biopsied, and subjected to extend medical examinations in search of answers. This was not the Redexians' first rodeo. They had visited other worlds with other species on numerous prior occasions. The Redexians were well aware that alien species could intentionally or innocently carry exceedingly harmful biological agents and diseases. Contact with aliens without precaution could decimate the Redexian crew and their mission. So the visitors were examined, probed, and sterilized of all harmful agents prior to boarding the mother ship, kind of like lab rats in an Earth medical laboratory. Let's see what this does to our rat buddies. No big deal. And we have four to play with in case we lose one.

Furthermore, all of the visitors' clothing and other objects brought on board had been sterilized and then examined for any hidden content. Spying and transmitting coded messages back home was anticipated. But the Redexians were the advanced society with more advanced technology. It was almost the reverse of humans visiting a colony of chimpanzees and taking proper precautions. Only after these Earth visitors were cleaned up and their gear inspected and rendered harmless were they allowed on board the mother ship. Naturally, to avoid any negative feelings, the Earthlings' memories of these events were thoroughly erased. They knew nothing about their extensive examinations or that they had been injected with various Redexian "bugs" to provide research on the effects on the "subjects."

In due course, Jacob brought these medical issues to the second-in-command's attention. As a result, Casey and Leah Anne were politely escorted to the mother ship's medical bay for examination and treatment. They were expected. Each had been secretly injected by the Redexians with alien bacteria to see what outcome could be expected and over what time frame.

The examinations led to the proper diagnoses and treatment so that the visitors could continue with their missions. The remaining two guests, Jacob and Chloe, were expected to appear before long with different symptoms from different injected biological agents. This sure was fun and produced quite a few laughs for the host's medical department. For them, this was standard procedure in getting to know their oh-so-mutually-beneficial new buddies. Say nice things and treat them like assorted lab rats.

Two days later, right on schedule, Jacob and Chloe were escorted to the medical lab for examination. Jacob had been experiencing increasingly severe headaches and vision abnormalities. Chloe had a swollen tongue and labored breathing. Each was examined, and their symptoms and their severity were recorded. The medical hosts chuckled to themselves prior to issuance of the appropriate medications. Not surprisingly, recovery was just around the corner. Each of the guests breathed a sigh of relief, feeling cured. Unfortunately, their hosts failed to inform them that further exposure to different bacteria and toxins were already scheduled. Good time to test for Earthling weaknesses. Duh, what did they expect?

Within a week of arriving on the mother ship, Leah Anne Bailey had prepared her first news article for transmission back to the *Washington Post* for publication. The article, accompanied by awesome photographs taken by Casey Foster received approval from the Second-in-command for transmission back to Earth. The news article was transmitted in the form submitted without revision. This was allowed, even though the Redexian had the ability to capture all incoming and outgoing electronic transmissions for review, modification, or deletion. However, in their judgment, these news article created no concern because the content was mere puffery. The first proposed news article transmitted for publication appeared as follows:

"Visit to the Redexian Mother Ship"
Byline: Leah Anne Bailey, *Washington Post*

For those of you following this extraordinary story, you may know that I and my three traveling companions, Casey Foster, Jacob Witwenova, and Chloe Anh Sing, were invited to visit the Redexian mother ship orbiting Saturn's moon, Titan. Some ten wonderful days ago the four of us boarded their shuttlecraft for a tour past the Earth's moon, our nearby sister planet Mars, past the great gas ball planet Jupiter with its great red spot, and on to Saturn's delightful moon Titan. We have had the special opportunity to travel where no Earthlings have gone before. We have seen, up close and personal, these incredible solar system wonders. All of this took place via our host's lightning-fast shuttlecraft, made comfortable for us in terms of atmosphere, gravity, food, clothing, and activities. Most incredibly, a voyage that would have taken many months, if possible at all aboard an Earth-manufactured spacecraft, was accomplished in a mere five flawless days of travel. Once I return to Earth I would love to contact my local AAA office to book further flights to exotic locations with this travel provider. But I don't think any are offered yet.

So, what have I learned from this experience? Clearly our hosts look different than us. This is natural, since they come from a world that is different from Earth. I've also learned that their customs and social interactions are different from our own. But while these differences clearly exist, there are also similarities. They have also been kind enough to show us marvels that we never would have been able to experience. Now we are safely on board their interstellar spacecraft and have been given access to its interior spaces and crew. It is of tremendous size and complexity, covering an area in excess of that which would be displaced by three modern naval aircraft carriers. This craft is sufficiently manned and provisioned for space voyages that take many years to accomplish without further replenishment of resources. How extraordinary. Better pack carefully.

So I have asked myself, why has this interesting species traveled to our world, Earth? What are they looking for? What do they hope to accomplish? And, most importantly, what do they expect from us? I don't have answers to these questions; I wish I did. But like you, my readers, I will wait and see what unfolds for all of us. I am sure we will learn of many marvels and be exposed to many sights and sounds that we have never seen before. I, for one, am excited by this prospect. I hope you are all excited as well.

Attached to this article you will see incredibly beautiful photographs taken by my colleague and fellow space traveler, Casey Foster. I hope these photographs will give you a glimpse of what we have seen. These wonders are all around us, and his photos bring home the beauty of nature. In closing this week's article, I would like to thank my fellow Earth traveling companions and our Redexian hosts for making this trip possible. Next week I will provide an update concerning my experiences on this incredible adventure. I look forward to our timely return to Earth with more news to share with my readers. Thank you for your interest in this unfolding story.

Leah Anne Bailey continued wandering around the ship interviewing any crew member she could buttonhole. Casey Foster almost skipped from portal to portal, deck to deck, bridge to engine room, and any other location he could wheedle his way into, snapping pictures as he went. Ambassador Witwenova practiced his Redexian language skills and sharpened his diplomatic skills. Each was tracked by the Redexian crew via hidden microchips implanted beneath their skin when they were rendered unconscious for their initial medical evaluations on the shuttlecraft. The Earthling generating the most interest was Chloe Anh Sing. She was much more stealthily in her snooping approach, ferreting out operational details of the mother ship and checking out its potential military capacities. She generated enough interest that a rotating crew of Redexians was assigned to keep a 24 hour watch on her whereabouts. Wherever Chloe wandered she was carefully observed. It became readily apparent that her task was to evaluate the potential military capabilities of the incoming aliens for her Earthling superiors.

After the first ten days of observing Chloe collect information, Captaion Oulah IV invited her on to the bridge for a blunt conversation. "I understand that your mission as a member of the Earth's contingent to our mother ship is to evaluate the sophistication of our technical capabilities as well as our military preparedness," said the Captain. "This is to be expected. When we meet with a new galaxy species we do our best to make a similar evaluation. It helps place into perspective what may be achievable by both parties. To round out your evaluation I have assigned one of my senior officers to escort you around our ship's bridge to explain its functional workings. This same officer will escort you through our engine room and explain the multiple methods we use for generating travel speed. His explanations will also touch upon the construction methodology and materials used to construct this incredibly complex mother ship. Secondly, I will personally demonstrate for you our military capabilities. Please keep in mind that, like Earth, we have a variety of military equipment and methods for delivery of them to their selected targets. We start with the most simplistic, low yield weapons and increase in complexity and delivery power until we reach the most devastating weapons. Of course, we always try our hardest not to utilize any of these weapons unless absolutely necessary."

With that introduction, Captain Oulah signaled his communications officer to illuminate the bridge viewing screen, directing the projection of an image showing the surface of Saturn. "Please keep your view focused on the surface of Saturn, approximately 1/3 of the way above its encircling rings," the captain said. With a hand signal, the captain authorized the firing of a single high yield photon torpedo at the directed location on Saturn's surface. In the bottom left corner of the view screen, the fired weapon was tracked from the mother ship as it approached and quickly reached the top level of Saturn's rotating clouds. At that instant, an enormous fireball spread out in all directions across the surface of Saturn. At intervals of every 10 seconds the view screen captured still photographs of the ensuing explosion.

When this lesson was complete and Chloe Anh Sing had observed its full impact, the Captain continued, "Please note that our instruments have estimated that this single photon torpedo strike has inflicted devastating though impermanent damage upon 17% of Saturn's surface. This corresponds to an area 6.375 times the entire surface of your planet Earth. Please also keep in mind that my weapons officer was instructed to fire only one high yield photon torpedo. One mid-grade photon torpedo would yield a force equal to 100 of your standard Earth atomic bombs. And if we chose a smaller target area, one low yield photon torpedo would yield the equivalent of 30 standard Earth atomic bombs. This would be approximately the same force as yielded by the meteor which exploded over Chelyabinsk, Russia, on February 15, 2013. We are able, if necessary, to deliver up to 25 such photon torpedoes to selected targets in any given five hour window of opportunity. In addition, we have developed high frequency laser beam systems with a capacity to strike and totally eliminate individual targets on the ground from an orbit of 150 miles.

"I suggest, continued Captain Oulah, "that you direct your Earth scientists to compare this small demonstration today to the astronomical event you referred to on Earth as comet Shoemaker-Levy 9, which impacted planet Jupiter on July 16, 1994. I will provide you with both video of that event and today's demonstration for your transmission back to Earth. Nevertheless, to reacquaint you with that event, you may remember that comet Shoemaker-Levy 9 fragmented into 21 pieces, which then impacted Jupiter's surface at speeds approaching 134,000 mph. These fragments ranged in size from being relatively small to the largest fragment approximating 1.2 miles in diameter. The scars created from these impacts were readily visible and larger than the well-known Great Red Spot on Jupiter's surface. Finally, to put this into perspective, the damage caused by the disintegrating comet's largest fragment, which struck Jupiter on July 18, 1994, created an impact area some 7000 miles across, releasing energy equivalent to 6,000,000 megatons of TNT. This represents a destructive power approximately 600 times your world's estimated total nuclear arsenal. If you will direct your scientists to compare our little demonstration today to that event, they will undoubtedly note the similarities. But just to make myself clear, when we travel around this galaxy we must be and have become prepared to defend ourselves and our home world of Redex. That is why we hope planet Earth and its citizens will join us as allies. Do you have any questions?" asked the Captain?

Chloe Anh Sing, special military agent from Earth, returned her gaze to the captain's now blazing deep set red eyes and as nonchalantly as she could replied, "Thank you for your demonstration. I anticipated as much." With that comment she took her leave, walking slowly and delicately off the bridge. Inside her jumbled brain, her working neurons were trying to fathom the massive damage she had just observed. "Nuclear schmuclear," she muttered to herself.

Later that evening, the four special agents from Earth were seated in their crew quarters for dinner. They had been informed by the second-in-command that five days remained before they started their journey back to Earth. Each member quietly discussed what they had observed, learned, and imparted to the mother ship's crew. As a team, they felt satisfied that they had accomplished their mission. Each had compiled detailed notes to share during their debriefing once home. The leisurely dinner was followed by music and a concoction of mildly alcoholic drinks, all provided by their generous hosts. Once it was time to settle in for the night, Leah Anne and Casey Foster retired to their shared private quarters. They had made it known to their hosts that they were a combined set, or a couple, as referred to on Earth. Unbeknownst to them, their late evening private activities were recorded and then broadcast live throughout the mother ship in full color video with surround sound to the Redexian crew. Some watched their antics with amazement, others with disdain. Most were merely trying to fathom what the hell was going on. It seemed similar to behavior noted by their home world biologists between mating Redexian puddle frogs. Most viewers seemed surprised that these two aliens seem to be enjoying themselves so much. They appeared to be in no rush to complete their choreographed behaviors. Creepy, amusing, and certainly different from normal Redexian experiences. A few Redexian crew members who thought of themselves as documentary experts forwarded their recorded observations of "that couple" back to their last duty station and then on to their relatives back home on Redex. Each realized this would take a great deal of time to arrive at its intended destination, but the bang for the buck seem to make it worthwhile. Perhaps these videos would become bestsellers, one of the top five video broadcasts from the field. This was similar to Earth broadcasts of adventurers prowling the Peruvian jungle searching for unusual wildlife, like a day trip in the African savanna. Crazy, special animals engaged in crazy animal behavior. Many Redexians wondered if this was some sort of aberration between these two and not a general practice of all Earthlings. Oh well, animals will be animals.

CHAPTER 12

RETURN TO EARTH

Captain Oulah IV of the United Redexian Frontier made the executive decision that the time had arrived for the formal return of planet Redex's explorers to planet Earth. The returning contingent would include the captain himself, his chief negotiator, his designated ambassador to Earth, his chief engineering officer, the expedition's lead medical officer, and a support staff consisting of five mother ship crewmembers. In addition, the captain decided to return to Earth the four visiting Earthlings who had been given access to the mother ship and crew. He had harbored some preliminary thoughts of keeping one or more onboard to serve as hostages, but further reflection led him to believe correctly that Earth would easily sacrifice each and every "visiting guest" if held hostage and dangled as bait. Of course, he could expect public displays by Earth politicians tearing their hair and wailing about this great unfairness concerning any hostage situation. But the reality was that none of these four would be deemed a significant loss to their home world. For that reason, and more importantly because goodwill at the early stages of formal contact with these alien galaxy members seemed useful, the captain decided to return all Earth visitors healthy, happy, and more informed about the Redexian mother ship and its crew's capabilities. Each would be suitably bugged for later information downloading and analysis. The captain's decision to return to Earth in five days was transmitted personally by him to Casey, Leah Anne, Jacob, and Chloe Anh. The Captain then requested his second-in-command, Weooh VII, to inform the balance of the Redexian Earth traveling team and the entire mother ship crew of their travel plans. Excitement ran high throughout the ship as each prepared in their own way for this historic formal meeting between neighborhood galaxy members. The unknown nature as to the outcome of this planned meeting raised the level of excitement for all participants.

To transport this contingent, the captain selected a mid-sized shuttlecraft for departure with sufficient supplies for a 30 day round trip journey. The mother ship was ordered to remain safely in orbit around Titan with the second-in-command delegated all operational authority. Just prior to departing, Captain Oulah IV had the following message transmitted by his communication's officer to Earth:

Gentlemen, please be advised that our Redexian shuttlecraft will be arriving in Roswell in five days. We are returning with our crew and the four Earth visitors whom we have entertained as our guests in preparation for these more formal meetings. We look forward to meeting with you and discussing issues of mutual interest. We anticipate presenting proposals which will need approval at your highest levels of government. Please plan accordingly. Your cooperation will be appreciated.

Signed, Captain Oulah IV of the United Redexian Frontier

Captain Oulah gave the order, and the shuttle departed at 1/3 impulse power from the mother ship. All hands on board the shuttle, as well as the mother ship, pressed their anxious faces against every available window portal and every available viewing screen. First, the captain ordered the shuttlecraft to slowly descend down towards Titan's surface so that he could visually inspect the proposed location for a substation. There below, on the frozen icy surface, the captain clearly observed a flat plateau cozily situated between a large liquid methane lake and the adjoining rocky hillside. It appeared that this potential site for a substation could provide vast quantities of natural resources for fueling and building projects. So after a half hour of traversing the site, the captain dictated into his personal notebook that if the economics proved reasonable, construction of this station could commence within the next 60 days.

The shuttlecraft then continued its flight towards Earth's rocky planet partner, Mars. Impulse power was switched to gravity-assisted flight, gradually increasing speed from impulse power to 10% of the speed of light. Titan, Saturn, and then Jupiter grew in size and detail and then diminished as the shuttlecraft passed by. Before long the carefully-laid trajectory began to reveal Mars, first appearing as a tiny red dot in the forward viewing screens. Minute by minute Mars became more distinct along with its various surface attractions. Upon arrival, the captain ordered the shuttlecraft placed in orbit around Mars at an altitude of 500 km. Circling overhead, without an obstructing cloud cover, the entire surface of Mars, including Mount Olympus and the long Martian Grand, came exquisitely into view. Once he felt comfortable with these initial observations, the captain ordered the shuttlecraft to orbit in a fixed position over the proposed observation base site. The report generated earlier concluded that Mars could easily support a permanent Redexian base capable of sustaining 1500 crewmembers. Each of the key indicators, including atmosphere, temperature, available water resources in the form of crystallized ice, and mild gravity made this location acceptable. It also had the distinct advantage of providing a favorable view of the Earth as well as the remaining portions of this solar system. Appropriate Redexian technology could be utilized from the surface of Mars to further scan nearby star systems to locate other habitable planets and, more importantly, to scan for any potential incoming hostile aliens.

Captain Oulah was also intrigued with the possibility of terraforming the surface of Mars to create a planet system more in keeping with Redex. Elevating the surface temperature by introducing carbon-based gases such as CO_2 would slowly raise Mars' surface temperature. Rising temperatures would then release frozen water locked for a millennium under the surface. Proper planning and engineering could then create natural lakes, rivers, and streams. Carefully introducing unique surface grasses, plants, and shrubbery could, over time, further add to a rising temperature, enhancing Mars' thin atmosphere. The captain also thought that Redexian technology might permit an increase in the existing level of planetary gravity, which in turn could help maintain and improve the atmosphere surrounding Mars. All of these possibilities led the captain to conclude that he would indeed order the construction of the primary Redexian observation base on the surface of Mars.

Next, Captain Oulah ordered the shuttlecraft onward towards Earth with its shining reflective moon. This trip would have taken an Earth spacecraft six months to complete using their current technology. But the Redexians were able to make this journey in less than two days using their graviton propulsion system. Upon arrival at the moon, the captain ordered the shuttlecraft into a stable concentric orbit. Below he could observe its rocky, crater-impacted surface, created in a much earlier time during the formation of this solar system. Thousands of incoming comets, asteroids, and various-sized space rocks had obviously impacted this moon, demonstrating the unmistakable destructive and yet at the same time creative nature of solar system formation. From this vantage point the captain turned his gaze towards Earth. It was a startling beautiful blue water world encircled by clouds sweeping across its surface. Unmistakable landmasses appeared, rising out of the water with large green swaths of vegetation ebbing into ice-capped mountain ranges. *A great place for a vacation*, he thought, *and a great place for another permanent outpost in this section of the Milky Way*. As set forth in the report prepared after the earlier inspection tour, the captain could see that the Earthlings, even with their present technology, could observe happenings on the surface of the moon and reach its surface. In other words, while the moon was an interesting location, there was with obvious risk of interference from the local Earth population. A small substation might add value, he suspected, but he would never risk a large construction project and Redexian crew on this moon.

Four days after leaving the Redexian mother ship, the captain had completed his inspection tour of potential observation settlements on Titan, Mars, and Earth's moon. He reviewed each of the written reports thoroughly and appended his own investigatory suggestions. A summary note, dictated into his personal notebook, formalized his decision that this solar system would indeed become a part of the Redexian protection zone. Now he needed to determine whether the local inhabitants on Earth would be useful as long-term allies or just obstacles he had to deal with as required. He honestly hoped that his intended meetings with Earth's leaders would convince him that a beneficial relationship could be established. He needed time to observe Earth's leadership and willingness to follow the Redexians' protection zone plan. Well, he had to start somewhere, and that somewhere was on tomorrow's horizon. He ordered the shuttlecraft to remain in orbit around the moon for another 12 hours while he and the rest of his crew finalized their arrival plans. And then, when the captain was satisfied that everything had been done to prepare for this visit to Earth, he ordered the shuttle pilot to proceed to the watery blue planet.

On planet Earth, the Group of 8 was making preparations to welcome the alien crewmembers and four Earth guests to the Roswell air base. They selected a greeting committee comprised of the chairman of the United Nations, Mr. Bak Sun Pang, as a representative of all of Earth's peoples; President Barack Obama, as Chairman of the Group of 8; Dr. James Westermone, as the authority on Earth currently most fluent in the Redexian language; and finally Sir William Jefferson Clinton Meek, the intended chief negotiator for the upcoming meetings between these two neighborly galaxy members. As it turned out, Sir William, known by his friends as Billy Bob, was an excellent choice for this position. He was the product of five centuries of English aristocratic inbreeding mainly focused in Hampshire County, directly west of London, England. His family had alternately squabbled with and served the reigning British monarchy throughout the ages, sometimes seeking autonomy and at other times seeking high-ranking court appointments. Sir William had been raised on the family estate, known as Framingham House, which consisted of a tidy 50,000 acres of prime pastureland presently supporting a prized herd of Angus cattle. Schooling was administered at the most highly distinguished private educational facilities in England, which were attended by only the upper crust. Following graduation from Cambridge, Sir William was shipped off to Paris for further educational opportunities at the Sorbonne. While many of Billy's classmates spoke French fluently and majored in literature, philosophy, or the fine arts, he spent his valuable time excelling in excessive drinking, gambling, and womanizing. In other words, he was perfecting the required background for a lifetime of high level negotiations conducted over dinner and drinks. His accent was nigh on perfect for a British aristocrat and stood him well with his peers. All of these attributes led him to be the British go-to guy for any discussions with the EEC, United Nations, pesky Iran, or the nut bag state of North Korea. A couple of pats on the back, a quick shot of 100% pure Irish whiskey, and Sir William was off to the current hotspot to negotiate a solution.

The Group of 8 also went to extensive lengths to provide tight security at the Roswell air base for the incoming visitors. Nothing would set back amicable relations with the arriving aliens more than the political assassination of an arriving Redexian ambassador. Under the leadership of the NSA, a 10 mile square area on the ground and in the overhead airspace was quarantined to all but prescreened and approved Earthlings. Security personnel, surveillance cameras, motion detectors, and defensive systems were placed throughout the area. Authorized snipers were positioned in various high spots to provide further security should any breach by unauthorized personnel occur. Now, after years of denial, Earth's peoples were ready to welcome real live, in the flesh visitors from outer space. A real extra solar spacecraft, which would have formerly been referred to as a UFO, was about to land and disgorge its big headed, red eyed, short in the poop, ear-wiggling buddies from planet Redex. Locked onto the Roswell air base's signaling beacon, the shuttlecraft honed in on its well-prepared landing station. Descending until it hovered over the landing target for a few seconds, its three landing gear were extended as the craft squatted down noiselessly, without kicking up so much as a fleck of sand. To the observers on the ground there was no visible sign of any cockpit area in the landing craft. It was a simple sleek metallic disc similar in size to a modern day Earth battleship. A few minutes later, a metallic ramp was extended from the underside of the craft and out walked the four living, breathing, smiling Earth agents previously sent to the Redexian mother ship. Each came out hands raised overhead, making friendly gesturing signals. Assuming that these were not replacement androids manufactured by the aliens, it was sure nice to see that the first official ambassadors to their galactic contemporaries had come home unharmed. One by one, Casey Foster, Leah Anne Bailey, Jacob Witwenova, and Chloe Anh Sing shook hands with the assembled members of the greeting committee. After that formality, all except Jacob, who would remain as Earth's preliminary ambassador, were quickly escorted to the nearby Earth welcoming center where they were isolated to check for foreign contamination. Each Earth agent was then extensively debriefed on their off-planet experiences.

Five minutes later, at exactly 10 AM local Mountain Standard Time, on March 15, 2016, Captain Oulah IV of the United Redexian Frontier, followed by his crew, exited the shuttlecraft and walked over to President Barack Obama, who was standing behind the welcoming lectern, presiding as chairman of the Group of 8. Chairman Obama presented a crisp military salute, which he had practiced numerous times in the Oval Office in front of its full length mirror. Captain Oulah, having been previously briefed by Agent Witwenova on this custom, returned the salute and nodded in the direction of his host. Chairman Obama flashed a cheerful smile at his visitor and began his short, well-prepared greeting speech, beamed instantly around the world by a worldwide television network, no advertising permitted.

"Dear visiting galaxy members from planet Redex, welcome in peace to our planet Earth as our guests. We have looked forward to this day for many years, hoping to find proof that we Earthlings are not alone in our galaxy and universe. Your arrival confirms that other beings inhabit our galaxy and have advanced sufficiently in a technological sense that we can make contact with one another. We look forward to sharing with you knowledge about our world and are hopeful that likewise you will reveal to us information about your world."

In response, Captain Oulah nodded towards the President and responded in near perfect English, "On behalf of our planet Redex, I accept your greeting and look forward to your hospitality. The united Redexian people, referred to jointly as The Redexian Frontier, have been exploring our sector of the Milky Way in search of new frontiers and helpful allies. We have come here in peace to share with you our thoughts and build a solid long-term relationship. We are hopeful that we have much to share with one another. We look forward to getting to know you and building a bright future for all of our people. Please let me take this opportunity to thank you for sending the four Earth emissaries to our mother ship so that we could start this process. Our interactions, though brief in time, have allowed us some initial understanding of your people and cultures. It was a welcome opportunity for us."

Simultaneously, President Obama and Captain Oulah moved to center ground, extended their right hands, which was becoming the standard greeting mode, and lightly touched their foreheads. While accomplishing this gesture, Captain Oulah, acting like a professional magician, slipped a custom self-inserting microchip beneath the skin on the President's index finger. Instantly, scrambled signals began transmitting from the microchip device back to the Redexian mother ship. *Nice to know what the other guys are talking about*, Captain Oulah reflected. Then, one by one, the remaining Redexian crew members moved forward to meet each of the Earth greeting committee members. Everyone shook hands, touched foreheads, smiled jovially at each other, faced the television cameras, and waved politely, each while trying to assess the other. Each was trying to determine whether peace and cooperation were more beneficial than aggression and defiance. Who held the winning cards? Who had sufficient leverage to come out on top of this hoedown? Who needed one more than the other? Who had more to gain; who had more to lose?

In a few minutes, the public portion of the greeting ceremony was completed. Everyone was still alive. No one had been shot by a hidden sniper, impaled by a quick sword, or vaporized into dust by a ray gun. Not a bad start from a historical perspective. President Obama then led the contingent inside the Roswell air base to the brand new conference center specifically designed for this initial get-together. The Group of 8 had chosen to present themselves around a large circular table carved out of exquisite granite in a height comfortable to all participants. A series of comfortable leather chairs was arranged for each of the guests, providing a King Arthur's Round Table-like setting. All equals here, right? Before taking their seats, the Redexian crew member chosen for his engineering background performed a quick electronic scan of the conference room interior looking for anything that might present a danger. Once he was satisfied that the area was safe, he signaled the captain that all could proceed. Situated around the round conference room table at equal intervals were trays holding various delicate snacks and pitchers of various liquids: water for the Earthlings and a variety of sweetened fruit juices for the Redexians. Again, the engineer discreetly poked a probe into each of the pitchers in front of the Redexians' drinks. Once satisfied, he again signaled the captain there was no evidence of poison or other damaging materials in the offered liquid refreshments.

Everyone present took a few moments to dabble at the refreshments while gathering their thoughts. Then, in a move somewhat reminiscent of Nikita Khrushchev slamming his shoe on a lectern at a much earlier UN conference, Captain Oulah nimbly hopped up from his chair and onto the tabletop. This provided a small advantage of height and a circular pathway to move in front of each of the participants. Now, looking down on the crowd, he began to speak.

"Gentlemen, I think it might be useful if I provided a short background summary of our planet, our people, and the reason why we have traveled so far to come to your world. Please note that our planet Redex circles its home star Fomalhaut comfortably within its habitable zone with many features like your planet, including surface water, land masses, mountain ranges, and vast grassy plains. Our star would be considered by your Earth scientists to be a red dwarf. Our planet is approximately 2/3 of the mass of Earth, which provides for a lower level of gravity. Our atmosphere, composed mainly of nitrogen, oxygen, carbon dioxide, and hydrogen, is somewhat denser than yours and results in less visible light reaching our planet's surface. Evolution on our planet led to the creation of intelligent life and sufficient planetary resources for us to develop an industrialized society.

"Our historical records reflect an ever-advancing planetary race with a civilization that is now a little over 50,000 years in the making. Along the way, our scientists developed astronomical instruments to begin searching the skies seeking answers to the creation of the universe. Our philosophers began wondering long ago whether our species was alone in the universe. To find answers to these questions, we began exploring the space outside of our planetary system approximately 2500 years ago. Our first satellites scanned for signs of microbial life. Further exploration let us look for signs of more advanced life forms, including both plants and animals. Down the road, with more sophisticated instrumentation, we found indications of intelligent life on a number of planets. As time went on, the political leaders of Redex decided that it was time to start sending manned missions to explore our nearby planetary neighbors. Our initial space technology only permitted exploration of star systems with accompanying planets within a 10 light years of Redex. Surprisingly, we found multiple planets with thriving life, including a couple with what we considered to have intelligent though not too advanced life forms. This was both enlightening as well as frightening. For once you conclusively prove that other life exists throughout the universe, the immediate question becomes how advanced are those life forms when compared to your own world? It makes you wonder what the intentions of those other life forms might be. It makes you wonder whether any potentially hostile intelligent life form might have designs upon your planet and your civilization.

"Luckily, so far these planets, with life forms potentially more advanced than on our planet, are many hundreds of light years from Redex. So now we scan the night sky, watch, listen, and plan potential warning systems and defense mechanisms. Our united Redexian people also determined that our best defense was to create a system of ever-expanding outposts to help alert us of any incoming hostile aliens. To help us with that goal, around 500 years ago we began placing outposts on friendly allied planets with interests similar to our own. It is for that reason that we Redexians initially sent satellites to observe your blue water world. The data returned from those satellites suggested a potential hospitable location for an outpost. So, culminating in July, 1947 by your calendar, we sent a small shuttlecraft to Earth to gain more extensive information. That information, beamed back from the unsuccessful crashed shuttlecraft, and the information collected by our satellites has led to our current visit. This is part of our overall plan to create sustainable outposts in strategic locations expanding outward from our planet Redex in all directions up to a distance of 25 light years. Later we hope to expand our defense network further in stages to 50 light years in all directions. Your planet Earth is one of the locations that we think may be useful. I hope that the information that we provide to you will lead you to believe, as we do, that a joint defense pact is in our mutual interest. It is standard Redexian policy to seek cooperation and allies where possible. That is what we are here to learn. I sincerely hope, for all of our respective benefits, that we will mutually determine that it is in our best interests to work together for the common good.

"To accomplish our goals, we have a short list of matters that we need to achieve. I will outline them for you briefly now and anticipate that we will discuss them in more detail shortly. Our goals include the following:

"Firstly, we wish to deploy three observation satellites in this solar system to collect information for transmission back to Redex and its outposts. Next, we seek to create a permanent observation base on the fourth planet from your sun, which we understand is referred to as Mars. Third, we wish to create a small recreational zone on planet Earth in the vicinity of Roswell, New Mexico, as a location for our crews to visit on a rotating basis. Fourth, we seek to locate and open a permanent embassy in a primary Earth city. Finally, we will develop small substations on Saturn's moon, Titan, and Earth's moon.

"I look forward to working with your people in a cooperative manner to achieve these goals." Having finished his remarks captain Oulah IV took a short "victory lap" around the circular granite table, nodding at each participant, and then plopped himself back into his comfortable leather chair.

Chairman Obama looked directly into the deep-set red eyes of his miniature, bulging-headed guest and responded without missing a beat. His many Earth squabbles with his political opponents, detractors on Capitol Hill, and international world leaders had prepared him for just such a moment. So deftly, like any top drawer politician, he responded, "Captain Oulah, thank you for your return visit to our planet Earth. Your remarks concerning our galaxy and your world, with its plans to create a defensive zone, have been most enlightening. I look forward, as do other members of the Group of 8, to reviewing your proposals. I will now defer my response to Sir William Jefferson Clinton Meek as our designated world ambassador to planet Redex. Sir Meek, he continued, any comments at this time?"

The hottest baked potato in the history of Earth's civilization had just been neatly dropped in Meek's well-dressed lap. He had the unenviable task of as serving as the prime negotiator with these little gray devils with the assistance of Jacob Witwenova in determining Earth's future. If he did a good job, his name would probably be inscribed in history's journals as a success alongside those of Caesar, Napoleon, and George Washington. If his work efforts turned out to be a flop, any remaining living Earthlings who had not been burned to a cinder would probably rank him as a big time loser alongside Nero and Hitler. But this was no big deal as far as Sir Meek was concerned. He was up to the task. He was prepared and ready for engagement. Heck, he was even well dressed, well mannered, and articulate to the nth degree. He was a British aristocrat with five centuries of haughty training. Time to roll the bones. Long live the Queen.

"Captain Oulah," Sir Meek began, "It is my privilege, on behalf of our planet and its civilization, to address you. Like Chairman Obama before me, I, on behalf of our world, welcome you and your crew members to our planet and to our solar system. It is indeed a pleasure to meet, at last, other members of our Milky Way galaxy. It is also enlightening to learn that there are other developing civilizations throughout our galaxy with whom we may eventually have the opportunity to meet. It seems that Redex's ambassadors have had previous opportunities to meet with other civilizations as you spread out from your home planet in search of knowledge, allies, and a common protective zone. We here on Earth are newcomers to this situation. But we look forward to working with you in an amicable, friendly, and jointly respectful manner to accomplish our individual goals. Please note that this initial meeting here in Roswell is intended merely as a formal public get-together to greet you and to advise our Earth people of your arrival. That was the reason for our initial greeting ceremony outside, which was televised live worldwide. The goals that you have now enumerated privately contain numerous matters which will require thoughtful examination by Earth's leaders as well as a careful response. I feel quite confident that the matters you have raised today can be addressed to everyone's satisfactions." Blah, blah, blah, blah… He intentionally droned on for a few minutes until everyone's eyes began to glaze over due to lack of substance. It was exactly what Sir Meek had in mind. And now for his punch line he concluded, "So, gentlemen, let me suggest that we schedule a mutually acceptable time and place in about three weeks in my hometown of London, England, to continue these important formal discussions. How would that suit you, Captain?" he asked.

Captain Oulah was not attending his first rodeo. He had been down this road before. He and his fellow Redexians had already established 10 outposts on other nearby planets, with eight of those being currently counted as allies with the remaining two worldwide civilizations fried to a crisp and obliterated. In short order the captain would make his preliminary determination regarding which direction he intended to follow.

"Sir William," he casually said, "I heartily accept your proposal for a follow-up meeting to confirm our plans. We can meet with the necessary world leaders in London, England, in 24 of your Earth hours. Please designate an exact location and time to begin these meetings. Thank you."

Sir William responded, "Captain, I'm not certain that I made myself clear. I doubt that the necessary world leaders can be assembled in London in your suggested 24 hour time frame. I'm sure you understand."

"Sir William," responded Captain Oulah, "I feel confident that you, as well as the other necessary Earth leaders, will use your best efforts to attend. If, however, this meeting cannot be convened within this 24 hour time frame, we will feel compelled to move forward independently with our plans until such time as your people become available. I would appreciate your formal response within the hour." With that, Captain Oulah IV stood up, bowed pleasantly to his hosts, pivoted on his tiny, little round feet, and walked back outside into the startling bright daylight, followed closely by his fellow crew. A short walk later and they boarded their waiting shuttle, withdrew the shuttle ramp, and promptly lifted straight upward without so much as a peep into a stationary orbit around Earth directly above Roswell, New Mexico.

A very short message was immediately transmitted down to Earth stating:

Thank you for our preliminary meeting. We await your response within the hour concerning a follow-up meeting to be held tomorrow in London, England.

Signed, Captain Oulah IV, United Redexian Frontier

The incoming alien space message arrived in both formal Newee as well as English. It was delivered promptly to the greeting committee members still seated around their conference room table looking somewhat perplexed. Each scanned their personal copy of the brief message and then looked toward President Obama for leadership. At this stage, it didn't take a rocket scientist to determine the best course of action was to attend a meeting with the little gray devils in London to see what could be accomplished.

Looking around at the group, President Obama stated clearly, "Gentlemen, we have nothing to lose by complying with the request for a prompt meeting in London, and potentially we have a considerable amount to lose by doing nothing. Specifically, Sir William, please make arrangements to a reserve a fashionable, favorable, quiet, and secure location in London for a meeting to convene at 7 PM tomorrow. I will make arrangements through the Group of 8 for the appropriate personnel to be present. I suggest that our world leaders meet at 5 PM at the selected location to review our negotiating position. I will request a concise briefing paper be prepared concerning the Redexians' various requests. Please let me know as quickly as possible the location selected so that our decision can be transmitted under my authority to the hovering shuttlecraft."

Sir William Jefferson Clinton Meek nodded towards the President while verbally indicating that he would comply. As requested, a few minutes after the meeting in the Roswell conference room was adjourned, Sir William confirmed to the President that the meeting would be held at his country estate, Framingham House, on its 30 acres of secure ground the following day. Without further ado President Obama had the following message transmitted to the orbiting shuttlecraft:

Please be advised that the meeting you requested will be conducted on the grounds of Framingham House in London, England. This meeting will commence at 7 PM Greenwich Mean Time (GMT) tomorrow. We look forward to an amicable exchange of ideas at that time.

Sincerely, Chairman Barack Obama, on behalf of the Group of 8

A few minutes later a less formal transmission was received from the shuttlecraft, as follows:

Can we assist by providing transportation to London on our shuttlecraft? It will save you some time. Please let us know.

Signed, Captain Oulah IV of the United Redexian Frontier

A further responsive transmission was then sent by President Obama:

Thanks, can you pick us up at the White House tomorrow at noon? We will transmit the exact coordinates of our London meeting place for your navigator's review.

Back came a further response:

We will pick you up as suggested. Let us know if Casey Foster, Leah Anne Bailey, Jacob Witwenova, and Chole Anh Sing also need a ride. No need to forward the coordinates for the White House or Framingham House; we found what we needed on Google Earth and locked in the target destination on our bridge navigation system. We will pick you up shortly.

Signed, Captain Oulah, United Redexian Frontier

CHAPTER 13

READY TO RUMBLE

Situated down the hall from the main conference room sat Casey Foster, Leah Anne Bailey, and Chloe Anh Sing, along with their debriefing team. The objective was to obtain as much information concerning the four Earth visitors' trip to the Redexian mother ship in as short a time as possible. Each agent was provided with their own debriefing person. Questions were fired at them with responses recorded accurately. Casey Foster's myriad photographs were downloaded, printed, and sorted according to category. He had brilliantly catalogued everything possible concerning the mother ship and its inner workings as a potential treasure trove of useful information. Jacob Witwenova also joined the debriefing group after he finished the private meeting. It seemed to him that no attempt had been made to restrict his access to any of the areas of the mother ship. The Redexian crew members had also been free to speak to him about any subject matter he was interested in discussing. In other words, his alien hosts had appeared unafraid that he would uncover anything damaging to their interests.

Similarly, Chloe Anh Sing explained to her military de-briefers that she had also been given free access to all of the inner workings of the Redexian mother ship. She had been allowed to inspect the engine room, where explanations of the three operational systems had been provided. She had been able to inspect various types of munitions and delivery systems. And most importantly, she had attended a meeting on the bridge with Captain Oulah IV as he demonstrated the immense power of one high grade photon torpedo that he unleashed on Saturn's surface.

The demonstration had been coupled with the captain's explanation that many more of these weapons, in various grades and strengths, could be delivered on target, one after another, in a short period of time. Clearly, these aliens had at their disposal weapons with overwhelming capabilities of mass destruction.

Leah Anne Bailey was likewise debriefed and asked to explain who she had been able to interview aboard the alien mother ship. She had been provided with access to the ship's officers and crew. All had spoken freely with her about their mission and their station duties. Nothing seemed to have been withheld. Leah Anne explained that in her opinion each of her informal interviews led to new information from a willing set of fellow galaxy members. It had been a great opportunity for her to collect information to be shared with the world's governmental leaders.

When the debriefing sessions were completed an immediate report detailing the findings was prepared for the Group of 8. The report's substance could be summed up in a few short lines: the visiting aliens were far more technologically advanced than we are here on Earth. The materials used in construction of the mother ship, shuttles, and armaments were in most cases not yet available on Earth. This could be explained by the fact that the Redexian civilization was approximately 50,000 years old, or 40,000 years more advanced than Earth's civilization. The Redexians had already been exploring the space beyond their home world for over 2500 years. Currently they had progressed far enough to place permanent outposts on a number of planets. The stated purposes for this space program was to seek new scientific information, to meet and understand other life forms on other planets, and to create sustainable observation outposts on outlying planets for security reasons. The debriefing group concluded that the chances for destroying the Redexian mother ship and its crew orbiting Titan was close to minimal. There were no Earth weapons or delivery systems that could reach the Redexian mother ship as it orbited Titan without obvious long term notice to the intended target to permit any reasonable chance of success. The only opportunity for possibly damaging the Redexians would be to attempt a biological and/or chemical attack on their crew members, either by trying to introduce such materials on Earth or at the mother ship. However, the consequences of such an attempted attack resulting in failure could lead to an overwhelmingly negative impact on Earth and all of its inhabitants. In other words, it wouldn't be wise to throw rocks at a potential enemy who could respond with a nuclear bomb. Play nice. Smile a bunch. Try to be helpful. Duck and weave.

For her part, Leah Anne had attended the Roswell meetings and was ready to move forward. She was hot to trot to prepare her next news article for publication in the *Washington Post*, enhanced by relevant photographs taken by Casey Foster. The two of them sequestered themselves next to the main conference room. Leah Anne started writing her next news article, and Casey Foster started selecting accompanying photographs. Both chuckled and smiled at each other. Within a short period of time Leah Anne's article began taking shape as follows:

"Getting to Know Our Galaxy Neighbor"
Byline: Leah Anne Bailey, *Washington Post*

Welcome back, my fellow Earthlings, to the continuing saga of getting to know our galactic neighbors from planet Redex. Recently my fellow travelers and I completed our incredible journey to and stay on the Redexian mother ship orbiting Titan. We have now returned to Earth with our Redexian shipmates, where I had the good fortune to witness the first public greeting ceremony at Roswell, New Mexico, between the visiting Redexian aliens and Earth's political leadership. It was, in my judgment, a startling good preliminary step in the process of two neighboring civilizations getting to know one another. Formal greetings, admirable cooperative handshakes, and gentle head touching were the order of the day. Brief opening remarks were presented by both President Barack Obama, Chairman of Earth's Group of 8, and Captain Oulah IV, as the representative of the United Redexian Frontier. Smiles from all participants were beamed instantly around the world by the on-site television crews. We now all know that we here on Earth are not alone in either our Milky Way galaxy or the universe as a whole. What I can add with wholehearted honesty is that our interaction with this new, intelligent species was a pleasant experience in which we were treated with respect. I remain positively hopeful that this relationship will grow and foster a cooperative interstellar understanding.

Following the public greeting ceremony, a private meeting of Earth and Redexian leaders was held inside the Roswell air base. During that meeting the alien guests presented a short list of their desired objectives. I am not presently at liberty to disclose any details concerning the Redexians' requests. What I can report to you is that further discussions will be held shortly in London, England. Happily, Casey Foster and I have once again been invited to attend these ongoing discussions. I will keep you informed.

What was it like traveling with and living aboard the Redexian mother ship? What was it like interacting with the Redexian spaceship officers and their crew? Did we feel threatened at any point in time or concerned about our physical safety? These are questions I can now answer for you based upon my own personal experiences. Firstly, the travel experience from Earth to the Redexian mother ship was amazing. We comfortably zoomed by Earth's moon, our red rocky neighborhood planet of Mars, and then swooshed by Saturn's multi-colored icy rings towards its moon, Titan, where the mother ship was orbiting. We were exposed to scenery never seen in person by human eyes, including the incredible sight of our unbelievably beautiful planet diminishing in size as we withdrew into space. I can only state as clearly as possible how precious Earth appears from the night sky. If nothing else I must state as emphatically as I can that we Earthlings must all do everything within our power to preserve our beautiful planet.

Traveling by and then orbiting planet Mars was incredible. Below our shuttlecraft we could clearly observe the main surface features of this planet. How wondrous, magnificent, and breathtaking! I am convinced that the destiny of Earth's people includes traveling to, colonizing, and developing Mars for our benefit. Then, just a few days after leaving Mars' orbit, we arrived at planet Saturn. The captain directed the shuttlecraft through the ice rings and the shuttlecraft proceeded until we arrived in orbit around Titan. Then the captain inched us forward until a hard docking took place and we entered the mother ship. It can only be described as being immense in both size and complexity. Imagine, if you will, a space vessel over three times the size and volume of a modern day aircraft carrier, staffed by 3000 crew members, traveling for many years with no place to refuel or refit. Everything, and I mean everything, must be on board for this lengthy voyage. Inside the mother ship, areas were set aside for three engine rooms, extensive crew quarters, farming and processing systems, extensive kitchen areas to process food materials into liquid refreshment, and of course the command station on the spaceship's bridge. There were also extensive areas set aside for leisure activities, education, and research. The ship is in fact a self-contained miniature traveling world with everything necessary stored on board. Comparing the Redexian mother ship to the current size and complexity of Earth's space-traveling capsules is simple. Earth's space vehicles are small and cramped. It's like traveling in an enclosed telephone booth. Our ships are merely life rafts to hopefully move you from one place to another while you remain alive. OK, these Redexians have had 2,500 more years to move forward with their space exploration, so it stands to reason that they are a little ahead of us in space travel. But I fully expect that someday we will be in a similar position.

After I attend the next formal meeting in London, I will again update you concerning where this process is leading. In the meantime, let's all enjoy the show. Thank you again for your continuing interest in this unfolding story. Please feel free to contact me at my Washington Post office with any of your comments or questions. Attached at the end of this article are the selected photographs taken by Casey Foster during our travels to the Redexian mother ship and while attending the public meeting in Roswell, New Mexico. I remain indebted to Casey for his incredible artistic talent in documenting my news reports.

Leah Anne's dictated article was then e-mailed to Kelly Oliveri to be finalized and forwarded to the *Washington Post* editor responsible for her news articles. Once governmental permission was obtained, the finalized article was published as a special news edition in the *Washington Post*. The front page story, highlighted by incredible color photographs, was greedily purchased by the consuming public. This made Leah Anne, Casey, and the *Washington Post* publisher exceedingly happy. The *Post's* ownership interests applauded these groundbreaking news articles and the corresponding rising newspaper advertising revenues. Everyone connected to the Roswell story was pleased.

The reaction of Earth's people on the ground still fit within Leah Anne's three previously designated categories. Those folks happily outside mainstream contact, living in faraway locations such as the South American jungles, extreme northern latitudes like Siberia and Alaska, isolated Central African republics, and desolate desert regions remained uninterested and out of touch. For them, the continuing saga of daily survival remained as their primary goal. Visiting aliens from other planets ranked low on their list of concerns. Snakes, gators, hippopotamuses, scorpions, lions, tigers, mosquito-borne diseases, and poor water quality had their attention. Until such time as any aliens popped up in their neighborhood, these folks would have little concern.

For the doomsayers, fervent religious followers, conservative preppers, and plain old haters, these aliens were now real. These good folks now had an opportunity to stare these red-eyed devils in the face on their television screens. They did not like what they saw. The Good Book, in whatever format or language, had made it clear to them that God had created man in His image. But these guys certainly did not look like us Earthlings and therefore could not possibly be created in God's image.

This opened a myriad of questions. If there was indeed one God who had created everything, including those other galaxies, stars, and planets, had that one God also created Redex and its aliens? If the answer to that question was "yes," had God indeed created an alien race prior to those of us here on good old planet Earth? Had God created a myriad of other life forms on other planets throughout our galaxy and the universe? If so, how special were we little Earthlings? Our importance as a special human species was dwindling fast. Had we suddenly entered a new Dark Ages? With this new reality in mind, a flock of current day evangelists of every stripe took to the street, pulpit, and television screen lamenting God's wrath towards Earth's citizens for their myriad blasphemous sins. Now we were all going to receive the punishment we so deserved. Out into the streets, you sinful people. Tear your clothing, flagellate your skin, lament, make holy offerings, pray for forgiveness, and promise, oh promise, to do better. This seemed to work for a while, until everyone grasped the truth that these visiting aliens were going nowhere soon. And just as importantly, even if they did leave, we now knew that they were still present on neighboring planet Redex, and apparently more aliens were present throughout the universe. We here on our little blue water world were going to need some new rules. Quick, line up the Pope, the chief Rabbi of Israel, the head Muslim Ayatollah, the leading Hindu practitioner, the Shinto master, and the Buddhist leader, the Dalai Lama. Maybe, just maybe, these religious leaders could get together and work out a common saving agenda. Help was needed. Good luck on that cooperative religious program. These guys and their predecessors had been beating the drums of hatred towards others for centuries. We are the way. We are the chosen people. We are following in God's true path. *They* are the blasphemers who should be wiped off the face of the Earth. Can't we just hit the major religion reset button? Now.

In the meantime, the newspapers, television programs, and online news sources continued to blast out coverage showing fervent groups of people lamenting the state of things and protesting to their respective governments for action. But what exact action could any of their governments take to assist them? So this approximate one third of the Earth's peoples was just plain upset, disturbed, and pissed off. Get used to it.

The remaining one third or so of Earth's people were happily content, for no real reason other than they had just plain old optimism. They felt comfortable. The new alien thing had arrived. All of their hoped-for dreams would soon come true. New educational opportunities, new scientific endeavors, new manufacturing possibilities, new medical discoveries, and an *Encyclopedia Galactica* would all soon be produced for everyone's enlightenment. Everything was going to work out just grand. We would all have sufficient food, clothing, entertainment, and energy resources to complement all of our Earthly needs. We had been taken in by happy-go-lucky, smiling benefactors to help us and protect us from any other off-world, hostile shitheads coming our direction. All we had to do was smile and be cooperative. Follow the new plan. Assist the Redexians in their endeavors within our solar system. Be helpful allies. Surely we could all do that. Surely we must.

Well, for the two thirds of Earth's population paying attention, this was all good theater. New and entertaining. There was something in this for everyone. Should we drink ourselves into a stupor under the barroom table or raise our glass of champagne to toast the upcoming nirvana? Perhaps it depended upon whether the glass was half full or half empty in your own mind's eye. Casey Foster and Leah Anne Bailey sided with those who thought good things were about to happen. Jacob Witwenova and Chloe Anh Sing were considerably more conservative in their viewpoints, having both been trained as spies and had personally witnessed many bad events. Across the globe, in 190 or more enumerated countries, all the world's political leaders took public positions running the full gamut of possibilities.

Fortunately for all the Earth people who had evolved into "intelligent organisms," one group of leaders was actually looking out for *everyone's* best interest. That would be the Group of 8, designated as the world's front runners on these issues. These guys were trying to keep their minds open. They had established committees, reviewed potential outcomes, prepared study papers, and were hatching plans for a worldwide response. The first public meeting between planetary neighbors had gone off without any highly unfavorable outcome. So President Obama, Chairman of the Group of 8, jumped up and hightailed it to Air Force One for the flight back to the White House. Secure phone calls to the other necessary parties would be made from the air. To speed things up, further requests to Captain Oulah to pick up the other world leaders across the planet for transport to London would be presented. It was a good test to see how cooperative these Redexians might be. Just dial up Air Redex and request transportation services. Time to move forward. The clock was running. Put on your game face, your uniform, and let's play ball. Happily, Captain Oulah agreed to assist with shuttle craft transportation.

Shortly after President Obama and his team scurried away on Air Force One, Casey asked permission from the air base commander to make a telephone call. With a wink towards Leah Anne, Casey phoned up his dearly beloved grandma Lucy Foster. One ring, two rings, and the phone was picked up with a cheery, "Hello, this is Lucy."

"Hi, Grandma, it's your favorite grandson," said Casey. "As you may know, I'm here in Roswell with Leah Anne. We will be staying for the evening and I was wondering whether we might be able to stop by to say hello and have a bite to eat?"

"Oh, that's such great news," gushed Grandma. "I'd love to have you both over. I've missed seeing you, Casey, and I'd love to spend more time getting to know Leah Anne better. When did you have in mind?"

"Any time that's convenient for you would be good. But there is a small glitch: we don't have any transportation. Is there a chance you could pick us up from the Roswell Air Force base?"

"Sure, Casey, that will be fine," responded Lucy. "Just let me take a few minutes to get tonight's dinner started and then I'll be on the way. I suspect I'll be there in a little over an hour. Will that work for you?"

"Grandma, that will be just fine. I can't wait to see you. Love you. Bye." Casey then swooped over to Leah Anne, put his arms around her waist, and swung her in a 360 degree circle, planting a big wet kiss on her soft, exposed neck. "Looks like I've made dinner reservations for both of us at grandma Lucy's for tonight. She'll be picking us up here in about an hour."

"That's a wonderful idea," said Leah Anne." I'd really like to spend some more time with your grandma and learn how you turned into such a nut bag. But, I think it's important that we don't overextend our welcome. You'd better make arrangements for us to stay downtown later this evening. And if you play your cards right perhaps I'll have a surprise for you."

"Now you're talking. I'll call the Sands Hotel in downtown Roswell and try to book the same room we shared on our last visit," Casey responded. "How does that sound?"

Leah Anne smirked, winked, and chortled, then drawled in her best Western accent, "Ride 'em, cowboy. Let's do it. It'll be just like a little private vacation for a few hours."

Without further ado, Casey dialed up the Sands Hotel and asked for the reservation department. "Yep," answered the drawling voice, "what can I do for you?"

"This is Casey Foster calling; I'd like to book a room for tonight. On my last visit to your hotel I stayed in the second floor corner suite with a king size bed facing the river. I'd like the same room again tonight. Is it available?"

"Let me take a look… Yep, it's here. I'll hold it for you, Mr. Foster. How many guests will there be in your group? What time can we expect you?"

"There will be two of us. I expect that will be there within the next couple of hours."

"OK, fine, we will see you soon," responded the desk clerk.

Casey turned around after making hotel reservations and saw his beautiful girlfriend, Leah Anne Bailey, *Washington Post* news reporter, looking like an angel. "Now, that's what I'm talking about," he said aloud. "Dinner at Grandma Lucy's, back to Roswell to stay at the Sands Hotel, perhaps a quick drink at the hotel bar, and then we ride into the sunset for the night. Giddy up!"

Leah Anne swished her way over to Casey and jumped into his arms. Planting a wet soft kiss squarely on his lips, she gushed, "This ought to be a night to remember. First Grandma Lucy's home cooking, followed by rolling in the Sand's king sized bed, and finished with a round of jamb the dart in the bull's eye."

About an hour later Grandma Lucy pulled up in front of the Roswell Air Force base in her bright red four-door Jeep Wrangler Unlimited, enhanced with a chrome front bumper, chrome side mirrors, chrome running boards, and chrome rear bumper. As far as Lucy was concerned, being a grandmother didn't prevent her from having some fun by driving quickly along the sandy mesas enjoying the desert views. When she arrived at the air base Casey and Leah Anne were waiting for her at the entryway. She stepped out of the jeep and was warmly welcomed with embraces from each.

"Casey," she asked, "do you mind driving back to my house while Leah Anne and I chat in the rear seat?"

"Nope, that works for me. I like driving, and it will be fun listening to you two jabber away," he said.

Twenty minutes later, having driven past numerous cacti and a few tumbleweeds, Casey pulled into Grandma Lucy's driveway. Entering the front door, the sweet smell of slow-cooking Southern-style chili greeted them. Mingling in the air, one could also catch a whiff of the still warm, freshly-baked cornbread that would accompany the meal. After a quick washing of hands and face, Casey and Leah Anne seated themselves at the dining table. Almost instantly, Grandma Lucy began serving the chili and cornbread, accompanied by homemade chips and salsa. A choice of cold Corona beer in tall glass bottles or freshly-steeped raspberry iced tea was placed in the center of the table. Lucy bowed her head and quietly recited a quick prayer of thanks for the safe arrival of her company.

Throughout the dinner all three exchanged updated information of what had taken place since their last visit. Of course, the trip from Roswell to the Redexian mother ship by shuttle was of primary interest, as well as the 20 days spent on board getting to meet the Redexian crew and observe the inner workings that incredible piece of machinery. Grandma Lucy was kind enough to also steer the conversation back to discuss Leah Anne's new job as the *Washington Post* science news reporter covering the Roswell alien story. She also had the good sense to ask Casey to entertain them by showing the photographs he had taken during the space trip. This dinner conversation was informative enough that it could well have served as a top scientific seminar on a first interchange between Milky Way galaxy members.

When the dinner had been completed, Casey cleared the table while Leah Anne assisted Grandma Lucy in washing the dishes. Fresh coffee was served in the dining room as Grandma Lucy approached the subject about which she really cared. "OK kids," she ventured, "was the trip to the alien mother ship fun or scary?"

"Mostly fun," answered Leah Anne, "but there was an element of suspense since we didn't really know what we were getting ourselves into."

"Knowing what you know now, would you do it again?"

"You can bet your cowboy boots and cowboy hat," responded Casey. "Where else could we ever get a opportunity like this one? I'd go again tomorrow."

"OK, you two," responded Lucy, "now for the really important question." Both Casey and Leah Anne's ears perked up, and their eyes were immediately riveted upon Grandma Lucy. *Oh boy*, they thought, *what's next*? Lucy began, "It seems to me that you two have been spending quite a bit of time together at work, during your news reporting trips, and I suspect during your mutual free time. You both appear to be bright, hard-working, and adventuresome in spirit. So the question that comes to my mind is: are the two of you planning to make your relationship permanent? After all, I'm an old grandmother and don't have forever to see my most favorite grandson, Casey, get married. There, I said it; the cat's out of the bag. How about it? Make an old woman happy. I'd love to plan a Western-style wedding."

Casey and Leah Anne each flushed a distinct shade of pink. Casey, as Lucy's grandson, would have to respond first. "Grandma Lucy, he said, "what a delightful way to put both of us on the spot. As you know, we have been dating for some time and trying to get to know one another better. The subject that you raise is of course extremely important. But in all honesty, it is not a subject that we have discussed. And it seems to me that Leah Anne might need more time before she could make any decision regarding such an important matter."

Then Leah Anne, took the bit between her teeth. "Grandma Lucy, while I'm not that sure about spending my whole future with your grandson, I can assure you that I'd love to spend as much time with you as possible. Your company is thrilling, and I enjoy every moment that we spend together. I promise you, though, that if Casey and I decide to go down the path you're inquiring about, you will be the first person to know. In the meantime, let me thank you again for your kindness and courtesy."

Grandma Lucy cocked her head to one side, looked the couple in the eyes, and walked back to the kitchen without an answer about marriage. Casey and Leah Anne had neatly avoided her question, but at least she had placed the subject directly before them, where it could no longer be avoided. The truth be known, both had been thinking to themselves along the same line for some time. Coffee was served and consumed with polite conversation for a while longer. Then Casey asked whether Grandma Lucy would mind driving them to the Sands Hotel in Roswell. Of course Grandma Lucy was happy to assist. She drove the young couple in her jeep in front of the Sands Hotel. Once there the nighttime hotel guests were met by the doorman. He grabbed their luggage and brought it inside to the check-in counter. Grandma Lucy waved goodbye and happily drove off toward her country home. *Nothing like starting the kettle brewing*, she thought.

Once inside, Casey nearly galloped over to the check-in desk, credit card in hand, which he casually tossed upon the countertop and said, "I believe you have reserved a suite for Casey Foster and guest."

"Yes, indeed I have, Mr. Foster. It's so nice to see you again. Just as you requested, I have reserved for you our best suite overlooking the

North Spring River. I'll send the bellboy up shortly with your luggage. Please let me know if there's anything else we can do for you."

"Well, I might as well arrange a wake-up call for tomorrow morning at 7:30 AM," said Casey. "We'd like to have time for breakfast before we head back to the Roswell Air Force base. Can you make arrangements for transportation from the hotel to the air base in the morning?"

"I'll take care of it for you," answered the clerk. "Now, if you don't mind, I hate to trouble you, but I would like to ask a personal question. Would that be alright?"

"I hope so," responded Casey. "What do you have in mind?"

"I just wanted to know whether you, Mr. Foster, and your companion are the two journalists covering this Roswell thing for the *Washington Post*."

"You bet," responded Casey, suddenly puffed up like a bullfrog sitting on his lily pad serenading the local shapely frogettes. "It's us. Leah Anne writes the alien news articles and I take complementary photographs. Have you seen any of our work?"

"You can say that again," responded the front desk clerk. "Everyone here in Roswell has been following the story closely. We all consider both the story and you as one of us. The alien story started here in Roswell, and I recall you spent time here growing up with Newton and Lucy Foster. So now everyone here claims to have been friends with your grandfather Newton and to have met you along the way. But let me take this opportunity to say how much I've enjoyed reading Ms. Bailey's news stories with your accompanying photographs. The shots that I've seen of your travels past the moon, Mars, and Saturn are incredibly eye-opening. The photographs that you have posted showing the alien mother ship's exterior and interior are mind-boggling. And the photographs highlighting the Redexian captain and his crew members are awesome. Perhaps, if it's not too much of an inconvenience, would you and Ms. Bailey mind signing one of the photographs that I've purchased showing the Redexian mother ship?"

"Certainly; that's no problem. Leah Anne, could you come over for moment please?"

Casey explained the request and both happily signed the color photograph. Indeed, they learned that the longer this story developed the more they were becoming celebrities. It was startling and unexpected, though also pleasant. Yet at the same time they could both tell it could start to infringe upon their freedom of movement and independence. But for now it sure was fun.

With a nod towards the front desk clerk, Casey and Leah Anne were escorted to their room by the bellboy. Once inside, with the door closed, Casey noticed a fancy bottle of French champagne sitting in a large silver, engraved ice bucket centered upon the room's desk. Dangling from the top of the bottle was a brief note welcoming these two special guests to the Sands Hotel and thanking them for their patronage. Casey grabbed the complementary bottle of champagne, unwrapped the cork, twisted the metal stays, and popped open the bottle as he quickly poured a bit into two waiting crystal champagne goblets. "It's good to be king," he bellowed, suddenly feeling full of himself.

"Don't forget the queen and her glass," responded Leah Anne.

Casey gently led Leah Anne over to the balcony doors, which he opened so they could step outside. They clinked their champagne glasses together as each sipped their reward. Overhead, standing out brightly in the dark night sky, stood Earth's moon surrounded by numerous twinkling stars. Hard to believe that not long ago they were both traveling by shuttlecraft up and around the moon, Mars, Saturn, and then off to the mother ship orbiting Titan. While other people could claim to be devoted world travelers, they could claim to be "out of this world" travelers. A designation for only a really, really, really small, special group of Earth travelers.

Leah Anne grabbed Casey by the arm, snuggled close, and gazed upward toward the sparkling stars. "Isn't this beautiful?" she said. "Here we are in Roswell, New Mexico, where you spent many happy summers growing up, looking upward and seeing the same incredible night sky as your grandfather Newton and his good friend Lone Wolf. And now we stand here looking up at these age-old stars enjoying this incredible view and wondering about what incredible things we have yet to learn. I couldn't be happier," she said.

"I'm not so sure about that," said Casey.

"What do you mean?"

"Well, babe, when you mentioned the bright twinkling stars overhead it reminded me that I have a surprise for you in my pants."

Leah Anne swung her eyes up into their sockets, thinking, *That's no surprise. I've seen that before.* However, without stopping, Casey reached into his back pocket and pulled out a small blue satin box. Slowly he opened it, extracted an incredible sparkling diamond engagement ring, and asked," Leah Anne, will you make me the happiest humanoid on Earth by marrying me?"

Leah Anne was flabbergasted. The time for this announcement was totally unexpected. She gazed at the engagement ring as a small tear rolled down her left cheek. Then she pivoted to face him and looked into his eyes, saying, "Hell yes, I'll marry you. I've been hoping you'd asked me." Words, for once, even from a professional news reporter, were now unavailable. She hugged Casey tightly and they moved back inside away from the exposed balcony. They sat quietly at the small table, slowly drinking their champagne while smiling at each other, speechless. Then, without any warning Leah Anne was hugging, rolling, kissing, licking, and caressing Casey. The frolicking was very mutual as the now engaged *Washington Post* news reporting team moved towards the king-sized bed. "Casey," Leah Anne whispered, "you had better be at your best performance level tonight, because I'm going to wear you out."

"Gee, that's a challenge," replied Casey. "We will see who screams for mercy first."

For the next couple of hours this new, soon to be permanent couple rolled and frolicked, with Leah Anne occasionally stopping to stare at her new diamond ring. Then a quick run into the shower by both and, after a thorough rinsing, activities of mutual interest began anew. As Leah Anne predicted, by early morning light Casey was pleading for mercy. While Leah Anne had been happy before, she was nutsy happy now.

"OK, OK, you win, I'm tired," said Casey. "I've had enough. Can we get some breakfast now? I'm hungry."

So after a full night's activities Casey and his new fiancé dressed and went downstairs to the Sands Hotel's dining room. Leah Anne flashed her new sparkling diamond ring to everyone within eyesight. Breakfast accompanied by a wide grin was a great way to start the new day. An hour later the engaged couple was delivered by the hotel staff to the front entryway of the Roswell Air Force base. Once there, they were greeted by Jacob Witwenova and Chloe Anh Sing as they all awaited the return of the Redexian shuttlecraft that would pick them up and transport them to the White House. Leah Anne then not so casually flashed her new engagement ring for all to see. Boy, that was fun she thought. All the new space agent spies were seemingly content. *What's next,* they wondered? *Who needed first class airfare when Air Redex is on call*? Casey and Leah Anne planned to call Grandma Lucy once they arrived in Washington.

CHAPTER 14

LONDON NEGOTIATIONS

Jacob Witwenova, Chloe Anh Sing, Casey Foster, and Leah Anne Bailey all stood in front of the Roswell Air Force base awaiting transportation to the White House. They were amicably chatting on the front lawn when the air base communication officer informed them that radar had picked up an approaching air vehicle. Arrival time was imminent. A quick glance skyward revealed the quietly-descending Redexian shuttlecraft. Without any fanfare the shuttlecraft hovered some 200 yards from the four awaiting Earth agents and then squatted firmly on the green grass lawn. As anticipated, the receiving ramp was lowered to ground level, permitting access to the interior of the shuttlecraft. Blue welcoming lights signaled that it was safe for the passengers to come aboard. Just like seasoned space veterans, the four Earthlings walked aboard to be greeted by Captain Oulah with the familiar handshake and head touching maneuvers. Brief welcoming exchanges were followed by the captain's order to the navigator to lay in the course for touch down on the White House lawn.

Unlike a standard jet aircraft, the Redexian shuttle shot straight upward using its graviton thrust system until it reached an altitude of 150 km straight above Roswell. Once orbit was achieved at that altitude there was no gravity to hold down the passengers. The navigator decided not to engage the artificial gravity system, allowing each passenger to float about like a hot air balloon on a pleasant summer's day. How fun. The navigator remained strapped down and on alert at his bridge command station. He notified his passengers that they could expect to arrive at their Washington, DC, location in a little less than one hour. They were free to float about at will and enjoy the view below until further notice. Using the available underside view portals, each watched as the shuttlecraft passed numerous patches of sparse desert, rolling plains, mountain ranges, blue-green lakes and rivers, and even an occasional small town. Eventually, larger, more developed cities came into view until at last the Baltimore/ Washington Metroplex loomed below, looking like one huge cramped urban development. Soon the onboard communication officer signaled the Washington national air center that they were arriving as scheduled. Air clearance for the White House was requested and granted after a quick check with the NSA. A variety of Air Force helicopters hovered nearby as the Redexian shuttlecraft lowered itself on to the awaiting White House receiving platform. Standing by the front gate area of the White House, hundreds of Washington locals and tourists were treated to the sight of this silver disc shuttlecraft arriving at their capital. Unlike the prior, more or less restricted Roswell visit, this one had been planned by President Obama to show off a bit more pomp and circumstance. Therefore, as the entry platform was lowered from the shuttlecraft to the ground, the Marine Corps marching band struck up "America the Beautiful." The President, Vice President, Speaker of the House of Representatives, and other Washington notables stood in a semicircle in front of the shuttlecraft awaiting the presence of the Redexian officers, as well as their four Earth "agents." As they emerged, the attending Marine Corps Honor Guard came to attention and saluted in their best military style. President Obama then walked forward, shook hands and touched heads with Captain Oulah, and led him courteously through a review of the Marines. They looked impressive, polished, and militarily adept. Captain Oulah, however, knew that one short blast from his carefully tucked away ray gun would neutralize them all in a moment. This was information he didn't feel was appropriate to divulge to the President. It was perfectly fine to let the Earthlings think that they held a big stick—for now. So together they reviewed the troops, smiled at the television cameras, nodded to the attending political representatives of merit, and walked over to the awaiting lectern for greeting speeches. Happily for all present, the speeches were short and simple. Hi there. How are you? Good to see you all. Let's all work together. Happiness and peace to all. Now it's time to boogie to London.

After a few quick, self-serving photographs were taken by the White House photographer, everyone going aboard entered the shuttlecraft, including the President of the United States. This was highly unusual, since the President almost exclusively traveled on Air Force One with his ever-present Secret Service contingent. But this was a new day with a new reality, and normal procedures had been set aside. Time to find out how much Earthlings could trust the new arrivals from planet Redex. And heck, if we had to, we could always replace a President, a few support staff, and four low ranking Earth "agents." So facing a 24 hour deadline to start the discussions concerning their proposed list of Redexian objectives, it was time to get moving. All aboard Air Redex.

The regular six-hour flight time from Washington, DC, to London, England was trimmed to a crisp 75 minutes. One could get used to quicker flight times, with no jet lag or recovery time. Before you could say "Jiminy Cricket," they arrived in London. The navigator focused on landing at the coordinates for Framingham House, located majestically on Buckhurst Hill adjacent to Earl's Lane. This quaint country estate some 30 minutes to the northeast of downtown London was initially constructed by the first Earl of Suffolk in 1575. Over the ensuing centuries it had been enhanced, expanded, re-landscaped, and stuffed with the accumulated wealth of some twelve generations of the aristocratic Meek family. The manor house comprised some 75 rooms on three floors, all dedicated to satisfying the lucky inheriting inhabitants and their guests. There was sufficient space for the aristocrats to enjoy the fruits of generations of English laboring servants. These regular serving folks worked downstairs and quietly went about their assigned tasks, dressed like strutting peacocks without saying a word to the haughty aristocrats unless directly addressed. They were pleased just to be employed.

Once his guests descended the shuttlecraft, Sir William Jefferson Clinton Meek greeted them personally, attired in his daytime informal tweed hunting suit. He welcomed them all to Framingham House and led them inside, through the receiving hall and into the daytime dining area. The serving staff waited patiently outside at parade rest and inside at attention with their backs against the dining room walls, white serving gloves at the ready. Upon Sir William's nod, the guests were all seated and High Tea was served. Piping hot Earl Grey tea was served, naturally, to his Earthly guests, accompanied by appropriate scones and cucumber sandwiches. The Redexian guests were served a more welcoming limited diet blended to their peculiar needs of lukewarm tea in silver serving bowls for appropriate slurping and licking. No singed purple-spotted tongues here. Amiable chatting about the history of Framingham house included discussions of the Meeks' involvement in local historical English society. Apparently, most of the Meek family had prospered with the developing British society. Many had held important positions in various courtly reigns. Later, as industrialization occurred, a few Meeks lowered themselves to the laboring class, although they restricted themselves to banking, medicine, and the practice of law. How common. A few other less astute clan members found their way into the clergy or purchased appropriate military commissions. Naturally, some of the more infamous members of the Meek family trundled off to the Americas, escaping well-earned stints in debtor's prison. No portraits of these unfortunate relatives would be found upon the walls of Framingham House. They had all probably perished in the wilderness, ravaged by bears or wild Indians. At the conclusion of High Tea, Sir William personally escorted the Redexian officers who were staying at the estate as his personal guests to their quarters. He had carefully arranged the entire west wing of the second floor for their exclusive use. Assigned to look after these special alien guests were two butlers, three serving maids, and a footman. Exactly what their tasks would entail was unclear at this point in time. The Redexians were also informed that with proper notice the kitchen could provide any additional food or beverage items requested. Captain Oulah thanked Sir William for his attention and indicated that any additional items would be brought for their use from their shuttlecraft. Other Earthly negotiating members would be staying on the east wing of the third floor with a similar level of service having been arranged. This demanding group was expected to hound the staff with repeated requests for attention. If guards were not posted at their hallway, and they were not, nighttime liaisons could be anticipated by the Earthlings. Horny bastards!

About an hour after High Tea concluded, the Group of 8 representatives and their staff met privately in the drawing room overlooking the formal gardens. Sir William, as the chief negotiator, and Jacob Witwenova, as the Earth's agent most familiar with the Redexians, were provided with instructions concerning these negotiations, the most important of which was that the final draft of any agreement that would need to be formally presented in writing to the Group of 8 for their approval. It was further decided that after introductions had been made, the actual negotiations would be led by Sir William. The other world leaders would attend for a while but had Earthly matters which needed attention. They did not want to give Captain Oulah and his team the impression that the political leaders on Earth needed to be present to talk to a mere ship's captain and Redexian ambassador. I mean, really, how absurd. The Group of 8 also instructed Sir William that certain quid pro quo arrangements for their assent to certain requests would be necessary. And of course there would need to be payment for any of Earth's materials and services that would be required. So, heads up, chins thrust forward, utilize the King's best English. It was time to commence negotiations.

At exactly 7 PM Captain Oulah IV, his chief negotiator Aounah III, and military advisor Neehoua IX were led into the auspiciously well-stocked library and seated around the hand-carved tiger maple conference table. Already seated and awaiting their entry was President Obama as chairman of the Group of 8 along with Sir William, Jacob Witwenova, and Chloe Anh Sing. For this occasion Sir William had changed, with his valet's assistance, from his informal hunting tweed suit into his well- tailored Braxton Street tuxedo with white tie adornment. He felt that if he was going to appear important he should look important. "Gentlemen and ladies," began Sir William, "please let me extend to each of you my heartfelt welcome to my family's ancestral home, Framingham. We have been honored throughout the generations to hold many such meetings in an effort to lubricate the interactions between distinct peoples. As we all know, this is the first formal discussion between our Redexian guests and Earth's representatives to discuss the requests presented to us by Captain Oulah. Let me inform you that I have been authorized by the Group of 8, on behalf of all Earth's people, to discuss this matter in detail. Furthermore, Jacob Witwenova and Chloe Anh Sing have had an opportunity to meet with our guests earlier on their visit to the Redexian's impressive mother ship. They will also assist me in these discussions. Without further delay unless, anyone has questions, I will begin this conversation."

Graciously, no one interrupted with any comments, although Aounah III continuously lapped up his tepid sweet tea from the silver serving bowl with relatively loud sucking noises throughout Sir William's introductory comments. Silence during another's introductory comments did not appear to be a Redexian social requirement.

Standing behind his King George library chair, Sir William turned to face Aounah III directly and stated, "My understanding is that your first request is for permission to station three observation satellites in our solar system to collect and transmit information back to your home planet Redex and to your various outposts. We have no objection to this request but would like verifying information regarding where you plan to place these three orbiting satellites, what type of information these satellites will obtain, and, of course, whether you are willing to share that collected data with us on an ongoing basis. Would you care to respond?"

"Sir William," answered Aounah, "you should be aware that these three satellites have already been placed in stable elliptical orbits around Saturn, Mars, and your moon. The data to be collected involves information regarding nearby star systems and their captive planets. We are also collecting any data that would disclose signs of alien life, as well as incoming space vehicles in this region of the Milky Way. This information is critical in our ongoing quest to provide a safety zone for Redex and our allies. As to your request to share this data, I believe that can be accomplished."

"Thank you for your response," said Sir William. *Crap*, he thought to himself. *Not even the courtesy to ask and get permission before dicking around in our solar system. How impudent.* But he did not let on to his displeasure. What was he going to do, tell them to retrieve their satellites? Yeah, like that would fly. So he merely said, "I'm sure that will be acceptable. I will leave it to our mutual staff technicians to work out the exact language on your request to station satellites and collect data in our solar system for our approval of the same.

"Your second request seeks permission to establish a permanent observation and servicing base on the fourth planet from our sun, which we refer to as Mars. Before I can respond, could you give me an indication regarding the physical size of the requested base, the number of expected personnel that will occupy the base, and its intended purpose?"

After shoving his silver bowl aside and wiping his lips with the edge of the tablecloth, Aounah answered, "The permanent observation base we intend to build on Mars will eventually house over 1500 Redexian staff in permanent headquarters to serve as our primary observation post in this solar system. To satisfy our needs we will require an area of land of at least 25 square kilometers. We anticipate that construction of this permanent observation base with supporting technical equipment, housing for support staff, landing facilities, and ancillary service stations will last for many months. We further anticipate that we will need to request certain raw materials and services from your people here on Earth to expedite this project. As for the data collected from our Mars observatory, we will feel comfortable in sharing that data with you as well."

At this stage, Sir William came to the realization, as had the Group of 8, that they had no reasonable way to stop the Redexians from utilizing resources throughout the solar system and building outposts where they saw fit. Rather, he would aim to negotiate reasonable requests in return for ownership rights and "proper payments."

"Thank you for your response," Sir William started. After whispering for a moment with Jacob Witwenova and Chloe Anh Sing, he said, "Earth's people have no objection to your request to build a Mars observation station. I suggest the land you wish to use for this observation station take the form of what we would refer to as a long-term lease agreement. In return for our granting leasing rights for this land, we would request that you also build out, with our assistance, a smaller nearby observation base that could house 50 Earth personnel. And, for the time being, our Mars personnel would need transportation to and from Earth to Mars, to be provided by you. Will this be acceptable?" he asked, holding his breath. Time to find out if there would be any quid pro quo!

"Yes, replied Aounah, "we have done this elsewhere in the past. We see no reason why Earth should not have its own observation base on Mars. We anticipated that this would be one of your goals considering the satellites you have presently orbiting Mars and your current attempts to explore its surface with remote controlled robots. It's also nice for a species to have a secondary home in its solar system as a backup in case something goes wrong on your home planet. We felt the same way 2500 years ago on Redex. We will need to further discuss mutual payments for mutual goods and services at the appropriate time."

Sir William continued, "As to your third request, I further understand that you are interested in creating smaller substations on Saturn's moon, Titan, and Earth's moon. Likewise, we are prepared to grant long term leases for substations on Earth's moon and Titan once the locations are designated and the purpose is disclosed. As to the moon, we would again request that a nearby base be developed by you for 50 Earth personnel, as well as short term transportation to and from its surface, to be provided by your people. Would this also be acceptable?"

"This can be accomplished," replied Aounah. "You have mentioned compensation for various projects. What do you have in mind?"

"We here on Earth are in need of readily available clean energy, readily available clean water, and the provision of safety for our planet and people from incoming asteroids, comets, and space debris. We, like you, plan to be around for quite some time and would not like to see our civilization destroyed by a large rogue space rock. Also to the extent that you may need our raw materials or services, they will need to be purchased at fair market values. Can you be of assistance in these matters?"

"Actually," responded Oulah IV, "since we are planning to share your solar system with ongoing contact with you here on Earth, we agree that providing protection from incoming space debris is an essential first step in cooperation. It has taken us many years and much expense to provide a level of protection to our planet from similar incoming space materials. We will be happy to assist you in two specific ways. First, we will assist in locating and documenting potential incoming debris that could cause serious damage to planet Earth, your moon, and Mars. Secondly, with your sharing of expenses we can provide protection from incoming space debris. Some of these space objects, if detected soon enough, can be destroyed or deflected. This is not a perfect scientific system, but it should help to avoid any major destruction. Please note that this will take some time to accomplish. It is not a foolproof system, but it can help. Again, our respective personnel can work on these details."

"On behalf of Earth," responded Sir William, "I thank you for your willingness to help us avoid potential destruction from incoming space debris. This is a subject which has recently been attracting a great deal of interest from our planetary scientists. Together I am sure we can devise a system to safeguard planet Earth, as well as any observation bases built on the moon or planet Mars." Unstated by Sir William was the fact that a recent NASA study performed under the direction of Dr. Omer Hoe found that Earth scientists had located approximately 90% of the largest planet-killing asteroids but only 10% of the still very dangerous asteroids up to 140 meters (460 feet) in size. A strike by a meteor of that size would completely destroy any large Earth city. And, more importantly, even if such an asteroid was detected in time, Earth currently had little to no means to deflect or destroy the asteroid before its impact with Earth. In short, Earth could really, really, really use some help in avoiding this kind of civilization-ending scenario.

Sir William went on, "I further understand that your fourth request would be to create a recreational zone near Roswell, New Mexico. Could you advise us concerning the size of this proposed recreational base, its purpose, and the approximate number of Redexian crew members who might be present at any given time?"

"I expect you have been informed by Jacob Witwenova and Chloe Anh Sing that the Redexian mother ship maintains a crew of approximately 3000 personnel. We plan on stationing almost 2000 of our crew members permanently in this solar system. About 1500 of those personnel will be based upon planet Mars, and a few dozen will be based on Titan and the Earth's moon. We expect that the remaining few hundred will be located on Earth in the various capacities. Furthermore, at any given time we would anticipate rotating somewhere between 100 and 150 personnel to the recreational space we build near Roswell. We have learned from our many space exploration expeditions that what we refer to as 'ground time' is always useful."

"On behalf of the Group of 8 and President Obama of the United States," responded Sir William, "your request to locate a recreational zone in the Roswell, New Mexico, area is tentatively approved. More details will be necessary regarding the specific location for the recreational zone, its intended use, and compensation for its ongoing use. Again, I feel that these are details that can be left to a smaller working group to develop a written plan for final approval. I expect, however, that the details will include some sort of long-term lease agreement, access to the recreational base by the local authorities, and coordination of construction and type of materials that may be located on the recreational site.

"Finally, I understand that the Redexian government would like to open a permanent Embassy in a primary city on Earth. Can you provide more details at this time?"

"Yes," responded Aounah. "In conjunction with my conversations with Captain Oulah, we have determined that the location for our primary Embassy will be in Jerusalem, Israel. I understand that we have already held some preliminary discussions with Prime Minister Netanyahu, and we have his permission for such an embassy. Our permanent embassy would be staffed by perhaps 15 to 20 Redexian diplomats along with our permanent ambassador. In addition, we will be providing a permanent ambassador to the United Nations. And as our presence on Earth develops, we may require additional embassies located in the capital cities of each of your Group of 8 nations."

Sir William reached forward, grabbed the crystal goblet set out before him, and poured himself a generous glass of sherry. Nodding to his guests, he continued, "Yes, we have indeed been advised by the government of Israel regarding your request to place a permanent embassy in Jerusalem. We have no objections to that or to your providing an ambassador to the United Nations. Each of the remaining Group of 8 member nations would also welcome an embassy in their capital cities. We favorably view this as an effort to establish a permanent, long-term, and mutually advantageous relationship. We are hopeful that all of our people will learn to treat each other civilly and with respect. Now that we have heard your requests and we have provided our response, let us turn the specific details of a written agreement over to our respective staffs. I feel confident that we will be able to resolve any details that come up during this process. Once we have a final draft agreement I will present it to the Group of 8 for formal written approval. Will that be acceptable?"

"Yes," responded Aounah III.

"Then let us adjourn while our staffs hash out the details," answered Sir William. "Finally, I have the pleasure to announce that we will be serving a formal dinner to all of our guests at 10:30 PM this evening. We look forward to seeing each and every one of you at that time. Thank you all for your attention. Please feel free to mingle and further discuss these matters."

"Before we adjourn," interjected Aounah III, "there is another matter that deserves our mutual attention. Our experiences both on Redex and other worlds that we have traveled to suggests that early stage developing planets like yours are likely to contain areas of serious conflict. The information that we have received from our initial satellite observations, shuttlecraft visit to Earth in 1947, and our more recent observations upon arriving in your solar system indicate that your planet has similar conflict issues. As we begin the process of developing permanent observation stations in your solar system and specifically here on planet Earth, these major conflict areas should be resolved. It is in no one's interest, in our opinion, to permit any such conflicts to grow and fester. Worldwide conflicts that we know about, such as your World War I and World War II, are to be avoided at all costs. More recently, we understand that nuclear activities here on Earth, if not contained, could create an even more destructive scenario. These obviously are not advantageous to the health of planet Earth, its inhabitants, or its visitors. We would like to discuss this in more detail in the ensuing days and seek solutions."

"Thank you again," said Sir William. "Your comments are certainly on point. The Group of 8 and the United Nations can provide details on present day Earth conflicts and nuclear issues. With that said, I again invite everyone to adjourn until dinner is served later this evening."

The planned evening dinner went forward uneventfully. Food and drink were made liberally available. The Redexians even provided pitchers of their sweetened fruit drinks, with and without alcohol additives. Everyone seemed to be getting along well as the serving staff discretely served rounds of refreshments. After dinner a pleasant variety of cigars were made available for smoking in the adjacent green tapestry-covered smoking room. Captain Oulah, accompanied by Jacob Witwenova, decided to sample a luxurious Cuban cigar. As they puffed side-by-side, Jacob asked the captain what his initial impressions were concerning Earth and its political leaders. The captain informed Jacob that although their customs were considerably different, in general he thought everyone could get along quite well.

At the same time, Ambassador Aounah sought out the Israeli leadership and requested a meeting with the Prime Minister for the following day. Following a quick secure telephone conversation with the Prime Minister's office, a meeting was scheduled for 10 AM the following morning. To expedite transportation, Captain Oulah indicated they could all travel by means of the shuttlecraft.

During the formal evening dinner, the respective Earthlings and Redexian support staff poured over surface maps of Titan, Mars, and the moon. They were trying to define the areas for each suggested observation outpost and any nearby Earth bases. With respect to the requested recreational zone near Roswell, New Mexico, local topographical maps were brought forth and studied. Embassy space was readily available at the United Nations. The respective staffs also were confident that the Israelis and Redexians could work out any necessary arrangements concerning a permanent embassy. So while the dignitaries ate, drank, and chatted, their respective staffs worked throughout the night clarifying details. Their plan was to present the Group of 8 and the Redexians with a proposed final draft of a written comprehensive agreement the following morning.

While all of this mingling was taking place, Casey Foster happily marched from group to group taking photographs for historical purposes. He composed photographs of various individuals standing to address the group, photographs of dignitaries shaking hands and touching heads, photographs of people negotiating the deal, photographs of dignitaries seated around the dining table, and photographs of groups mingling in important discussions. He also took careful notes to make sure that he had proper names and proper spellings to go along with each of these photographs.

Nearby, Leah Anne continued her process of taking detailed notes regarding the entire get-together. She had been interviewing various members of the respective delegations throughout the day. She requested specific quotations from Sir William, Captain Oulah, Aounah, and President Obama regarding their thoughts on the meeting between these two civilizations. Mostly benign quotations were offered, which she duly noted. Leah Anne's planned to write an updated news article for the *Washington Post* and perhaps later to write a novel regarding the historic interchange between these Milky Way neighbors. So she sauntered from one group to another smiling pleasantly, asking questions, and taking notes. Leah Anne was having a heck of a time. She was enjoying her new occupation as a news reporter and the time it allowed her to spend with Casey, day or night.

As the sun rose over Framingham House the following morning, Captain Oulah stood in front of the waiting shuttlecraft enjoying the surroundings. This English countryside manor, bathed in the glow of morning sunlight, brilliantly showed off its formal gardens, rolling green grass fields, and background hilltops. It was a stunning view. *One could get used to living in surroundings like these*, he thought. *Maybe a similar countryside manor should be allocated for Redexian use*. He wondered how he would look in a miniature formal tuxedo. Before long, the Redexian crew and necessary guests trickled in for the trip to Jerusalem. Once all were aboard, the captain signaled the navigator to proceed.

The shuttlecraft hovered over its landing site, and when its gravitational thrusters were engaged it immediately shot straight skyward until reaching a stable orbit at an altitude of approximately 150 km directly over London. Then the navigator entered the coordinates for the Israeli Prime Minister's residence in Jerusalem, Israel. During the flight the shuttlecraft followed its laid-in waypoints and traveled quickly to its next destination. The communication officer contacted the Prime Minister's office and received permission for landing. Shortly thereafter, the shuttlecraft carefully lowered itself straight down, landing upon the securely guarded backyard area. At least a dozen members of the Israeli Defense Force surrounded the landed shuttlecraft with their Uzi machine guns pointed skyward. Upon the captain's orders, the landing ramp was extended.

Out from the shuttle walked the arriving contingent, who were immediately met by Prime Minister Benjamin Netanyahu. Smiles, handshakes, head touching, and a mutual chorus of "*Shalom*" was uttered by all. Official photographs of these proceedings were snapped. The Prime Minister walked side-by-side with Captain Oulah and Aounah as he escorted them to his private quarters. This was quite unusual, since almost all matters of state were handled in the Prime Minister's state office. Everyone else was excluded from the private residence meeting, including security and support staff. This would be indeed a private meeting among just these three individuals.

Inside, the three spoke about the need for peace in this volatile region, the recent conflict between the state of Israel and the radical political group Hamas in Gaza, the antagonism towards the state of Israel from Iran, and the growing radicalization of many religious groups in the region. Each of the three expressed a deep-seated desire to create a peaceful solution between the Israelis and Palestinians. It was time for final action to be taken to resolve the decades-long conflict. To achieve such a resolution, it was necessary to bring together each of the essential parties who could make such an agreement. To these ends, the names of one dozen principals was prepared who had the power and authority to strike a deal. The Redexians pledged to set a time, date, and place for each of these individuals to get together to hammer out a final peace deal. Time was running out to voluntarily enter into a peace agreement.

The Prime Minister and Redexians remained in deep conversation for over an hour. Those outside could faintly hear conversations taking place in English, Hebrew, and the Redexian language, Newee. When at last the Prime Minister and his guests emerged, they took their places at two previously-arranged lecterns in the downstairs formal library. A small assembled crowd of news journalists, photographers, and television crews were present to record the outcome of this unusual private meeting. Prime Minister Benjamin Netanyahu was no stranger to international events. He had been front and center on almost every aspect of Israeli developments over the last 30 years. He had served as Prime Minister of Israel on several occasions and had a solid reputation for being thorough and direct. Throughout the world he was admired by some, love by a few, and considered a strong, determined opponent by many others. There were only a few individuals on planet Earth who were more recognizable. His words, when spoken, were taken seriously by diplomats, statesmen, and everyday people in Israel and beyond. When he spoke, people listened.

"Thank you for attending today's historic meeting between our State of Israel and our new guests from planet Redex," said the Prime Minister. "I've had an opportunity to meet with Captain Oulah and his planet's ambassador to Earth to discuss their interest in placing an embassy here in Jerusalem. I am pleased to announce that we have agreed to their request. We have mutually selected a site near our state headquarters in Jerusalem for the construction of a Redexian embassy. I understand that this location will serve as their primary Redexian Earth embassy for transaction of all international and interstellar political relationships. It is indeed an honor for us to welcome these fellow galaxy members. We look forward to working closely with them to create a favorable environment for their endeavors. Let me stress to one and all that I personally believe this to be a great opportunity for all of us here on planet Earth. These neighbors, whom we are just getting to meet, have an extensive history of growth and development on their planet. We shall have an opportunity to learn from them what they have achieved in creating a stable, peaceful planet. Furthermore, the wonders to which they have been exposed will hopefully be shared with us. We have all begun to learn that their advanced technology, science endeavors, and social relationships could be most helpful to us in developing our own Earthly society.

"Now I have the honor and privilege to introduce to you their ambassador from planet Redex, Mr. Aounah III. Ambassador, would you like to say a few words?"

"Thank you, Mr. Prime Minister," Aounah said. "It is a great honor for us to be allowed to build a permanent embassy here in Jerusalem. We have looked forward to accomplishing this goal ever since we first learned of the state of Israel. The history of Israel and this region is of great importance to our Redexian people. It seems that your new State is carrying on many of our traditions including the current use of one of our sacred languages, Hebrew as it emerges as one of Earth's vibrant cultures. From this vantage point in the holy city of Jerusalem, which we also understand to be a melting pot of three of Earth's great religions, we hope to interact peaceably with all of Earth's peoples for all of our mutual benefit and safety. Peace be unto each of you. Shalom."

Everyone present nodded their various sized heads in an accepting manner to these remarks. So far so good. No one vaporized yet. No major city destroyed yet. No mass kidnapping of virgins for pleasure purposes. Just plain old getting along stuff, so far. Nice! And we can make super large size yarmulkes to fit those bulging, wrinkled kepi's.

CHAPTER 15

MOVING FORWARD

The lights burned brightly throughout the night at Framingham House as the joint Earth and Redexian staff members diligently worked on preparing a final mutual cooperation agreement. The attending household footmen, valets, and maids regularly brought snacks and drinks to fortify these multilingual interstellar workers. Drafts one through four were compared, modified, enhanced, and buffed until the final agreement was ready for translation into English, French (the language of international discourse), and standard Newee. At last all were satisfied that the proposed agreement set forth the terms discussed and tentatively agreed to by their respective principals. Details had been added where necessary, with intentional vagueness included where actual working conditions might require some latitude among the parties. By first morning light, a neatly-stacked set of agreements was ready for examination by Barack Obama, chairman of the Group of 8, and Captain Oulah on behalf of the United Redexian Frontier. These two took their time completing their breakfast libations before entering the library together at 9 AM to review the final documentation.

President Obama, accompanied by both Sir William and Jacob Witwenova, reviewed the agreement in English. Captain Oulah, assisted by his chief negotiator Aounah, reviewed his documentation in standard Newee. As far as both leaders were concerned, the documents looked satisfactory and were ready for signature. However, Chairman Obama, as agreed to on behalf of the Group of 8, submitted the final proposed accord in writing with his recommendation for acceptance to the Group of

8 for their approval. Within a short period of time he received approval to finalize the deal. So with a flourish Chairman Obama and Captain Oulah signed three sets of final documentation, which were then stamped and sealed according to standard United Nations protocol. The two principals had the common sense not to delve into questions regarding enforcement of the agreement, jurisdiction, or penalties should deviations take place. This could be left for later if questions arose. Perhaps matters in dispute would be settled by a drinking competition, or personal combat, or a pillow fight. Who knew?

To commemorate this historic achievement, the Secretary General of the United Nations, Ban Ki-moon, on behalf of its 193 member states, plus 2 tagalong observer states, issued a formal communiqué that read:

For the first time since the inception of the United Nations Charter on June 26, 1945, I am pleased to announce the signing of a formal agreement between our Earthly member states and the United Redexian Frontier, a sister civilization from planet Redex, orbiting its star Fomalhaut, located a mere 24 light years from our sun in the Milky Way galaxy. This agreement calls for cooperation between our galactic neighbor and ourselves in observing nearby star systems, collecting information about those star systems and searching the heavens for other signs of life. To coordinate our future joint efforts, the Redexian Frontier will be opening an embassy in Jerusalem, Israel, and will send an ambassador to the United Nations headquarters in New York City. A recreational center near Roswell, New Mexico, will also be constructed for visiting Redexian crew members. As quid pro quo for this agreement, Earth shall receive an observation base on planet Mars as well as our moon. This is an exciting time for all of us as we engage in our peaceful cooperation among close galactic neighbors.

Based upon the prior meetings, it also came to the attention of UN Secretary Ki-moon that the Redexians were concerned about the nuclear ambitions of both North Korea and the state of Iran. Further trouble in Africa, the Middle East and the Israeli/Palestinian ongoing dispute, the Syrian civil war, and the various proxy wars being fought throughout the region also received their attention. The Redexians suggested preparation of a position paper outlining the matters in dispute as well as the political leaders most knowledgeable about these matters. As a result, Secretary Ki-moon, in conjunction with the Group of 8, pledged to prepare a position paper within the next 20 days. Captain Oulah suggested that once the paper had been reviewed he might be able to offer some suggestions regarding a resolution of these trouble some problems.

Leah Anne Bailey, along with Casey Foster, had been following each of these matters closely. Leah Anne continued taking scrupulous notes of the meetings, the final agreement, the statement issued by the United Nations Secretary General, and her own observations regarding the status of events. Casey Foster had continued taking dozens of corroborating photographs. Now the two of them huddled together both figuratively and literally as Leah Anne prepared her next *Washington Post* news article. She produced an outline for her article while Casey selected his most illuminating photographs. Together they spent the evening in the Framingham House conference center hammering out the details on Leah Anne's next article.

"Moving Forward"
Byline: Leah Anne Bailey, *Washington Post*

Day by day, this Roswell story becomes more intricate and interesting. I am pleased to announce that the Group of 8 leadership met with the United Redexian Frontier leadership near London, England, to review the proposals for joint cooperation between our respective civilizations. I had the good fortune, along with Casey Foster, to be invited to attend. These meetings were held at the private country estate of Sir William Jefferson Clinton Meek, at his 500 year old ancestral country estate, Framingham House. I am able to report that the meetings were friendly and cooperative. The requests by our visiting guests from planet Redex were reviewed in detail and clarifications were sought where appropriate. These requests have now been approved as set forth in a formal signed cooperation agreement between Earth and the Redexians.

In return, the Redexians have agreed to construct an observation base on planet Mars for Earth use, as well as a small observation base for Earth to use on our moon. To provide Earth with protection from potential incoming asteroids and other space debris, the Redexians will collect systematic observational data in conjunction with Earth scientists and then provide the means to deflect or destroy any such dangerous objects approaching Earth or Mars. Of course, it remains to be seen how well these plans will be carried out. It remains to be seen what level of cooperation will exist between our neighborly civilizations as these construction projects go forward. It also remains to be seen how we will compensate each other for our mutual efforts, services, and materials. But I am convinced that, like any other preliminary interaction between people, goodwill and hard work can make the end result satisfying.

I, for one, am thrilled by the prospect that Earth can become a safer planet from incoming dangerous space debris. This is a matter which we have only recently become familiar with as our scientists have now documented prior vast devastating events on our planet. We all know now about such losses, such as Earth's dinosaurs, as a result of these rogue incoming planetary rocks. I am also thrilled by the prospect that in short order we Earthlings will begin to occupy off-world observation bases on our moon and planet Mars where we can learn more about our solar system and the Milky Way. It is my hope that as our Earthly species slowly moves out among the stars we will achieve more safety for our race and more knowledge of our place in the Universe. What an exciting time for all of us to experience.

As a disclaimer, I need to briefly mention that many of our 16th century preliminary contacts between our European ancestors and our South American ancestors proved devastating to the local culture. European greed, lust, and struggle for worldwide power and gold resulted in the eradication of an many South American cultures. I am hopeful that this current interaction between different species in our galaxy will provide more mutually beneficial results. Only time will shed light on this outcome. But everything that I have observed so far leads me to be optimistic.

Attached again to this article are the magnificent supporting photographs taken by Casey Foster. You will be able to see for yourself the location of the meetings at Framingham House in London and the interactions between the Group of 8 participants and the personnel from the United Redexian Frontier. By now, I expect that your review of the photographs taken by Casey of our alien visitors are becoming more commonplace. Perhaps before long these Redexian visitors will appear more similar than different to us. Hopefully, over time we will learn to see them as part of the expected diversity of the Universe.

Once again, Leah Anne's dictated article was e-mailed to Kelly Oliveri to be finalized and forwarded to her *Washington Post* editor. Government permission was again obtained, and the finalized news article was published in the *Washington Post* the next day, highlighted by the spectacular color photographs taken by Casey. Leah Anne's news readership continued to grow as the story "grew legs." The resulting correspondence and e-mails flooded into the *Washington Post*, and *Post* management bathed in the reflected limelight. Ownership bathed in the increased sales and profits. The *Post*, as expected, loved a good, long, popular, newspaper-selling story.

Back in New York City, the United Nations' international conflict staff prepared a report on the world's current leading trouble spots. The list of the potentially dangerous conflict areas was led by the emerging nuclear states of North Korea and Iran. The report detailed how many nations had been in contact with North Korea over a lengthy period of years trying to curb North Korea's nuclear ambitions. Coupled with the expanded production of nuclear materials, the North Koreans had engaged in what they termed a "military first" objective in which national resources were first devoted to military achievement. Particularly troubling was the fact that North Korea was also developing ever more sophisticated missile delivery systems upon which a nuclear device might eventually be mounted. Continuing negotiations with North Korea had not arrived at any achievable denuclearization results. More worrisome were the confrontations between North Korea and its neighboring states, which were continuous and escalating. To further exacerbate the tense situation, the North Korean citizens were restrained by a military state in which few if any rights were available to them. A few North Korean leaders had all the power, privilege, and property, while the remaining population was subjugated to the will of these few dominant figures. It was clearly a situation that could get out of hand, with devastating results unless nuclear disarmament and a change in political leadership could be achieved.

Likewise, the United Nations staff report highlighted the current negotiating position between Iran and the other world nuclear powers. Iran had taken the position for years that it was entitled to develop its nuclear capacity for "peaceful purposes." Its surrounding neighbors viewed Iran as trying to secretly develop nuclear weapons. Iran's current program of developing nuclear materials in locations that were not being monitored and could be safe from attack led many to view its proposals of denuclearization with skepticism. Given the nature of Iran's involvement in other extremist activities in neighboring states, its objectives were subject to intense scrutiny. It was apparent that all concerned knew that this nuclear issue needed a prompt resolution or significant outside coordinated intervention.

Other significant disputes meriting inclusion in the UN staff report included the decades long Israeli/Palestinian dispute over territory and rights among their people. This was a conflict rooted in the United

Nations' 1947attempted partition of the Palestinian territory into two separate sovereign states of Israel and Palestine. However, as soon as the United Nations had voted to create these two distinct states, a generalized war throughout the region sought to destroy the state of Israel. Subsequently, there had been many other armed conflicts between the Palestinians and Israelis. On the one side stood the state of Israel, which had expanded its territory as a result of these prior conflicts, and on the other side stood the divided Palestinian response from both Hamas, controlling the Gaza Strip, and the Fatah movement, controlling the West Bank. To further exacerbate the problem, Israel had been confronted by Hezbollah, based in Lebanon and supported by Iran. What a mess. All attempted negotiated solutions had failed miserably. War, negotiations, hoped-for solutions, failure, and more war all led to a continuing cycle of despair. No end to this conflict seemed to be in sight.

The United Nations staff also highlighted the four year civil war centered in Syria, with pro-government forces facing off against a variety of home-grown combatants and international terrorists. To make matters worse, many outside governments had taken positions concerning which side they favored for success. Massive aid and arms shipments had been sent to each of the warring sides hoping to tip the balance from one party to another to spread the reign of terror throughout large portions of Syria and Iraq. As the conflict spread, Earth's leadership had taken notice. Something needed to be accomplished to bring this matter under control. It was not going to be easy. It would be a long-term, messy, expensive project.

Also meriting inclusion in the United Nations' staff report were the current raging battles in Ukraine between government forces and Russian-backed separatists. It was a conflict growing in intensity, involving some of the world's major powers with both political and economic interests at stake. Meetings, negotiations, resolutions, and proposals had been offered and avoided by all. Sanctions were imposed, counter sanctions were applied, and everyone in the region was under stress.

The staff report pertaining to Earth's leading "trouble spots" was final-ized and handed over to the United Nations leadership to be polished. A review of the report illustrated that Earth and its many inhabitants didn't look particularly civilized. Perhaps another few centuries of development might help to calm down us gun-toting, missile-launching, ever on alert, pissed off war mongers. Well, those Redexian guys wanted to know what was happening. This UN report should give them some sort of idea. Lucky them.

The finalized report on the leading world trouble spots was deliv-ered to Sir William at the Jerusalem residence of Prime Minister Benjamin Netanyahu. The Prime Minister was engaged in discussions with Sir William and Captain Oulah concerning the construction of the Redexian embassy, which would be located on Daniel Oster Square, a block away from the Prime Minister's residence on Smolenskin Street in the Rehavia neighbor-hood. How cozy . Final architectural plans would need to be drawn up and submitted for Israeli government approval. It seemed that the Israeli government and the soon to be nearby Redexian embassy neighbors had agreed, in principle, to connect their two locations by means of a secret underground tunnel. These two parties had further agreed that an ad-ditional secret underground tunnel would exit the Redexian embassy and emerge approximately 3 blocks away at a vacant warehouse, where a mid-sized shuttlecraft would be permanently stationed. This would provide easy availability for transportation from the Redexian embassy to other locations on Earth or the planned observation bases on the moon and Mars. For whatever reason, it was becoming apparent to all that the Israeli government and the soon to be permanent Redexian visitors were devel-oping a close political relationship.

Once the United Nations report was received, Sir William, Prime Minister Netanyahu, and Captain Oulah reviewed its content. Together, they discussed which trouble spot deserved the most pressing attention. While many of the matters in the UN report presented various degrees of unsettling behavior, by far the most troubling was North Korea. This politically isolated Asian nation seemingly operated totally outside the normal bounds of civilized behavior. It constantly threatened its neighbors and had progressively developed sophisticated military weapons. Of particular concern was its nuclear program, which had developed sufficient nuclear materials to build a handful of first generation nuclear weapons. Should its political leadership become further unglued and carry through on its threat to unleash nuclear war upon its enemies, enormous damage might be inflicted in the area. Repeated efforts at negotiations had been a complete failure. North Korea's only relevant ally, China, had been unable to halt the development of North Korea's nuclear program, even in conjunction with other world powers.

Three North Korean leaders, Kim Jong-un, as Supreme Leader, Pak Pong-ju, as Premier of the North Korean cabinet, and Choe Hyong-sop, as chairman of the Workers Party Standing Committee, made the decisions that became enforceable state policy. These three, individually or together, would need to be convinced that the time for change had arrived. So it came to pass that North Korea was selected as the test case for ramping down Earth's trouble spots. An action plan for approval by the Group of 8 and the United Nations was prepared. Once approved, the Redexians were chosen to take the lead role on implementing the plan. That seemed somewhat foolproof, since what could the North Koreans do with respect to action taken by planet Redex or its visiting aliens?

The time had also arrived for the Redexians to start their ambitious construction projects, including their observation bases, Jerusalem embassy, and Roswell recreation center. To begin the process, Captain Oulah transmitted a coded message to second-in-command Weooh VII:

Second-in-command, be advised that we have achieved our intended preliminary agreement with Earth's political leadership for the construction of a recreation center near Roswell and observation bases on planet Mars, Earth's moon, and Titan. We have also agreed to establish our primary embassy location in Jerusalem, Israel, and to send a Redexian ambassador to their United Nations headquarters in New York City. Attached to this coded message you will find a complete copy of the final agreement in standard coded Newee. Review the agreement thoroughly and place a copy in the mother ship's main computer and another in my private safe. To move forward with our plan, you are hereby ordered to move the mother ship from its present orbiting location around Titan to planet Mars. This undertaking should be initiated within 12 hours. Once you have achieved a stable orbit around Mars we will move forward with our plan concerning construction of the Martian observation base, embassy location in Jerusalem, and the recreational center near Roswell. Forward to my attention the most recent surveys and architectural plans for the Martian observation base, Jerusalem embassy, and Roswell recreational center. I expect that construction will commence within the next 20 days. Advise receipt of this message and compliance.

Signed, Captain Oulah, United Redexian Frontier

The captain's message, traveling at the speed of light by radio transmission, was received on board the mother ship four minutes after being sent. Commander Weooh received the message and promptly responded:

Captain, I have received and reviewed your coded message. As you have requested, all will be accomplished promptly. I have notified our engineering and construction departments to finalize preparations for construction of the Mars observation base, Jerusalem embassy, and Roswell recreation center. Attached to this message you will find the architectural and survey plans for each. I anticipate arriving in orbit around Mars within 72 hours. I will notify you upon arrival and entry into a stable orbit. Please advise if you have further orders at this time.

Signed, respectfully, Commander Weooh VII

Sir William had another item of interest that he wished to raise with Captain Oulah. It concerned the binder with metal discs found by Newton Foster and Lone Wolf at the site of the initial shuttle crash near Roswell in 1947. These discs had been preserved by Lone Wolf until their recent hand-off to the United States government by Casey Foster. Despite efforts by numerous Earth scientists, these discs remained a mystery as to their operation and content. Sir William had been provided with four of the discs, in two different sizes, to discuss with the Redexians. It was hoped that, given the recent agreement reached between these neighbors, the contents of the discs might be explained.

"Captain Oulah," began Sir William, "it has recently come to my attention recently that some additional materials were found at the site of your earlier shuttlecraft which crashed in Roswell, New Mexico. In particular, earlier this week I was provided with four metal discs that were found near the crash site. We are unfamiliar with the purpose of these discs and their content. I am hopeful that you might be able to explain the purpose of these discs and what they contain."

With that comment, Sir William handed Captain Oulah two of the larger metal discs and two of the smaller metal discs. Captain Oulah took the discs in hand and gave them a quick visual inspection. "Sir William," he said, "it appears that the discs you have presented to me are standard versions of recording devices that we use on our spacecrafts. The reason for the two different sizes is that the larger version is utilized on the mother ship main computer system, while the smaller versions are used in transportable electronic devices. As to their content, I cannot elaborate until they are played back for content. I suspect some of the materials relate to the operation of the crashed shuttlecraft, its on-board technical systems, navigational information, and recordings of collected observational information. After my technical crew reviews these materials we will be able to share the information with you. If we are lucky, the larger discs might contain information concerning our home world and some of the planetary systems closer to Earth that we have visited. Let me see what I can do. Usually these metal discs are stored within a service binder on the shuttlecraft and number between 10 and 15. Have you recovered any additional discs?"

Sir William Jefferson Clinton Meek looked directly into Captain Oulah's deep red eyes and without missing a beat lied by omission: "These are the only discs provided to me. Let me inquire as to whether or not there may be any additional discs. I will let you know as soon as I obtain an answer."

"Thank you," responded Captain Oulah, bringing this discussion to completion.

Captain Oulah made the operational decision to remain on planet Earth for the start of the embassy and recreational center construction projects. He anticipated that local Earth contractors could provide the bulk of on-site construction services and raw materials. With the assistance of Prime Minister Netanyahu, acting as an intermediary, Captain Oulah hired a local Israeli contracting firm which met all Israeli security requirements. The outside of the Redexian embassy would be constructed to match the appearance of local Israeli government buildings. It would appear to be a two story structure with a rooftop observation deck. However, the bulk of the embassy would be constructed underground. This would provide more privacy and a much greater level of security.

Two days later, a construction team from Elad Elaho Corporation arrived at the Daniel Oster Square site for initial ground preparation. Once the site was leveled and enclosed with a 10 foot high privacy fence, the real work began. Most importantly, the contractor began digging a 300 foot deep shaft for the installation of a high speed elevator. Once the bottom of the shaft area was reached, the contractor began digging a horizontal tunnel towards an empty warehouse three blocks away. The main embassy building would contain two above ground floors and ten below ground floors separated by 20 feet of reinforced concrete roofing. While some interference at the ground level might be possible, clearly no one would reach the underground embassy facilities without explicit permission. Once the main embassy structure was finished, mother ship personnel would complete the interior space with appropriate security and electronic instrumentation. The embassy would blend into its surroundings and be functional inside. The building would also contain sophisticated transmission systems for sending messages to various Redexian outposts and then back to Redex. The business of entering a new solar system and establishing a presence had begun without incident.

With the embassy construction underway, Captain Oulah traveled to Roswell with Sir William and Jacob Witwenova to start construction of the recreational facility. All three were familiar with the Roswell base, and all three had toured the underground facility where the shuttlecraft had been reconstructed. They had been provided access to the various materials collected, analyzed, and stored. The Roswell Army/Air Force base had been renamed as the Walker Air Force Base from 1948 through 1967. In 1968, according to the United States government, Walker Air Force Base had been closed. The military base had then allegedly been converted to continue operations as the now private Roswell Air Center, which provided limited access for private air carriers for the purpose of transportation and research. Many of the prior government buildings had been refurbished for private use. And, of course, below ground, unknown to the public, there remained the secret government research and storage facility managed by General Sealls.

Captain Oulah decided that this airport, located within 3 miles of downtown Roswell, would be insufficient for the large recreational facility he planned to build. Instead, the captain chose to build the Redexian recreational facility within the Snow River Cave National Park system, located 40 miles west of Roswell. This 1500 acre parcel was easily reached from Roswell via New Mexico State Road 70, otherwise known as the Billy The Kid Trail. This parcel was further enhanced by the fact that it was located just north of the Mescalero Apache reservation which could provide an easily available labor pool for construction and servicing of the recreational facility.

Once second-in-command Weooh arrived at Mars and inserted the mother ship into a stable orbit, he sent a message to Captain Oulah:

Captain, the mother ship has arrived safely at planet Mars and is inserted in a stable orbit 500 km from the surface at its equator. Please provide updated orders.

Signed, Second-in-command Weooh VII

Captain Oulah responded:

> Your message has been received. Send down to Roswell, by prompt shuttlecraft, our security chief, head engineer for construction, lead architect for construction, and our leading language expert. Also immediately dispatch a mid-sized battle cruiser to be stationed over the Korean Peninsula. I expect to be returning to the mother ship along with certain special guests within the next five days. Make appropriate arrangements. More directives will be issued shortly.
>
> Signed, Captain Oulah of the United Redexian Frontier

With construction underway, Captain Oulah turned his attention to the initial pacification of Earth's major trouble spots. The plan to tamp down Earth's major trouble areas had been agreed upon by Sir William, Jacob Witwenova, and Prime Minister Netanyahu and was then forwarded to the Group of 8 and United Nations task force for approval. It recommended as a first step a proposed "peace meeting" between North Korea and South Korea to be convened in the South Korean capital city of Seoul. The plan was approved and then presented to both the North Korean and South Korean governments as a useful way to discuss and hopefully resolve any remaining differences. The UN proposal wisely contained sufficient incentives to convince North Korea's Supreme Commander Kim Jong-un, its Premier Pak Pong-ju and the chairman of its Communist Standing Committee, Choe Hyong-sop to attend the peace conference. The South Koreans would be represented at the peace conference by their first freely-elected female President, Park Geun-hye, and their Chief of Security, Kim Jang-soo. To balance the negotiating scales, the Chinese agreed to send their head of national security, Lo Wan Soo, and their leading military logistics expert, Chloe Anh Sing. In short order, all of these international dignitaries, with appropriate levels of protocol, were assembled at the South Korean presidential palace. Pomp and public display were a main feature of the initial get-together, with incredibly tightened security provided for all. Televised broadcasts of the meeting were sent around the world as the leaders shook hands, smiled, and presented meaningless short speeches. When the appropriate public fawning and self-serving statements had been completed, all assembled dignitaries were ushered inside the main conference hall for the expected hemming and hawing. Any progress seemed unlikely to the public. Seating took place by seniority and level of self- proclaimed authority.

Unbeknownst to almost all assembled, a mid-sized Redexian shuttle-craft landed, as planned, in the presidential palace backyard within minutes of the opening meeting. Without fanfare a Redexian security team, ray guns at the ready, enhanced by a specialized United Nations security team, marched inside to the conference center and took immediate possession of all of the assembled dignitaries. Protest and gesticulations were of no use. All were promptly escorted outside and onto the awaiting shuttlecraft. Once the dignitaries were on board, Captain Oulah gave the order to proceed. The shuttlecraft shot skyward, departing the South Korean presidential palace for orbit. A quick tourist-like flyby of the moon for close-up viewing had been scheduled to mollify the passengers. Then the shuttlecraft zoomed at 3/4 solar system speed directly to the Redexian mother ship now orbiting Mars. No itinerary was provided to the "guests". Drinks were on the house. Everyone had first class seats. Free viewing screens were provided in order to observe the quickly receding planet Earth and its accompanying captive moon. Once in orbit, the Earth appeared to these guests as a precious little blue globe floating in darkened space. The guests enjoyed the view but wondered what the hell was going on. The North Koreans in particular were befuddled. They had always thought they were totally in charge. But that wasn't the case on this shuttlecraft trip. New rules. No violations. Sit down, be quiet, and behave yourselves—or else!

Whoa, this was certainly a new twist on international and interstellar diplomatic wrangling of the highest order. The people back on Earth were merely informed that the principals meeting in South Korea would be engaged in private discussions without interruption until such time as an agreement regarding stability in the region could be reached. No mention was made of the mandatory jaunt into outer space by the assembled dignitaries. Time, and not much time at that, would reveal how well this off world approach worked. Game on!

CHAPTER 16

SNATCH AND COMPLY

The Redexian shuttlecraft shot through the cold, dark, almost empty interstellar space towards its mother ship, orbiting planet Mars 500 km above its equatorial surface. The on-board dignitaries were informed that they were on the way to a safe, quiet, out of the way location for the North Korea and South Korea peace negotiations. This location would enhance their ability to speak freely in order to find a "mutually acceptable" peace resolution. Once their initial belligerence simmered down, all aboard came to realize that they had no choice other than to cooperate. The captain took the occasion of this two day trip to Mars to individually acquaint himself with each of his guests. He asked them privately what their position was with respect to resolving the outstanding disputes. After a couple of days of private conversations the captain felt comfortable that he had reached an overall understanding of the present problems. However, it was also clear to him that many of the more troubling issues were not being addressed. He intended to make sure that all issues were placed on the table and that an enforceable resolution satisfactory to the Redexians was reached. From his point of view, the Redexians were about to make a substantial investment in terms of time and resources in this solar system and they needed to resolve any disputes that could negatively impact their long term objectives.

As the shuttlecraft traveled ever more closely to Mars, its surface features became more visible. The guests were also treated with a view of the visually stunning smooth plains on Mars' surface, such as Daedalia Planum and the vastly interesting Vastitas Borealis, an extensive low land plain containing obvious signs of water ice. In plain view to the approaching shuttlecraft passengers were the two circling moons of Mars. This included Deimos, orbiting Mars at about 14,500 miles above its surface, and the much larger, mineral-rich Phobos, orbiting some 3,700 miles above the planet's surface. How intriguing.

On the third day after leaving Earth, the shuttlecraft was piloted towards the docking station on the Redexian mother ship. However, Captain Oulah decided that his guests would be treated with a close flyby inspection of the enormous mother ship before boarding. He wanted them to witness firsthand the complexity of this enormous interstellar traveling machine. While Earthlings were now able to manufacture and operate first generation space crafts, he wanted them to compare their achievements with the Redexians' incredibly intricate piece of space-faring machinery which had transported it crew safely 24 light years from its home world. This flyby would visually confirm to the guests the advanced state of these aliens' scientific accomplishments. It was kind of like the native Americans witnessing for the first time the arrival of Columbus on their shores with his three enormous sailing ships. It focused their attention like a laser beam. *Who are these guys, and how advanced are they* everyone wondered?

After the outside observation maneuvers were completed, the shuttlecraft navigator positioned the vessel for a hard docking with the mother ship. Once satisfied that all was in order, Captain Oulah opened the shuttlecraft hatch, and everyone aboard transferred to the mother ship. There awaiting the arriving passengers stood second-in-command Weooh VII in full military uniform. A sharp salute with accompanying head bob and wiggling ears was tendered to his captain as he stood ready to receive new orders. In return, the captain returned his salute and head bob with wiggling ears. How attractive and polite by both officers.

"Second-in-command," said the captain, " direct each of our guests to their quarters. Then make arrangements for a guided tour of the mother ship's interior for our guests. Once this is accomplished, meet me in an hour, along with our staff officers, in the bridge conference room." The captain, having finished his remarks, bowed to his arriving guests and quickly made his way to the command station on the mother ship's bridge. Once seated in his command chair he scanned his adjacent computer screens for all current relevant information. He then asked each of the bridge officers to report on the current status of the mother ship. He needed to know exactly what was going on throughout the spacecraft.

As ordered, the well-trained, attentive officers were all assembled in the bridge conference room to meet with their captain. "Gentlemen," he began, "our arrival in this new solar system has gone off as planned. We have made initial contact with planet Earth's political leaders. We have sought and gained approval from Earth's leaders to place 3 satellites in their solar system, build observation bases where we desired, establish an embassy in Jerusalem, Israel, and construct a recreation center for our crew near Roswell, New Mexico. Perhaps we could have accomplished all of this without cooperation from Earth's leadership, but I am pleased that these accomplishments have occurred with their expressed approval. Prior experience on other worlds has taught us that allies are more useful than a captive species plotting to get free. We will now proceed with all due diligence with these Earthlings' assistance to reach our goals for this solar system as set forth clearly in our orders from our leaders on Redex. We will follow those orders to the letter. As you know, Redex seeks to establish multiple observation bases throughout our area of influence in the Milky Way. Our people need advanced notice and protection from other possible incoming hostile alien species. These Earthlings, properly handled, can assist us in these goals. But to make our investment in time and resources feasible we need to eliminate any major threats to our plans. So correcting the behavior of our " these on board guests from North and South Korea will serve as our first test case.

"Keep in mind that planet Earth and its people can become a valuable resource for us," he continued. "They, with our guidance, can help us observe the surrounding interstellar space and find any of its other occupied planets. They can assist us in providing raw materials and labor as we build and man our observation bases in this solar system. And Earth can serve as a defensive ally or as a more primary target for any incoming hostile alien species instead of planet Redex and our people. As such, you officers are to treat each of our guests with civility. Of course, they are to be observed carefully, and reports on their behavior and conduct will be made available for my review.

Shortly I will initiate what has been termed as peace negotiations between North Korea and South Korea. This is the first step in achieving our objectives to tamp down the violence prevalent on Earth. Nuclear resources in the hands of unstable governments will not be permitted. Threats of generalized warfare, which would envelop a significant portion of Earth's people and resources, will not be permitted. Rest assured that with our leadership staff working together we will succeed, as we always do. I will keep you all advised. Dismissed!"

The Redexians were not the only ones planning for their future in the Milky Way. Back on Earth, the Group of 8 convened a meeting to discuss the status of recent events. In keeping with a prior arrangement, President Barack Obama chaired the meeting. He began, "Well, gentlemen, we have been able to enter into a signed agreement with our galactic neighbors for mutual cooperation in creating multiple observation bases on Mars and our moon, a defense system for Earth from incoming destructive space debris, and a joint defense pact to work together as allies against any hostile incoming alien forces. Furthermore, in an effort to curtail some of Earth's nuclear trouble spots, the Redexians have also agreed to work on a Korean peace agreement and de-escalate the North Korean's nuclear program. To start this program, the Redexians have picked up the North Korean and South Korean peace delegations in Seoul for transport to their mother ship. They will start by arranging for the North and South Koreans to sign peace agreement. Once this is accomplished, attention will be directed to North Korea's nuclear program. It will be interesting to see how well this turns out. But on the other hand, we all agree that a backup clandestine defense strategy must be prepared. And now, would any of you like to comment?"

The Chinese delegate began, "We are hopeful that this new alliance with the Redexians may prove mutually beneficial. This is especially true regarding their pledge to assist us in formulating and building a planetary defense system to protect us from dangerous incoming asteroids, comets, and space debris. We also applaud their planned efforts, which might restrain and wind down some of the Earth's leading conflict spots. Nevertheless, we remain cautious regarding how helpful these new allies may turn out to be. Experience has taught us that today's ally may become tomorrow's sworn enemy. And when a potential enemy has extreme military power backed by extensive resources, caution must be exhibited. For that reason our Chinese defense experts, alone and in cooperation with our group, continue to plan for possible defensive military actions as a last ditch effort for self-preservation of our Earthly species. We realize that failure to succeed completely in any such attack could lead to our complete annihilation. We will proceed most cautiously."

The German delegate rose and said, "We, like you, hope for a long term peaceful coexistence with our new Redexian neighbors. But we also have a history of entanglements in many worldwide military conflicts. Success in military conflict requires research, planning, production of superior military equipment, and coordinated, meticulous efforts to implement a military plan. This alien situation presents an incredibly tough nut to crack. Our potential opponents have a vast technical superiority and a wide array of means to deliver a crushing blow to our planet. Just as worrisome, this opponent could call in overwhelming backup forces from their other bases in our galaxy and from their home world. Woe be unto us if we attempt a military attack and fail. Having stated this, I still feel it to be essential that we continue to work secretly on backup military plans. For if we get attacked and are not prepared, we shall surely all perish. Our government believes the best approach is to fight a delaying guerrilla response. This might be sufficient to inflict enough damage over time to cause these aliens to withdraw. The German government pledges complete cooperation to the Group of 8 to protect our human species."

In an interesting move, the Israeli delegate hopped to his small feet, standing straight up but still at least 10 inches shorter than most of the other delegates. "All of you around this table are familiar with the continuing

Israeli fight for survival. Ever since the creation of our nation state in 1947, the same year as the now-confirmed crash of the Redexian alien shuttle-craft in Roswell, New Mexico, we have prepared for and been engaged in nation-saving wars. We are a small nation dedicated to our own survival. Planning and fighting against terrorist groups has been our specialty. Planning and fighting against neighboring nation states has been our background. Preparing for and fighting against outside unfriendly nation state coalitions has been our fate. We have been forced to dedicate much of our national resources to preparing ourselves for these conflicts. So far we have been successful. The irony of this situation is that we presently have a close working relationship with these new Redexian galaxy neighbors. We welcome this opportunity to work together with them in cooperation and peace to build a safer planet. We welcome the opportunity to join with such an ally to help protect all of us from incoming space debris and other potentially unfriendly alien visitors who might arrive in the future. But rest assured that we Israelis, like all of you, are Earthlings first. We will do whatever is necessary to protect our nation state, our people, and our planet. We pledge to remain committed to the Group of 8 for protection of our world and our species. Let us all pray that it doesn't come to that. *Shalom.*"

President Barack Obama, chairman of the Group of 8, gained the attention of the delegates and walked to the podium. "It's interesting how, in times like these, our world's leaders, each leading a nation state with independent needs and desires, can come together when threatened from an outside source. Americans feel the same. We cherish our freedom and independence. We plan to never be under the yoke of foreign interests. And if an outside species tries to destroy us, we will respond fully. All of the resources and manpower of our nation are available for our joint defense. This is a policy, currently in place, that will never be waived. So, like my other fellow delegates, I am hopeful that this new relationship works out. But together we need to continue planning for the worst. I am also looking forward to seeing what results can be achieved on the Redexian mother ship regarding the North Korean nuclear program and peace negotiations. It would be nice to have a positive result. But as we wait, I suggest that our joint defensive committee continues to work on plans for our mutual defense. All in favor of continuing our cooperative efforts with the Redexians while at the same time developing a defensive military plan please raise your hands."

The vote came in promptly. Nine in favor and none opposed.

"Thank you for your help, gentlemen. We are adjourned until further notice," said Chairman Obama.

"Excuse me, Mr. Chairman," interrupted the Russian delegate as he turned to face Chairman Obama. "I'm afraid I need to present a short statement before we adjourn. It may surprise some of you to learn that our national security department has been working closely with the Israeli Mossad security agency over the last few months to provide protection to Earth's population from possible alien military action. We have quietly arrived at a couple of potential solutions."

Everyone's attention was immediately riveted upon the new Russian speaker. Wouldn't it be nice to have a foolproof solution in your back pocket to roll out when needed? Wouldn't it be easier to sleep at night knowing that there was a way out of this conundrum if and when the time came? Wasn't the world a much more enjoyable home before these aliens came knocking at our door? So they refocused their attention to listening to their Russian comrade, whom most of them distrusted.

The Russian speaker continued, "Our joint efforts have proposed two separate paths for potential destruction of the Redexians. The first solution would be to introduce lethal biological disease pathogens into their population. This could be done either here on Earth at the Roswell recreation center or through infecting the Redexian crew members on their mother ship. To accomplish this we are developing specialized lethal strains of the Ebola virus, which can be administered unnoticed. We are also developing three lethal strains of smallpox and variations of the European plague, which could be passed along to the entire Redexian mother ship crew.

"We are aware that this biological plan has several shortcomings. First, it will take some time to infect the entire alien crew. Secondly, it will take some time for them all to die. And thirdly, we cannot assure a 100% kill rate. In addition, since all deaths will not be immediate, there may be time for the Redexians to send distress messages to their outposts and home world. So we cannot guarantee that there will be no retaliation against planet Earth once these pathogens start killing the Redexians.

"Our second plan, which I consider more likely to succeed, would be to introduce a killing agent into their drinking supplies. More specifically, we feel that radiation poisoning with polonium would be the best bet. It's fast acting, irreversible, and almost impossible to detect. Polonium will kill them all. And since they are small, it will kill them pretty damn quick. We are also studying methodologies to take control of the mother ship and its military resources. For unless we can disable or take control of the mother ship we can be destroyed almost entirely in an instant. We are also aware, as you should be, that the longer this problem goes unsolved the more vulnerable we become. Once the Redexians establish a self-sustaining base on Mars, with outposts on our moon and Titan, we and our Earth resources will become expendable. We will be unnecessary for their prime objective to operate observation bases to provide a protective zone for their home planet. For the time being, we agree with Chairman Obama and the rest of you that taking action at this time is not in our best interest. However, we will remain on high alert while continuing our defensive strategy. I suggest you all do so as well."

Chairman Obama looked intently at the Russian delegate and thanked him for his comments. "Gentlemen, I appreciate all of your ideas and willingness to work together to protect our planet and people. Again, I suggest we adjourn at this time."

Aboard the Redexian mother ship, Captain Oulah was ready to move forward with the Earth pacification project. He had intentionally selected North Korea as the test case. The ongoing nature of the dispute between North and South Korea, buttressed by a belligerent nuclear armed regime not responsive to world opinion needed, to be reined in. These bad boys had been in control of this nation state for over 50 years, led by the public face of the Kim family, currently displayed in the round, semi-bald, weird haircut-displaying head of Kim Jong-un. It was time to face off with these backward intransigent commies. So the Captain informed his second-in-command to assemble all Korean and Chinese peace participants in the main mother ship conference room. Thirty minutes later, at exactly noon standard Redexian time, all arrived and were seated at the conference room table. This proved rather interesting, since the conference room and conference table looked more appropriate for a kindergarten class. The Redexians were small, light, and flexible, and these physical characteristics resulted in corresponding furniture accommodations. However, everyone present was smart enough not to joke about the miniature furniture situation. No midget-tossing jokes here. Protocol demanded politeness, usually.

"Thank you all for attending this peace conference," began Captain Oulah. "We are here to discuss and reach a peace agreement between North Korea and South Korea. My understanding is that the hard-fought war between each of your two nation states was completed in 1952. And yet I have been led to understand that presently only an armistice agreement has been signed. So we will discuss the conflict status and remain here until a peace agreement is finalized and signed by each of your political authorities. To assist in this process I have requested that the United Nations conflict staff prepare a draft peace agreement. Now, before each of you there is a draft peace agreement, which can be reviewed in Korean, Chinese, or English. We will take a short fifteen minute break while you remain in the conference room to read this document. Then I will first ask the North Koreans for their thoughts, followed by the South Koreans, and finally the Chinese. Let's proceed."

Kim Jong-un, as Supreme Commander of North Korea, decided not to wait until he had reviewed the proposed peace agreement. "Captain," he said belligerently, "North Koreans do not negotiate under duress or at a time and place not selected by our government. Your proposal that we pursue this matter right now is unacceptable. Perhaps we can arrive at a mutually satisfactory timetable to reconvene when the proper preparations have been achieved."

"Sir," responded Captain Oulah, "the time for making further arrangements and preparation is over. No one will be leaving our command ship until this agreement is finalized and signed. Let me assure each of you that I expect this to occur soon. Failure by North Korea and South Korea to arrive at and sign a peace agreement will leave us no choice other than to impose our own solution to wrap up your deadly, time-consuming, mutually destructive, and unnecessary war. Do I make myself clear?"

A collective grumbling and eye-rolling maneuver could be observed among some of the participants, but no one ventured a further comment. Each looked down at the draft agreement placed before them and started reading. The captain wondered whether some of the wording had been sufficiently simplified for each of these under-educated participants to understand. He didn't really care one way or another. These guys were going to discuss, negotiate, and sign a peace agreement.

After a fifteen minute break, Captain Oulah began, "Now I would like a representative from North Korea, South Korea, and finally China to make a brief statement with respect to this proposed peace agreement. Would you care to begin, Mr. Kim?"

"Let me go on notice," responded Kim Jong-un, "that our delegation is here as a result of subterfuge. We are being held against our will. Sovereign nations from planet Earth, especially our country of North Korea, do not negotiate under these conditions. We will not have a peace agreement dictated to us by an outside third party. However, having said that our honorable chairman of the North Korean Communist Standing Committee Mr. Choe Hyong-sop will respond on our behalf." That was certainly news to Mr. Choe, who had not prepared to provide any statement and now had no choice. Well, the only reason he was still alive was that he had faced situations like this many times before in North Korea. He knew how to bob and weave artfully while appearing to hold the country's hard line position.

Mr. Choe stood behind his dinky chair, military suit bedecked with medals granted over years of dedicated service to the Kim regime. His straight black hair was tucked neatly under his military cap. "Let me begin by confirming the comments just presented by our illustrious grand leader Kim Jong-un. We are not here to negotiate while surrounded by a sea of hostility. Our South Korean neighbors have transgressed against us for many years and denied us our well-earned rights. We are also surrounded by a sea of other nation states who wish us ill. For that reason alone, we have developed the most powerful military force in our region. We are ready to defend our rights to the last of our united people. But since we are all present we will now listen and respond to any reasonable peace proposal." Without looking at his grand leader, Choe slid into his small chair and looked at his folded hands.

Next to speak was Kim Jang-soo, chief of South Korea's national security. "Thank you for your opening comments, Mr. Choe," he began. "I am pleased that you have illustrated for our hosts and other attendees the belligerence that we normally face when trying to communicate with North Korea. Unlike you, we are here to resolve all of our differences and sign a peace agreement without further delay. As to the proposed peace agreement before us, although I need to discuss it with my fellow principals, it looks pretty solid upon first examination."

In somewhat of a surprising move, Chloe Anh Sing, as the military expert present on behalf of the Chinese government, spoke next. "We Chinese believe that it is time to bring this Korean Peninsula conflict to a final conclusion, as summarized by a signed peace agreement. This certainly appears to be the intention of our Redexian hosts. Let me also advise each of the delegates that I have had the pleasure of spending a fair amount of time on this mother ship previously as a guest. During that time I had the opportunity to meet with and become acquainted with Captain Oulah of the United Redexian Frontier. I can assure each of you that Captain Oulah does not make idle threats. He has indicated that we will remain here until we negotiate and sign a peace agreement. Therefore, I am convinced that this will in fact happen soon. I suggest that each of you get comfortable with that idea. We Chinese are available to consult with anyone interested in hearing our thoughts on ending this conflict. The proposed peace agreement document is a mere three pages long. After all, how much space does it take to declare that all hostilities are ended, that the current borders of neighbors are to be fixed in place, and that the peace agreement would take effect at midnight? Read it, review it, talk about it, see if any changes need to be addressed, and then it will be time to sign it!"

While the peace delegates continued to bicker over the proposed peace agreement, Captain Oulah walked to the command station on the bridge of his mother ship. He ordered the communications officer to connect the bridge to the Redexian battle cruiser stationed over the Korean Peninsula. Moments later he was informed that the connection had been achieved. "Commander," asked Captain Oulah, "are you on station over the Korean Peninsula as ordered?"

"Aye, Captain, we have followed your orders to the letter. We are available to commence any action required pursuant to your orders. How do you wish us to proceed?" responded the commander.

"Have you collected the necessary information concerning all targets that we have previously identified?"

"Aye, Captain, all targets have been identified precisely as to their exact locations and entered into our onboard shuttlecraft computers."

"Arm all weapons and stand down on alert status," the captain ordered. "I will be back in touch with you shortly."

"Aye, Captain, we await your orders for immediate implementation," said the battle cruiser commander.

Captain Oulah, satisfied that all was in place for action, returned to the main conference room where he observed the North and South Korean delegates squabbling. The Chinese delegates, huddled close by, observed the lack of progress. These guys didn't look ready to agree to or sign anything. It was clear to the captain that more persuasive action would be necessary before an agreement could be signed.

"It seems to me," interrupted the captain, "based upon my observation of your current discussions, that no agreement has yet been achieved. Let me assure you that this matter will be brought to a satisfactory conclusion and an agreement will be signed shortly. Perhaps, we can move this matter forward by your viewing a short demonstration tape that our knowledgeable Chinese delegate, Chloe Anh Sing, has previously witnessed."

With a wave of his hand, a view screen dropped down in front of the assembled group. Queued to the screen was the recent Redexian demonstration of delivery to Saturn of one high grade photon torpedo. Wow, that's some explosion! Move over, Hiroshima and Nagasaki. The assembled group watched silently. To further press home his point, Captain Oulah then signaled for the video operator to queue up the tape showing the bombardment of Jupiter by the a breakup of the Hale-Bopp asteroid fragments. Once the delegates had viewed both tapes, the captain explained what they had seen." Gentlemen, I have previously explained to Chloe Anh Sing that the first video tape demonstrates the impact of one high grade photon torpedo delivered from our mother ship to Saturn's surface. That explosion caused a temporary devastating effect to over 17% of Saturn's planetary surface. It is similar in destructive capability to the second tape I just showed you, where a large broken, asteroid impacted Jupiter's surface. Our one high grade photon torpedo is capable of delivering an explosive force 600 times Earth's complete nuclear arsenal. And our mother ship is capable of delivering many multiple photon torpedoes to any target on planet Earth upon my command. I have advised Earth's political leadership through your Group of 8 that we prefer a cooperative, mutually beneficial relationship with Earth's people. However, to protect our interests, we will take appropriate action when necessary. So I will ask you directly, gentlemen from North Korea and South Korea, are you ready now to end all hostilities and sign the peace agreement right now?"

"On behalf of the South Korean nation," said President Park Geun-hye, "we know that it is time to put all past disputes behind us for the benefit all of the people on the Korean Peninsula. We are ready to sign the agreement before us without any further modification or delay."

Kim Jong-un had been raised in the corridors of North Korean leadership. He had watched his grandfather and father before him rule North Korea with an iron fist. He had learned that a united North Korea could not be dissuaded from taking the action that leadership decided to follow. He had been taught that the North Korean military could defend their nation against all transgressors. He was also not convinced that the Redexian aliens could and or would implement any threats against his nation. Why would they? How could they? So he stood and stated, "Captain Oulah, thank you for your efforts and demonstration. Unfortunately, our peaceful united North Korean nation is unable to sign a peace agreement without discussing it in our North Korean cabinet and its political standing committee. I do give you my solemn word that upon my return to our capital in North Korea that we shall give due deliberation to this proposal. I anticipate that we can have an answer for you within a matter of weeks. I feel confident that you will find this acceptable. Thank you for your efforts. I believe that we are all headed in the proper direction."

Captain Oulah faced the North Korean commander and ordered the large view screen at the front of the conference room illuminated. He then ordered his communication officer to connect him to the Redexian battle cruiser stationed over the Korean Peninsula. "Delegates at this peace conference," he said, "I have previously ordered one of our mid-sized Redexian battle cruisers to take up a position over the Korean Peninsula. This battle cruiser is on station and has collected information concerning each of North Korea's military installations, missile batteries, nuclear facilities, and political headquarters, including the presidential palace. Each of these targets has been acquired and entered in to our computer system. At this time, I will let you all hear my communications with the battle cruiser. Commander, can you hear me?"

"Aye, Captain," responded the battle cruiser commander in English.

"Commander, do you have the presidential palace in North Korea and the primary North Korean missile batteries locations targeted?"

"Aye Captain. These targets are all ready for action. How do you wish to proceed?"

"Commander, you are hereby ordered to eliminate all of these targets immediately. Do you understand these orders?"

"Aye Captain," responded the battle cruiser commander. "Your orders have been received, understood, and are hereby being implemented."

With that, the Redexian battle cruiser fired five pulsating, high-intensity laser beams towards the selected targets. One laser beam was directed at the North Korean presidential palace and the other four at North Korea's primary missile launching stations. Seconds later, as each delegate watched from the mother ship's viewing screen, it was obvious that all targets had been obliterated. In addition, all the people located at each site were also terminated, including the entire Earth-bound Kim family dynasty. Nothing remained but leveled, burnt ground at each of the five sites

"Commander," responded to Captain Oulah, "I will be back in touch with you shortly. Remain on station for any further action necessary. And if North Korea launches any of its other missiles or takes any overt offensive military action, you are ordered to intercept and shoot down any such missiles and destroy the rest of the Korean military infrastructure." Understood?

"Aye Captain, as you have ordered, we will remain ready to implement all further orders."

The room full of delegates aboard the mother ship was stunned. They had all realized that their hosts possessed vast military capabilities. This attack and destruction on the North Korean targets got their undivided attention.

"Redexians never like to use force unless it is absolutely necessary," explained Captain Oulah. "But in this particular case, the ongoing dispute between North Korea and South Korea has created an area of unease throughout the entire Korean Peninsula and its surrounding nation states. It will be brought to an end now. I understand that the South Koreans are ready to sign the peace agreement and move forward. I ask you North Korean delegates whether you are ready to sign this peace agreement now?"

Kim Jong-un was ashen-faced. He could not and would not speak. His "ultimate power" had just been decimated. He suddenly remembered how much he liked his earlier schooling days when he lived in Switzerland. It was quiet, peaceful, with nice food, access to easy money, with plenty

of drinks available. Good looking girls were everywhere, and most importantly, he had no obligations, duties, or responsibilities. This Supreme
Leader stuff was suddenly getting old.

Pak Pong-ju looked at Kim, saw that he was useless, and spoke softly
on the Supreme Commander's behalf. "Captain Oulah, your demonstration merits our undivided attention. If you will permit us to return to our
private quarters for a few minutes, we will be able to return with what I
anticipate to be a favorable formal answer. Will that be acceptable?"

"Of course," responded Captain Oulah graciously. "Consider this
meeting adjourned for one hour. We will reassemble here in this conference room after you have had an opportunity to reflect upon our current
situation. But before you are all escorted to your separate quarters to con-
fer, I have a few more matters which you may wish to discuss. In addition
to signing a peace agreement, I expect to see the borders between North
Korea and South Korea opened. And since peace will have descended
upon the Korean Peninsula, I expect that the demilitarization zone will
no longer be necessary. Accordingly, all mines, fencing, barbed wire, and
other military equipment in and adjacent to the zone will be removed. In
addition, since peace will have arrived on the Korean Peninsula, there will
be no reason for North Korea to maintain any nuclear materials or nuclear
capacity. Accordingly, all current North Korean nuclear materials will be
destroyed by us. No new nuclear materials will be produced. And since
peace has now arrived, the North Korean military structure will immediately be downsized in both materials and manpower to a reasonable level
for a country of its size. Having accomplished these goals, the next step
will be to arrange for the re-unification of North Korea and South Korea
into one democratic state. This will be especially necessary considering
that the Kim dynasty will no longer remain in place. Please consider my
comments. Everyone is excused at this time. We will reconvene in one
hour to sign the peace agreement."

With that, each of the peace delegations was escorted by the Redexian
crew to their separate quarters, where they were quietly locked in. There
would be no rambling about the mother ship until these matters were

concluded. Of course, the Redexians could hear and see everything occurring during this break, since each of the quarters was carefully bugged with multiple video and listening devices. The chatter coming from the North Korean suite was quite interesting. None of them had ever been subjected to this kind of treatment by any outsiders. They had been the kings of their domain for many years. Kim Jong-un in particular remained stunned and mute. He had never been treated in this fashion except occasionally as a young man by his distant, overbearing father. Accordingly, it was left to the Chairman of the North Korean standing committee to move this discussion along. He, in conjunction with Pak Pong-ju, conferred about their potential options. They had few at their disposal and none upon which they could rely. They presently had no means to communicate with any of their on the ground leaders, which meant that no action could be taken until they were returned to North Korean soil. It was also obvious just by looking at their supreme commander that he was not going to be of any help or assistance. The ball was in their court. They would need to make the decision together and then implement those choices.

Kim Jong-un politely excused himself from his supporting cast and entered the restroom facilities. It was not quite as luxurious as his presidential palace facility, but it was satisfactory. All the necessary items were present, and the room was rather toasty, as he liked it. A glance towards the mirror over the sink confirmed that he looked like a whipped Shar Pei dog. In due course he sat on the facility, contemplating his next move. He was unaware that the doors to their suite had been locked. He was further unaware that the door to the restroom was now locked as well. He was unaware that a video was being taped of his actions within the restroom. And if he had been aware that he was being videotaped he couldn't have imagined why that would be the case.

Suddenly, on the direct order of Captain Oulah, his future was decided. The exterior wall of the restroom slowly raised like a garage door into the ceiling, resulting in some rather dramatic changes. The temperature promptly dropped from a cozy 72° inside to the outside temperature of approximately -250°. Mighty cold. In addition, the vacuum of space quickly sucked the Supreme Leader outside without the benefit of a protective space suit. Not much oxygen was available, nor air pressure to keep a body happy, healthy, and alive. The combined loss of heat, oxygen, and air pressure led to the inevitable result of one big dead former North Korean leader. He had been reduced in stature to a mere ice cube consigned to cartwheel through space forever. A one person frozen asteroid. He, like every last soul of his family in North Korea, had been permanently eliminated. The Kim dynasty was over, done, and finished for all time! Once the Supreme Leader had taken his leave, the outside panel swiftly slid back into place, and the previous cozy atmosphere was replaced. The restroom door slid open and revealed no one inside. Kim's comrades had heard a gurgling cry from the restroom and looked inside to see it vacant. They quickly looked out of their porthole and saw their former Supreme Leader floating off into space, pants at half mast, dead as a doornail. Nice haircut.

It was time for the North Koreans to select a new democratic leader. So ever vigilant Choe Hyong-sop slipped off his tie and quietly eased up behind Pak Pong-ju, still watching his former illustrious leader float away. Choe then carefully slipped the open end of his tie loop over Pak's unprotected head, and quickly strangled the unsuspecting Premier to death. Bye, bye comrade! Of course, all of these unusual events in the North Korean suite had been captured by the thoughtful redexians on the hidden recording equipment in beautiful, color, 3D super enhanced videotape for later replay.

North Korea suddenly had a new, though as yet unelected, democratic leader in the soon to be democratic State of North Korea. So much for all for one and one for all. Top dog wins! Choe Hyong-sop wondered whether he would need a political action committee?. How would he raise the money to win the first election? Well, he would solve those problems or people would die. He looked forward to being the first democratically-elected President of North Korea, with all of its perks. Capitalism was starting to sound downright great, especially for those at the top of the food chain! It was time for him to consider what kind of a deal he could strike with his South Korean counter parts on a re-unification plan along with his personal and very private compensation. The time had arrived for all Koreans to sign the peace agreement.

For now, all was proceeding exactly as Captain Oulah had planned. As a result, he had almost an hour before he needed to reconvene his considerably more cooperative peace negotiating teams. So the captain excused himself from the command center on the ships' bridge and returned to his own quarters. With a push of his buzzer he sought the presence of his twin serving girls, along with appropriate liquid refreshment. He felt that he had earned an hour of down time. *It's good to be king*, he thought to himself. *Onward, United Redexian Frontier.*

Down below on the little blue water world no one yet had a clue as to what was occurring on the Redexian mother ship. Those new "allies" would be informed of the status by Captain Oulah once the Korean peace agreement was signed. He calculated that would occur very soon, just as he planned.

Peace on Earth, good will to all, especially Redexians.

Let New Colonial Earth move forward!

ACKNOWLEDGMENTS

I am indebted to the following people for their assistence and support in bringing Return to Roswell, Book II to completion. First to my wife, Kathi who remains an inspiration in her efforts to keep me focused on the story line and final results. She also continues to work tirelessly on editing and processing the manuscript. Keary Ryan Rosen played the major role in designing the art work for the front cover. Tim Symonds added his professional talents to the overall book cover design. Professional editing services were provided by Kevin Anderson & Associates. Nevin Weiner, Esq. a long time friend continued to provide legal services, as needed. Readers at various stages of the drafts and final manuscript include Homer Hoe, a golf wizard, Dorothy McAden, and William Meek. Manuscript preparation was assisted by Lisa Barbic Vince, number one, Jill Barbic, going to the Ball, and Laurie Myers, whose talents are considerable. Createspace has been instrumental in moving this process towards publication.

Finally, I would again like to thank all the big headed, red eyed, silver aliens that have visited Earth in the past and are planning to return again shortly. Their efforts have made this second book in the Return to Roswell trilogy possible. Book III is in the works. Let the New World continue!

ABOUT THE AUTHOR

Martin A. Rosen was born in Chicago, Illinois and raised in Winnetka, one of its northern suburbs. He received his Bachelor of Science degree from Indiana University in Business and Finance in 1967. In 1971 he also earned his J.D. from Indiana University where he was a member of and had an article published in The Indiana Law Review. He has practiced law for over 45 years in Washington D.C., Denver, Colorado and Sarasota, Florida. He resides in Florida and Vermont with his wife and two Labrador Retrievers, known as the Chocolate Factory.

www.ingramcontent.com/pod-product-compliance
Lightning Source LLC
Chambersburg PA
CBHW022128050726
47590CB00002B/452